Yesterday Once More

Award-Winning Short Stories

Volume II

by

Steve Whisnant

With Photos & Illustrations by

Guest Artists

Yesterday Once More

Steve Whisnant

SkyMacSyd Publishing

Visit the author's website:

www.stevewhisnant.com

Yesterday Once More

Copyright 2009 by Steve Whisnant

Trade paperback edition ISBN 978-0-9767244-3-8

Cover photograph by Stewart Matthews

Special thanks to the Arkansas Department of Parks & Tourism for allowing the use of several images.

1st Edition
February 1, 2009

Printed in Canada

SkyMacSyd Publishing
P.O. Box 56363
Little Rock, Arkansas 72215

In Memory
Trish Johnson-McDuffie, Author

Acknowledgement & Dedication

To my grandmother, Rayda Stanley

My success at winning contests for the stories in this anthology would not have been possible without a little help from my friends (okay, a lot of help). They are: Members of Fiction Writers of Central Arkansas (FWCA), Ozark Writers League (OWL), Northeast Texas Writers' Organization (NETWO), White County Creative Writers (WCCW), Penpoint Writers' Group, and Arkansas Pioneer Branch of the National League of American Pen Women. Others include, specifically: Jim Bell, Joe David Rice, Ellen Withers, Dean Kelsey, Clark Dorr, Dorene Harris, Trish Johnson-McDuffie, Dusty Richards, Betty McPherson, Mike McMinn, Pam Withroder, Madelyn Young, Helen Austin, Laura Parker Castoro, Clovita Rice, Rhonda Roberts, Lorna Stone, Carol Hodges, Barbara Longstreth Mulkey, Victor Fleming, Marsha Camp, Regina Williams, Jeanie Horn, Allen Lee, Linda Fisher, Peggy Vining, Luella Turner, Jennifer Di Camillo, Paula Martin Morell, Del Garrett, Margaret Ponder Thompson, John Achor, Dr. Ed Simpson, Judi King (Aunt Judi), Barbara Stanley (my mom), Page and Tom Mann (my mother-in-law and father-in-law), and my family—*especially* my wife, Mary.

I would like to also thank my copyeditor, Diana Ross, for editing the final proof before printing.

SkyMacSyd Publishing
P.O. Box 56363
Little Rock, Arkansas 72215

SkyMacSyd Publishing
P.O. Box 56363
Little Rock, Arkansas 72215

Contents

CHRISTIAN

LITERARY (And Other Stuff)

WESTERNS

Artwork Contributor Bios

About the Author

Foreword

When I first met Steve Whisnant I thought, what a nice young man. As our friendship grew I said, what a talented young man. The more I learned about him the more I admired him, his love of people, his enthusiasm for life, his appreciation of other writers and their talents, and his drive and determination to become a successful author.

Steve is already a dedicated, prolific writer. He has a special willingness to share what he has learned with other writers, his life is one of service.

He served two years as President, and two years as Vice-President, for Fiction Writers of Central Arkansas and did a wonderful job of encouraging each member when they received notice of their work being accepted for publication. He made new members feel welcome to the group and encouraged them in their trials and efforts.

Steve is a very busy person, a family man with a wife and three daughters, including twins. He gets up early each morning before his day job as a field representative for the Vital Records Division of the Arkansas Department of Health. His work is an asset to his writing because he travels throughout the state and meets people from all walks of life. He hears the stories of those he assists in filling out birth and death certificates. He listens carefully and often makes mental notes of how some of their stories can be utilized and incorporated into some of his yarns. His tales have a human element, unique with his technique and emphasized in his short stories.

Steve was recently a featured author in the Arkansas Author's Day with many of the most well known national writers with Arkansas ties. He was then invited to speak at the Ozark Writers Live festival with other popular local authors. His experiences have led to numerous speaking opportunities at libraries, bookstores, and conferences on topics of publishing and writing. He also speaks to genealogy organizations on topics of vital records and book printing.

Presently, the name Steve Whisnant is being heard all over the south. This is not luck! Steve has become a top-notch author. The future will someday proclaim him as a best selling author.

Sincerely,

Peggy Vining, Poet Laureate of Arkansas and
2008 Governor's Arts Awards Recipient for
Lifetime Achievement Award

Introduction

I consider my first published anthology, *Yesterday Again*, a success, because all the printed copies sold. With this glorification (pun intended), it's only natural that I would want to offer the world my second collection of award-winning short stories. My goal is to take you on an emotional roller-coaster ride, leaving you wanting more. Perhaps a third anthology?

For the most part these stories are clean, adult tales. However, with apologies to family and members of my church at Calvary, I do reserve the right to use a "bad" word at times. These vernacular misfits are used less than what one reads in most well known novels (my wife insisted I not include my award-winning erotica tale).

I wrote in the introduction to my first anthology that I hope my progeny will think it cool that granddaddy penned a book. Well, here's another collection for them to consider my "coolness". All but a few stories won contests and/or were published.

Enjoy!

Steve Whisnant
Husband, father of three girls, and writer

P.S., Oprah, I'm available for an interview—have your people call my people.

Paranormal

A Little Hope
(Yesterday Once More)

Introduction

I subtitled this story *Yesterday Once More* simply to link a story in the anthology to the book's title. Clovita Rice, an award-winning writer/poet and friend, suggested the trend of "Yesterday" in my future anthologies, and I liked it. My first collection, now out of print except for a few bookstores and used on Amazon, was called *Yesterday Again*. Let's see, what shall I name my third anthology? *Yesterday, Not Just the Day Before Tomorrow?* Probably not.

A Little Hope won 2nd Honorable Mention at the 2005 Ozark Creative Writers' Conference in the Paranormal Romance Award contest. Sponsored by Jeanie Horn, a wonderful award-winning writer and advocate for struggling authors, she wanted a paranormal romance story, no witchcraft, occult, or devil worship.

AWOC.COM Publishing then accepted the piece in the Ozarks Writers League (OWL) annual anthology, *Echoes of the Ozarks: Volume II*. This was my first story to be accepted in someone else's anthology.

The Vision by Sherrie Shepherd

A Little Hope

Call me Gabriel if you like—you know, like the angel.

For reasons unknown, God has given me the power of telepathy. But, I can't tell anyone. How would you like to be in the presence of someone who always knew what you were thinking?

Now, I say 'God' gave me this power, but I'm uncertain. It's my faith, perhaps. Anyway, I sort of stay underground and shy away, in general, from nosy people. In the beginning, I did use my ability to earn a small fortune—a little insider trading, if you will—so I travel the country waiting to see where my future takes me.

Like now, for example. I have just pulled my travel trailer off the freeway in Clarksville, Arkansas. My dog Toto will rest while I enjoy a meal. The billboard on the interstate read: Take next exit for an 'all-you-can-eat' buffet.

The Catfish House looks like a renovated gas station. At 3:00 in the afternoon, few patronize the place, leaving me almost alone. With a plate of fish, hush puppies, and all the extras, I sit, say grace, and then dine while enjoying the surroundings.

A truck driver picks his teeth after a full meal. It's impossible for me to avoid the temptation to project my telepathic power into his mind and pull out his thoughts. He's waiting to have his rig unloaded at a warehouse down the road, after which he will travel to Fort Smith to have it reloaded and then on to Oklahoma City to spend Christmas with his family.

Across the room I see an old woman staring at her plate; melancholy emanates from her soul. Even without reading her mind I can hazard a guess. Recently widowed, she's lost all hope.

My calculations are confirmed after utilizing my faculty. Such a tragedy; we humans and our mortality.

It was cancer, of course. The big "C". She watched the hospice nurse do everything in her power to alleviate the pain. What a relief it was to her when the coroner and RN pretended not to notice at the death scene investigation that her husband self-prescribed more pain medication than required.

She knew of his plans; they had discussed it. They held one another for an hour before she closed the door and turned on Mozart. Background music might help.

"Please, leave the room," he had told her. "It is time. I love you so much."

For over fifty years they shared their loving lives…. Enough! I must stop invading her mind.

But wait, I sense another event about to unfold. She plans to join him, soon.

Surely something I say can make a difference. Stepping from my table, I cross the room toward the buffet. It will take me past her.

"Ma'am," I say. "My name's Gabriel. Don't mean to pry, but you appear sad. Is there anything I can do?"

"Oh, no thank you. That's very kind of you to ask."

"You remind me of myself when my parents died—your demeanor, I mean."

"My husband passed away a few weeks ago and…. It's been difficult."

Her twisted, arthritic fingers cling to a glass of tea; moisture dribbles onto her hand and down to the table into specks of salt lying atop the surface. Leathered, cracked skin covers her face. I can feel her many years of hard labor on a nearby farm. Yet, I sense that she never complained.

"When I saw you from my table over there," I continue, "I suspected it might be your husband. I'm so sorry. I watched my mother go through the same thing when my dad passed away. She lost her will to live and died within six months. Don't want you to do that."

"Well, you're very kind for showing concern. Thank you for asking."

I return to my table and bite into a ketchup-doused hush puppy.

The window by my booth looks out past rolling pastures toward the Ozark Mountains on the horizon.

I plan to take Highway 21 outside Clarksville up to Jasper where I will park my travel trailer along the Buffalo River. Just a few days of relaxation before heading to Big Bend National Park in Texas. An old Mexican friend, who ferries tourists across the Rio Grande, and I will share tequila.

Returning to my seat with a second plate of food, I notice that the widow continues to stare outside. I wonder what she sees, so I look into her mind.

She's conversing with him, or Him—I'm not sure yet.

I close my eyes and focus. In her psyche she's with her husband. He's sitting next to her!

Please take me with you, she thinks. *I miss you so much.*

Only He can decide that, she thinks, or is it her husband?

I'm not sure if she's talking to herself.

The waitress approaches. "Are you okay, Mrs. Michael? Can I refill your tea?"

She ignores the worker, who leaves in a hurry.

I have nothing left in this world. I'm ready to be with you for eternity.

Remember what the Bible says about husband and wife in Heaven. Our relationship will be different.

I don't believe that! Our love will be stronger.

We'll see … but when He's ready for you.

I have nothing keeping me here. The kids in California call, but it's not the same.

Her mind feels dangerously out of kilter; I fear she may go into cardiac arrest if she's not calmed.

The waitress and her boss approach; the widow never looks up. "Mrs. Michael, are you okay?"

I see the widow's eyes roll up; her head falls to the table.

"Call 911!" the supervisor demands.

As the waitress runs to the phone, her boss pulls the woman from the booth and lays her flat on the floor. He begins CPR—too late.

A translucent figure arises from the widow's body, but only I seem to notice. I assume it's her soul.

Near the window by where she sat, another image materializes. He walks right through the table and up to her. Husband and wife are together again.

They embrace and kiss.

Being with you and Him is His plan, right?

Part of it, the male spirit thinks.

They walk past the wall and into the parking lot. I can see them stop by a tree near a field.

The sound of an approaching ambulance can be heard. I throw money for the bill onto the table and walk outside, fully expecting the couple to disappear. Leashing Toto, we head toward a trail leading to a small forest of pines and a distant pond. Cattle graze on a nearby slope; the scent of honeysuckle plays with my acute senses.

The reunited pair seems to change; their images appear younger and more vibrant. Toto barks in their direction but they don't seem to notice us.

Our love and faith brought us here, he says.

They kiss and now I see them as they might have looked when first married. A happy couple with their lives before them.

What a joy it was to raise three fine children with you, she says. *They grew up so fast. I know it was hard on you when they moved away, but they took it very hard when you died. They loved you so much … you were such a great father.*

We'll all be reunited. Death is just a step.

All those years we were together, and after you passed away, I would stare at the valley from my kitchen window and let time pass, wondering about life and my future.

"Hush, Toto!" I shout, looking down at my noisy pet.

A paramedic pulls a stretcher from the ambulance and glances toward my barking dog. I wave; he then rolls the wheeled cot into the restaurant.

When I turn around I see the couple strolling through the field, hand in hand. A breeze makes the tall grass swirl like surf atop the ocean.

I want to follow, but stop. My bride of many years bubbles to the surface and I remember! The wreck, screaming, sirens. An EMT found her on the shore where the road curved along a bridge. The car had flipped several times before finally resting against a giant oak.

My head was injured, they said. After twenty years of love and one grown child, I still called her my bride.

Toto breaks free and runs toward the fading images. Just as my pet leaps, the apparitions fade and I sense an altered blotch of light ascend toward Heaven. All is peaceful—except for my yapping dog.

* * *

In the travel trailer, parked outside the restaurant, I pull a box from the closet. Photographs of Elizabeth and me at our wedding bring tears ... many tears. We often held hands and kissed many times, always before bed and at sunrise. The hurt felt like a knotted rope around my heart.

Wind brushes the curtains aside and a stream of light illuminates the inside of my home on wheels. It feels like a whisper in my ear and I imagine she's telling me all will be okay.

For years I blamed myself. The deer ran out from nowhere. In time, with the help of several specialists, I regained most of my cognitive functions but knew I could never return to work. The internal dialogues from others too often invaded my mind. Doctors said it was from the injuries, but I knew.

All hope lost.

Gabriel ... don't give up.

I close my eyes and project my thoughts, like I did when our child threw a fit and the screaming grew painful. Elizabeth's faith was weak and I imagined her in the throes of Hell.

How often I have struggled with the idea. Surely He knew of her kindness, but eternity? I cannot fathom such a vengeful Lord toward His children. With all my books on the subject, I have read many accounts and hope Hades is just an idea dreamed up by man to scare the masses. We *will* be together again ... we must!

A storm brews in the distance and a faint murmur grows behind me ... always behind, even as I turn to listen.

Two souls intertwined forever, as mates, it seems to say. *Our essence is forever.*

It's her! My Elizabeth has reached out.

But I must admit, hallucinations were difficult to distinguish from reality after the wreck. An angel once appeared on the windowsill and spoke. The doctor said it was in my mind.

As children, Elizabeth and I lived down a dirt road from one another. We'd meet halfway and play in the fields chasing cows, or swim on the creek. Our life forces were tied together as one.

"Can you hear me?" I yell.

The wind picks up and my open door slams shut. Toto begins to bark.

"I'm so sorry for what I've done." The tears feel warm against my cheeks. *There is a reason for everything.*

Was it her or just the gale increasing outside? I glance out my window.

Lightning flashes on the horizon, and I see her standing by the trail. *I am always with you.*

She waves and then her image fades.

I step outside and Toto runs past, and sniffs where she had stood. I know.

"Let's go, Toto. We're off to Jasper. I want to show you where my bride is buried."

Friendship Made in Heaven

Introduction

Friendship Made in Heaven won 2nd Place at the 2003 White County Creative Writers' Conference, Short Story contest. The requirements were, "Fiction, any genre."

The story was then accepted for publication in *The Storyteller* magazine's April/May/June 2005 issue.

Like most writers, I'm always keeping an eye out for new story ideas. While conducting a workshop for my day job at Bradley County Medical Center, in Warren, Arkansas, a maintenance employee helped me locate the conference room where I would give the presentation. When he learned I like to spin yarns, he told me about a local event that many called a miracle. Using his story and my embellishments, I created the following tale. I apologize for not remembering his name, but he was a character.

Friendship Made In Heaven

Darn, it's hot, Stan thought.

He unloaded his laptop, projector, and boxes of paperwork from the state car and used a dolly to roll the works of his trade into the Bradley County Hospital.

The sultry summer day caused sweat to cling to his suit. As liaison for Vital Records within the Department of Health, he traveled the state and conducted workshops with employees responsible for the completion of birth and death certificates. For several weeks he had made phone calls and sent e-mails and faxes to set up the training session.

"It's burning up," he said to a stranger holding the door as he wheeled his handouts and computer through the narrow passageway.

"That it is. Can I help you?"

"I'm looking for the conference room."

"Follow me."

Stan noticed the dark green jumpsuit of the gentleman and thinning gray hair. His attire and facial features reminded Stan of his grandfather years earlier.

The small hospital was getting a face-lift and construction equipment lay scattered along the hall.

"My name's Ray—I'm in charge of maintenance."

"Stan Beckman."

The two exchanged handshakes. After Stan explained his workshop, Ray said, "You must have an interesting outlook on life ... having to deal with death and all."

"We receive about a hundred death certificates a day ... you can't sit there and think too much about it or it gets to you. I'm also a writer in my spare time. So I get good ideas from this job."

"A writer, huh? Well, I have to tell you about the miracle that happened around here."

"A miracle? Please forgive me if I'm skeptical. What happened?"

"I need to help move some things for a patient who recently passed away.

I'll come back and then we can talk. How's that?"

"Sounds good. My presentation won't start for an hour."

"See you in twenty minutes."

The training room was just large enough to allow walking space around a conference table. Windows looked onto a courtyard surrounded by the hospital. Several patients sat under an awning and smoked as kids who looked to be in high school mowed.

Stan turned his attention to the room and made a few seating adjustments. He then prepared his laptop and projector and placed handouts on a counter against the wall. Ray was running late so he decided to dally in the hallway.

"Excuse me, young man," he heard while passing a patient's room. "Can you help me sit up?"

Stan stepped to the doorway and smiled at the elderly lady on the bed inside. Dark veins ran throughout her loose wrinkled skin and gray hair pressed against her head where she had lain on it.

"Sure." Gently placing one palm behind her back, he used the other arm to tug her up by pulling her hand. She slowly moved her legs until they dangled over the bed.

"Thank you. I've been that way too long—gonna get bedsores, you know?"

Before he could reply he heard a noise behind him. He turned and saw another elderly patient enter the room dressed in bedclothes. Stooped with osteoporosis, she moved slowly with a walker.

The woman Stan had assisted spoke, "It's about time you got here, Lucille."

"Oh, hush. Don't you go giving me a hard time, *Mrs.* Turner."

"Well, I've been waiting for you for days now ... maybe months."

"I got here as fast as I could. You just shush."

Stan stepped back and watched as the two hugged.

"She didn't give you a hard time, did she son?" Lucille asked.

"No ma'am," Stan said. "I was just helping her sit up in bed."

Lucille looked back to her friend. "Are you ready?"

"I've dreamed of this day all my life."

Stan waited for them to struggle their way into the hall. He smiled as they poked along and disappeared around the corner.

"There you are," Ray said from the conference room down the corridor. "Did you find everything you need?"

"Yes, sir."

After the two men sipped water from a fountain in the hallway, they relaxed in executive-like chairs encircling the conference table.

"So, you get a lot of good ideas as a writer from your job?" Ray asked.

Photo by Carolyn Boyles

"Sometimes ... especially from coroners. I always pick their brains for a good mystery."

"Let me tell you what happened here a few years ago." Ray straightened up in his seat and rested his elbows on the table as he leaned over. "There were these friends who were born and raised here in Bradley County on farms near one another. Their families attended the same church and the two girls became friends in Sunday School."

Ray paused until a page over the intercom ended. "To make a long story short, the two girls remained best friends for eighty years. Did everything together, I heard. When they married, their husbands became good friends. Anyway, years flew by and the ladies were widowed. I guess their friendship helped them survive their husbands' deaths. In her mid-seventies, Martha had a stroke and was in and out of the hospital. Her friend nursed her back to health.

"Then their luck reversed and Lucille's health went downhill and her children put her in a skilled living center. As the years went by, they saw each other every day. Like clockwork you could find them in the gardens together at noon down at the nursing home. Then Martha had another stroke and no one expected her to live much longer.

"Here's the miracle I told you about. The night Martha died in this hospital, her family was by her side. No one knew Lucille's health had also taken a sudden change for the worse. When her son called Lucille to tell of Martha's death, a nurse answered the phone. They found out that Lucille had also just died. Friends all those years and they died at the same time. Check the paperwork, it's documented."

"Wow, that is very interesting!" Stan said. He then glanced at the hallway and remembered the two old ladies. "What was Martha's last name?"

"Turner."

Stan's heart skipped a beat and an eerie feeling wrapped around him. He stood and walked to the entranceway. Down the hall he saw the room where he had assisted the elderly woman out of bed a few minutes ago.

"You won't believe this," he said. "I just met a woman named Mrs. Turner and her friend Lucille in that room over there."

Ray smiled. "I believe you. And you wouldn't be the first. Of course, it's been several years since their deaths."

"I'm serious. These ladies were alive—I saw them!"

"Follow me."

The two walked to the room and Stan gasped when he saw a chapel with a cross on the wall above a podium supporting an open Bible.

"No, no, no," Stan said. He rubbed his hand through his hair. "There was a bed over there. Both ladies were in here."

"The hospital moved the chapel here a few years ago when the families of the ladies paid to have the room dedicated to their memories." Ray pointed to a plaque fixed to the wall.

It read, "In Loving Memory to Martha Turner and Lucille Jones."

Stan's perceptions of reality were boarding on chaos. "This is all a joke, isn't it?"

Ray smiled at the confused look on Stan's face. "I'm a good Christian," Ray said. "I believe the Lord has made a miracle here."

"I saw those ladies!"

Stan hurried to a side exit and sat on a ledge outside. He needed fresh air. Ray gave him a few minutes and then followed.

"I hallucinated," Stan said. "That's what I did."

Ray pulled a faded newspaper clipping from his billfold. "Did they look like this?"

"That's impossible!"

"Stan. I've never experienced it myself. But I know others who have."

"They saw the two women?"

Clinching his fingers tightly and breathing hard, Stan kept turning his head back and forth in deep thought, trying to make sense of it all.

Ray placed his hand on Stan's shoulder. "The apostle Paul interpreted his sign one way and did great things with it. Others interpret their vision differently and end up in mental health facilities. This is good, Stan. See it for what it is."

Squinting his eyes, Stan noticed two figures on the far side of the parking lot, watered like a mirage in bright sunlight. Then they disappeared as if over a horizon; in his heart he knew it was the two friends.

Stan stood to tell Ray. "I think you're right. A miracle did take place here...."

Only then did he realize Ray had vanished. A man in a hospital uniform carrying a toolbox walked out the glass door.

"Pardon me," Stan said. "Did you see Ray walk by? I think he's head of maintenance."

"No sir, that's me. I'm head of maintenance. We don't have a Ray that works here. Used to a few years ago, but he died."

24   Yesterday Once More

Mysteries

Last Supper

Introduction

Like many writers, I have a sick sense of humor. I wrote *Last Supper* in my mind during communion at a former church I attended in 2005. A critique group I had been a member of for over five years helped me edit the piece and offered insight into the surprise ending.

Last Supper won an Honorable Mention in the July/August 2005 issue of *ByLine* magazine for the New-Talent Short Story contest, an open genre category. There were 112 entries nationwide, with the top three winners from Virginia, Arizona, and California.

After entering the story unsuccessfully in a few other contests, it was accepted for publication in 2007 by *Amazon.com Shorts* under their mystery category. You can download authors' writings there for 49 cents. Daniel Slater, director for *Amazon.com Shorts*, said in my acceptance letter, "Great story, thanks for the submission. Happy to accept it."

Last Supper

DISPATCH: "Hey, Spradlin. Just got a 911 that people are running from the Resurrection Church over on the corner of Second Street."

SPRADLIN: "I'll check it out."

* * *

Turning onto Second, Officer Spradlin saw frantic men and women in suits and dresses scurrying about. Several people appeared to be assisting others lying motionless on the ground.

As he pulled into the church parking lot, the officer witnessed a woman comforting a crying girl in the shade of nearby pines.

A man ran toward him. Spradlin rolled down his window.

"Officer! Somethin' terrible happened. We need medical help."

Tilting his head sideways, Spradlin reached up and pushed a button on the radio microphone attached to his collar. "Kevin ... we need an additional ambulance, pronto."

"Roger," the dispatcher replied.

In a yard beside the church, the officer saw a woman in a black dress lying on the ground. She wasn't moving and another female knelt alongside her, weeping.

Jumping from his patrol car, Spradlin followed the man to the main entrance and into the foyer. Hysterical cries echoed from the worship chamber.

"This way, officer."

Spradlin stood at the threshold leading into the sanctuary. Nothing had prepared him for this, not even his tour of duty in Iraq.

Lying in the aisle and between pews were maybe forty to fifty bodies. Vomit splattered the floor; air hung heavy with a sour stench.

"What the hell happened?"

"We don't know … we just don't know."

"Is there a gas leak?"

"No, sir, I don't believe so. The children and adults with them are all okay. I was in the nursery and heard screaming. When I ran into the hallway, those two women there," he pointed, "were grabbing their throats and spitting up. They had just crawled from the worship hall."

Speaking into his radio, Spradlin said, "Kevin, I need *all* available officers and ambulances. We have a freakin' Jonestown massacre down here!"

* * *

Detective Kelsey liked to wear the tan, waterproofed trench coat in the cool fall weather; gave him that Columbo look. Peter Falk had been his favorite actor for years and many family and friends said they looked much alike.

"Sixty-two," Carson told Kelsey, slapping the daily paper onto his desk. "The latest died overnight at Crittenden Memorial. Two others at Baptist Hospital in Forrest City are doubtful. Please tell me you have something, anything, for me to satisfy the newshounds."

Kelsey admired the trophies in Carson's display cabinet, then strolled along the back of the State Police Director's office. He pulled out a pack of cigarettes and thumped it against the back of his hand.

"Put those away," Carson demanded. "This facility is smoke-free. You know that."

"I know, just like to predict what I can get away with."

"Save your *experiments* for the bad guys. Look, surely this was not some mass suicide. What happened?"

Running his fingers through his thinning, gray hair, Kelsey said, "We know the preacher is dead, and all the deacons—except for Meyer, who was 'out sick' that day. His wife and teenage son are two of the dead. Several members of the church told me that Meyer often helped prepare the grape juice for the communion ceremony. Are you familiar with the ritual at their church?"

"I think so. Except in our church the congregation shares one chalice. We don't all have our own tiny containers and drink at the same time after a prayer."

"Tricky rite, don't you think? Transubstantiation, I think they call it. Or consubstantiation. The doctrine that, in the Eucharist, substances of bread and wine are changed into the body and blood of Christ. Remarkable history on the subject and causes a lot of bickering between the different churches—some deadly."

"I'm sure the press will love the police director giving them a theology lesson. Stay focused. Do you have anything on who might have done this?"

"I have no doubt the tox results will show poison mixed into the grape juice is what killed everyone."

"And you think maybe Meyer had a hand?" Carson asked.

"There's talk he and his wife had trouble. He was responsible for purchasing the grape juice … although it's unclear who might have placed poison into the containers. Nevertheless, I believe that we will find this an open-and-shut case."

"There's a media circus out there, and the governor wants a quick arrest. If the case is 'open-and-shut,' then get on it."

"I've already made plans to follow up with Paul Meyer."

Depravity Cost by Lance Waters

Kelsey pulled his Oldsmobile into Meyer's driveway. The mileage reimbursement helped pay for the old clunker, or at least for its maintenance. The unsteady state of the vehicle often led his interviewees to a less than favorable opinion of the detective. This misconception was part of Kelsey's facade.

Taking his time and looking about, he approached the front door and knocked. Introductions were made and he was allowed in.

The house overlooked the St. Francis River below Crowley's Ridge. Inside, through a large window, Kelsey admired the narrow tree-covered channel.

"I'm sorry about your loss, Mr. Meyer."

He turned and walked toward the couch where Meyer sat. Kelsey held a framed family photo. "I'm known for being blunt," Kelsey continued. "Most people like that about me—or so I'm told. We have over sixty deaths, all apparent homicides, and you responsible for buying the grape juice used in communion—"

"This had better not be going where I think it is! My family's dead. Those cops already got a court order and ransacked my house. It took me all evening to clean up their mess."

"I feel for you, but I have statements reporting an affair between your wife and the preacher."

"You should talk with Reverend Nixon's wife, then. She had the same access to the refrigerator. Don't you find it interesting that her 'allergies' prevented her from drinking the juice?"

"But you arrived that morning and poured the grape juice yourself. Then suddenly went home sick."

"Food poisoning."

"Of course. I read the report."

Kelsey replaced the picture atop the mantle, returned to the window, and watched a small boat work its way up river. An old black man could be seen fishing from the bank on the opposite side. "You may want to consult your attorney, Mr. Meyer."

"But I didn't do anything!"

"Threatening e-mails were found on your computer, Mr. Meyer. Did you not tell Reverend Nixon to stay away or else?"

"What man doesn't try to protect his wife?"

"But she was a willing participant."

Meyer suddenly stood. "You must leave! Any further questions should be addressed to my attorney."

"What did you mean in your e-mail…" Kelsey took out a piece of paper, "…'I'll expose you to the world for all your lies'?"

"Nixon was a charlatan, a fake. His last church forced him out for mishandling funds. I wanted to audit our books but he resisted. He knew I knew. And he increasingly made references to the end of the world. All he did was spread fear."

"Reverend Nixon had no criminal record. Perhaps you should have found another church."

"Yes, I can see you know very little about church politics. We like to take care of these 'events' ourselves, and discreetly."

"How convenient. Nevertheless, adultery is a sin, is it not? You might be surprised how strong a motivator for revenge it is. I'm sure you have a biblical quote from scripture on the subject."

"You rotten little … look, he had affairs with several wives! The deacons were the only ones who knew."

"Coincidentally, all the other deacons are now deceased."

"I'm the only one who had the gall to stand up to him."

"You had breakfast with him that morning."

"We have a prayer breakfast sometimes before Sunday service. I'm sure this is where I got food poisoning. I went home right after…."

"After you prepared the grape juice."

"Get out!"

* * *

Six months later, Kelsey's wife put down her Stephen King novel and watched her husband hang his coat in the closet, then undress and prepare for bed.

"I missed the evening news. Did they find a verdict?"

"Guilty … it was open-and-shut."

"Well, then. I look forward to reading the Gazette tomorrow." She smiled and reached for his hand. "Come here and kiss me, my famous hero."

The next morning, the paper read:

Record mass homicide in U.S. history

Local church deacon leaves a trail of clues
By Gage Spencer

Marianna, AR—A string of clues led to the conviction yesterday of Paul Meyer for capital murder in what officials are calling the worst mass homicide in U.S. history outside the Oklahoma City Bombing and 9/11. The jury strongly recommended the death penalty and experts agree it will most likely occur in this case. Even the governor, who is on record as being against capital punishment, has openly expressed the opinion that execution is appropriate.

According to the prosecuting attorney, Kevin Mann, cyanide was found in the communion drinks and linked to Paul Meyer through Internet usage. The motive appears to be revenge after several affairs and possible stolen church money came to light.

Paul Meyer claimed Reverend Nixon was misappropriating funds and carried on sexual relationships with church members. Mrs. Nixon said this was false. "He was a faith-

ful husband," she said. "Paul Meyer had access to the church's bank account also. He's covering for himself."
Detective Kelsey with the State Police said….

"Good morning."

Stirring the cream into her coffee, Mrs. Kelsey looked up at her husband as he entered the kitchen. "Good morning. I was just reading the paper. All those broken families … maybe the survivors can rest now that justice is served."

"Yeah … and Paul Meyer became a grandparent during the trial. His oldest son from a previous marriage will be in debt for years helping to pay for his dad's defense. Damn lawyers cost a fortune. I bet Paul gets the death penalty."

"Why would someone do such a dreadful act? Child abuse … heredity?"

"I'm sure some of it's upbringing, but I'm also of the opinion that there is a bad sequence of DNA, and no matter how good the parents are, that child will turn out evil."

"I'm proud of you. Your investigation helped bring a killer to justice."

"Well, there wasn't much to it; Paul Meyer wasn't very smart. The trail led straight to him. I think he wanted to get caught."

* * *

"Mr. Kelsey, you have a phone call."

Entering his corner office and removing his tan coat, Kelsey told his receptionist, "Okay, send it through."

On the second ring he answered. "Detective Kelsey."

"Detective, this is Dan Pace. It's been a few years since we last talked."

"Yes, Paul Meyer's attorney."

"Paul's son, Larry, and I would like to meet with you. Mr. Meyer is flying into Memphis from Stanford tomorrow and we can drive over."

"I don't see why—"

"We have something we would like you to see."

The next day, at Pace's request, Kelsey arranged to have a computer and large monitor set up. He placed the equipment on a stand in front of a worn, leather couch. Kelsey stood as the attorney and his former client's son sat.

"Larry," the detective said. "I'm sorry about your dad, but I was only doing my job. A jury found him guilty."

"I understand, but I told everyone all along that my dad was innocent." He began to tear up. "And now I have the proof."

"But he was executed six months ago; how could something surface now?

I was very thorough in my investigation."

Larry's head fell into his hands and he sobbed.

Pace handed Kelsey the DVD. "Play this."

The detective slid the disk into the CPU and the monitor displayed a picture seconds later. The scene jiggled as the person holding a video camera walked about.

"That's the kitchen at the church," Kelsey remarked.

"Keep watching."

A hand reached out into the frame and yanked open a refrigerator door and grabbed a large plastic container of grape juice. The screen faded and then popped back on. The camera had been placed so that it pointed toward the juice sitting on a counter. Aging hands slid into the picture holding a brown bottle, and the sounds of someone whistling led the detective to turn up the volume. The safety cap was twisted off and contents poured into the juice.

"This could have been made at any time—"

"Keep watching," the attorney said.

The next scene showed a plate of eggs, sausage, biscuits and gravy wrapped inside plastic. A single piece of tape stuck to the outside read, "Paul Meyer's Plate."

A voice boomed through the speakers and Kelsey quickly turned the volume down. Whoever was holding the camera said, "Paul should really enjoy his breakfast this morning. He and the rest of the deacons should be here in about thirty minutes."

"I don't like this," Kelsey said. "Explain—"

"Keep watching!"

The screen went blank. The next shot was in Reverend Nixon's office. He sat at his desk and the camera was placed on something stationary directly in front.

"Thank you, *Paul*, for helping me fill all the containers with grape juice before services this morning."

An eerie laugh sent chills up Kelsey's spine.

"If my plans worked, then Paul's son should be getting this DVD after his father's execution. That's right, this is a confession! I poured the poison into the communion containers. And you probably want to know why? Because I'm not who I appear to be, and Paul found out. He knew about the money and my past. He knew about my affairs—including with your step mom, Larry—and he was planning to expose it all. How foolish it was of him to tell me before going to the church's elders or local police! To hell with you all! The world *will* remember me."

The screen suddenly went dark and the room filled with silence, except for Larry's sobs.

Kelsey finally responded. "But how...?"

Dan Pace answered. "The reverend sent the disk in a package to an attorney out West the same morning, after the videotaping. Nixon had his last will and testament set up so that the package was a gift to Larry—not to be disclosed until he graduated college."

Kelsey looked at Larry, but words were lost. The young man continued to wipe tears from his face.

Finally, Larry replied. "You know the worst part? I spent thousands of dollars trying to save my dad, and I had the evidence to free him all along. I dropped out of school to work full time on his defense, all through the appeals process. Had I been able to stay in school I would have graduated before his execution. It's my fault!"

Awaiting Manner of Death

Introduction

Awaiting Manner of Death won 1st Place in the 2007 Arkansas Writers' Conference's Grif Stockley Award. The criteria required, "Story about a true crime which does not have to have been solved or brought to trial."

Popular Little Rock author Grif Stockley sponsors this contest. He is known as a tough editor and rarely hands out prizes if he feels the stories need work. For this reason I consider the award one of my most cherished to date.

Although it's unknown how many entries were in this competition, Stockley gave only a first and second place prize. I'm proud to say that my fellow writing friend, award-winning author Del Garrett, won 2nd Place.

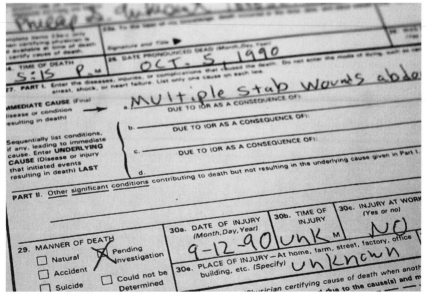

Photo by Stewart Matthews

Awaiting Manner of Death

Because the event that follows is an on-going investigation, I have disguised my identity, location, and details, to prevent compromising the case. For the purpose here, we will call me a County Coroner.

Like many coroners in Mississippi, I am a full-time funeral director. In 2006 I took over the low paying job when the previous coroner stepped down and county voters elected me. My forensic expertise is limited to what I can learn from the State Medical Examiner. In Mississippi, anyone can become coroner if he or she is elected. With no financial incentive, what doctor desires to get out of bed at 3:00 a.m. to pronounce a residential or nursing home death?

This is why most coroners are funeral directors, EMT, or, yes, even auto mechanics. The real expertise lies with the four Medical Examiners in Jackson, who will advise us if we call. Difficult death scenes are referred to the M.E. who takes over the case to complete necessary autopsies and other investigations into the cause and manner of death.

So it was with interest when I received a call in February 2007 from the Mississippi Department of Health, Vital Records.

"We need your help," the Field Rep said.

"How's that?"

"Your predecessor, before he decided not to run for coroner again, was trying to help us get a 1990 death ruled upon. It's still pending."

"Pending! 1990?"

"Right … paperwork fell through the cracks and I found the death certificate recently in a folder; still pending."

"Why didn't Pat unpend it or rule the death Could Not Be Determined?"

"Let me give you the details," the Field Rep said. "Item 23, the Cause of Death, says, 'Multiple knife wounds to abdomen and chest.' Item 26, Manner of Death, has Pending checked. It was signed by the emergency room doctor—"

"Was the coroner notified back in 1990?" I asked.

"The death certificate says yes, but it's typed in—probably by the funeral director. All medical cause of death information is handwritten by the doctor, except for item 35 where it asks if the coroner was notified. This is typed and looks like the same typewriter as the deceased's personal information at the top of the DC. I think the funeral director keyed it in."

"Did anyone ask the coroner at the time if he was notified?"

"That was three coroners ago, no one knows. I've only been here seven years, so the death took place almost ten years before I became Field Rep for Vital Records."

"How am I going to investigate?"

"Pat didn't help me much on this case, but before he stepped down as coroner, he said the Bolivar County Sheriff seemed secretive about releasing details to him."

"I'm Coahoma County Coroner, why would Bolivar officials be involved?"

"Pat told me the stabbing happened along the Bolivar County border and the victim was brought over to the hospital in your county where he died as an inpatient."

"Why did the ER doctor sign the death certificate for a possible homicide? This should have gone through the coroner and to Mississippi's Medical Examiner."

"I agree, which is why this is an interesting case. It appears the ER doc came up to pronounce because the attending was not there. I'm looking forward to seeing what you find."

"Thanks."

I'm a little disappointed that this case is not closed. Obviously there are questions that need to be answered. Did the dead guy accidentally stab himself or try to commit suicide? I've heard of slashing one's wrist, but with a knife to the stomach and chest? But 'multiple' times? Red flags are waving all over this event.

In a file cabinet I found the folder with paperwork Vital Records had faxed to the previous coroner, Pat. It included a copy of the death certificate with handwritten notes. At least Pat made an attempt to investigate.

Dr. Kelly, the emergency room doctor who signed the DC, still worked part time at the hospital. I stopped by to visit him. All he could tell me was that yes, he signed the certificate, but figured that since the form stated the coroner had been notified, the coroner would rule on the manner of death.

"Why did you sign it, then?" I asked.

"Funeral director pressured me—said they needed a copy of the certificate or the crematory wouldn't cremate."

I looked at the form again and hadn't noticed that item 20a on the DC showed the deceased was cremated on October 16, 1990.

What the hell, I thought. It's against the law to cremate a pending manner of death unless the coroner or Medical Examiner gives a letter of approval. The DC did say the coroner back in 1990 was notified, so maybe he had been. I could find no record, however.

I looked at the dates again and saw where the ER doctor signed on October 8, 1990. Why did it take the funeral home eight days to cremate?

Dr. Kelly was of little help; obviously he had scant training in medical school on how to fill out a death certificate.

Next, I contacted the Bolivar County Sheriff's office. The clerical girl there remembered my predecessor calling, but said files going back seventeen years were unavailable. She was unable to assist.

Hospital medical records were of little use as well. Surely the deceased did not stab himself! The interval between onset and death stated "23 days." Could he have stabbed himself accidentally three weeks before he came to the ER, and slowly died over that period of time?

Or did someone knife him and hold him hostage before he escaped? So many unanswered questions.

The same funeral home owned the crematory where final disposition occurred. Surely they would have questioned the facts before cremating. And why did the funeral home hold the body so long? Cremations usually take place within two days after death. Otherwise, family members must pay to have the body embalmed as well as storage costs.

I'm starting to think the victim accidentally stabbed himself and waited three weeks before going to the hospital. Seems stupid, but dumber things have happened.

Yet why am I having so much trouble getting details? Perhaps I've watched too many movies with cover-up themes.

When I call the funeral home, the director explains that he will search his old files, but the parlor burned four years ago, destroying many records from decades of services. I remember that now, and we are both skeptical any paperwork survived.

A few days later the Field Rep called for an update. I said, "Bolivar County Sheriff's office found a former deputy who remembers the case. They're trying to contact him now."

"If you're unable to rule on this manner of death, I could contact the CEO at the hospital and make him responsible. State law mandates that the administrator in charge of the facility is responsible to get the death certificate complete. His doctor screwed up accepting the certificate, so maybe the hospital attorneys will get involved. It's an idea."

"Give me a little more time. I'll talk this over with Dr. Estes, the Chief

Medical Examiner. See what he suggests. We may ask the Attorney General to get involved."

That state employee for Vital Records is okay, but he can be pushy at times. Of course I realize he's only doing his job.

A coroner in another county told me that the Director of Vital Records threatened him with handing a case over to the prosecuting attorney if the coroner did not rule on a two year old pending death certificate.

I know this coroner and how unorganized he is. Two years is a long time when the state average for ruling on pending causes and manners of deaths is now at three months. Ever since the state legislature pumped more money into the state Medical Examiner's office, investigators are able to complete autopsies and other tests in record time. This is good news for families who don't have to wait a year or longer anymore, as they used to.

Insurance companies often won't pay until they know the medical information related to death, and this can be detrimental to many families if that's the only income they'll have.

Last month I ruled a gunshot wound to head as a suicide. Everyone agreed, including the sheriff's office, that the man intentionally shot himself. The surviving spouse is raising hell and called our local Senator. She's claiming it was an accidental shooting.

No doubt that either her insurance states beneficiaries lose benefits if the manner of death is a suicide, or she has a double indemnity policy where she gets paid twice as much for an accidental death. Now the legislator is trying to get the Health Department director to see about getting my ruling overturned. Good luck, without a court order. And I'm not changing it.

No one said my job was easy.

Yesterday I had to pronounce two hospice deaths at home, and the day before I worked a motor vehicle crash on Highway 1. Tractor-trailer versus minivan—wasn't a pretty sight.

It's like damn if you do, damn if you don't. Government wants me to report all the HIV and AIDS cases along with other related causes of deaths such as alcoholism or drug uses. Families beg me to leave it off, give the deceased one last note of decency. I do the best I can.

Now I'm stuck dealing with a case that occurred seventeen years before I took office. I may just wash my hands and tell Vital Records it's up to them. How in the hell could the officials at the time let this one slip by?

Pending Death

Introduction

Pending Death was published in the July/August/September 2006 issue of *The Storyteller* magazine. I fictionalized elements from the previous story, *Awaiting Manner of Death*, to write this tale. Regina Williams, the magazine's editor, wrote on my acceptance letter, "Good Story!"

Authors are often told, "Write what you know (and read)." As Field Representative for Arkansas' Vital Records Section, I work with coroners, hospice nurses, funeral directors, medical examiners, midwives and others who are responsible for filing birth and death certificates. This area is rich with new plot material, as the current story will demonstrate. I mention that so if you have aspirations to become a writer, I hope you learn from my examples to help you succeed. When you are interviewed on C-SPAN or Oprah, reference my name.

Pending Death

"Here, check this pending death certificate. I think the doctor who signed it is now dead. See if you can get the coroner to rule on the cause and manner of death."

Dwight Pierce took the document from his supervisor and scanned the date and county of death. "It's fifteen years old! That coroner is no longer in office in Sebastian County … can the current coroner rule on the manner and cause of death?"

"Sure. He's elected; he can rule on it. I don't care how old it is."

"How did this DC stay pending all these years? You'd think someone, a family member, would have complained. Insurance usually won't pay on a pending case until after the investigation."

"Fell through the cracks, I guess. I found the folder in the back of my desk drawer. See if you can get it fixed. Try the state's Chief Medical Examiner if the County Coroner won't cooperate."

* * *

Several weeks lapsed; Pierce sat at his desk within the State Health Department. Troubleshooting was his main task. Funeral directors called him when they couldn't get a death certificate signed by a doctor. With a hundred deaths daily, scattered around the seventy-five counties of Arkansas, he never knew what new crisis would crop up.

Alex Curruth, Sebastian County Coroner, had agreed to review the pending death certificate for a George Brotherton.

Since Pierce had not heard back, he called the coroner. "What did you find out about that death certificate?"

"Brotherton died in the ER at Sebastian Memorial Hospital. I had the records faxed to me after they were retrieved from off-site storage. The director of medical records was not happy having to send someone to get them. This is a strange case."

"How so?"

"Brotherton was stabbed by someone who has remained nameless. I'm told he talked to a nurse who took notes, but her information has vanished. My predecessor was aware of this case, apparently. Before he passed away and I was appointed the new coroner. But I can't find his notes anywhere. The ER doctor who signed the DC pending committed suicide six months later."

Pierce sighed. "Can Brotherton have a 'Could Not Be Determined' manner of death from stab wounds? We know it can't be 'Natural.'"

"Afraid so … if we can't prove 'Accident,' 'Homicide,' or 'Suicide.' I'll ask around. There are a few names on the faxes I have."

The next day Pierce walked into his office with a hot cup of coffee. His mind was preoccupied with a hangover when the phone rang.

"Hi, Curruth," he said.

"Hey, buddy," the coroner replied. "I'm not going to be able to help on that DC of yours."

Curruth's tone took Pierce by surprise. And 'buddy'? They had talked often over the past few years. The coroner never referred to him as buddy. "Is everything okay?"

"Yeah … yeah. It's just out of my hands."

"Should I call the state's Chief Medical Examiner? Maybe he'll rule on it."

"I don't care, okay! Just leave me out of it."

When they hung up, Pierce scanned the death certificate again. George Brotherton seemed unimpressive, like an invisible man at first glance. Education showed he dropped out at the tenth grade. Pierce printed out Brotherton's birth certificate from the vital record's file. No father was listed, although the death certificate had a James Tedford listed as dad. Mom had been unmarried at her son's birth.

James Tedford … James Tedford, he thought. *Why does this name sound familiar?*

He typed in the name and retrieved a fourteen-year-old death certificate for the father. "Gunshot Wound to Head" and "Homicide" were listed as the cause and manner of death.

Does everyone connected to Brotherton die?

Glancing at the occupation block, Pierce noticed that Tedford had been a State Senator. He Googled the name on the Internet and found stories of corruption never proven, and investigations that ended when Tedford died.

Pierce also searched for the mom, and found she, too, died in a strange drowning soon after her son's funeral. Although Tedford was listed as father on Brotherton's death certificate, no public document connected the three.

As he stood to refill his coffee, the phone rang. "Vital Records."

Someone on the other end took deep breaths but remained quiet before asking, "Pierce?"

"Yes."

The phone went dead. "Oookay," Pierce thought out loud.

* * *

"What's the status of that Brotherton's pending death certificate?"

Pierce wiped his hand down his face, took a sip of coffee, then told his supervisor, "The coroner won't touch it, and the Medical Examiner's office wants nothing to do with it, either. Brotherton's father was a State Senator.... Should I call the County Judge or District Attorney?"

"Sure. Keep me updated—gotta go. I have a customer with a complaint."

Before he could look up the number to call, his phone rang. "Vital Records, this is Pierce."

"Pierce, this is Governor Vance. I'm getting complaints that you are overstepping your authority and investigating an old death?"

Recognizing the governor's voice, Pierce said, "No, Sir. We have a pending death certificate and I'm just trying to get it completed."

"Leave that to the experts."

"But no one wants to touch the case."

"Then let it lie until they do."

"It's been fifteen years."

The dial tone sounded like bees swirling around his head after the caller slammed the phone down. Pierce later relayed the story to his boss.

"The governor wouldn't call you directly; he'd have an assistant call, or contact me. Don't worry about it."

"You still want me to follow up?"

"Yes. And tell the judge or DA about the call."

That afternoon Pierce ran into the former State Registrar of Vital Records. "Do you remember a pending death certificate for George Brotherton?"

"Are you kidding? I've been gone for ten years, and we got over 28,000 certificates each year."

After explaining the situation, the former Registrar replied, "Now wait a minute … I think I do recall that one. It had remained pending for a few years before I resigned to start my current job. I had Lisa Brooks, your predecessor then, investigate. We couldn't get the County Coroner, nor the Medical Examiner's office, to do anything. I think Lisa was working on it when I left the job."

Pierce returned to his desk and stared at the folder that contained

Brotherton's file. With dry lips and racing heart, he contemplated the call to the local Sebastian County officials. Would the DA investigate? And was that the governor or not? Sounded like his voice.

For his entire life he had prided himself that he would do the right thing. Weasels who didn't testify against criminals frustrated him. It was their civic duty!

After talking with the secretary for the Sebastian County DA, he faxed them a copy of the pending death certificate and said the coroner had some medical records that might help.

The DA seemed receptive, but the events of the case continued to play in his mind. Turning on the Internet, he Googled the DA's name and the governor's.

Horrified, he read that the two men campaigned together years ago when the current governor was the DA for Sebastian County. *I never knew...?*

"Shit, shit, shit," he whispered.

An eerie feeling crept over him and he typed his predecessor's name, Lisa Brooks, into his Vital Records' database.

A scanned image of her death certificate flashed on the screen.

Cause of death said, "Overdose of Prescription Drugs."

Manner read, "Could Not Be Determined."

Pierce pushed away from his desk and stared at the image on the screen. The case had been referred to the Medical Examiner's office. The M.D. who signed it was no longer employed by the state.

* * *

The sun shone hot on the cloudless Arkansas day. Donna McKenzie walked into her new job with a grin from ear to ear. The sign outside that pointed toward a glass door read, "Birth Records & Death Records."

"Welcome," her supervisor said. "Let me show you to your desk. Once you get settled, I'll introduce you to everyone. Then we can get down to business. I have one special project for you. Your predecessor had been working on it before.... Well, I'll tell you about it later. I have his folder of notes."

What Happened to Youth Missing in 1982?

Introduction

<u>Note</u>: This newspaper article was originally published in the *Sherwood Voice* on April 10, 2003, and is reprinted here with their permission.

The clip could be included in the nonfiction part of the book, but the mysterious nature of events lent itself to this section. What I learned from writing this piece is that I probably will never want to be an investigative journalist. It's not easy calling law enforcement agencies to discuss issues they'd prefer you didn't, or talk with a parent about his or her child's death. I gained a lot of respect for these reporters, such as Arkansas' award-winning journalist Mara Leveritt. She's been inspirational in my career, and I'm glad we have her.

In 2003, the former *Sherwood Voice* editor Warren Watkins asked me to follow up on the mysterious death of Mike Haynie from twenty years earlier. Here is the article.

What Happened to Youth Missing in 1982?

Twenty years ago last January, a hiker stumbled across a skeleton in a remote area of Saline County, Arkansas. The bones were all that remained of Michael Wayne Haynie of Sherwood, 5-9, 145 pounds, with fair complexion, blue eyes, and black hair, who had disappeared 10 months earlier. His death remains unsolved.

On March 2, 1982, wearing blue jeans, a beige pullover T-shirt and tennis shoes, Haynie disappeared after leaving for work at the North Little Rock Ramada Inn. The same day, an employee of the state Game and Fish Commission saw Haynie's intact green Chevrolet Monte Carlo on Hwy. 9 in northwest Saline County, 50 miles from Haynie's home, but did not report it until the next day.

When police found the car, it was behind a pile of gravel 200 feet from its previous location and had been vandalized. The state crime lab discovered specks of blood on the windshield, although it was not enough to determine at the time if it was Haynie's blood type. The keys were still in the car and there was no trace of forced entry or a struggle.

For the next ten months family and friends had to wait for clues to turn up. Haynie's parents reported no ransom demands and no response to a $3,000 reward they offered for any information leading to their son's safe return.

Then on January 13, 1983, a hiker found the skeletal remains. According to Saline County Sheriff James Steed, the remains were discovered three miles from Haynie's car. A 20-gauge shotgun belonging to Haynie lay at the scene. The skeleton was taken to the state crime lab.

The funeral on Tuesday, Jan. 25, 1983, was an extremely emotional time for everyone, according to Patrick Haynie, the boy's father, who now lives in south Arkansas.

Later, the state crime lab medical examiner, Dr. Fahmy Malak, ruled the manner and cause of death as undetermined, indicating he was unable to conclude whether the death was an accident, suicide, or homicide. Patrick

Haynie remained dissatisfied with the ruling, and stated his son would never commit suicide.

Why his son traveled to the remote area of Saline County was never clear, although Patrick Haynie said his son had hunted turkey in the vicinity before.

Sherwood alderman Keith Rankin was in the same class with Mike Haynie at Sylvan Hills High School. "He kept quiet and was not a trouble maker," Rankin said. "He never bothered anybody and was a good guy." Rankin did not believe Haynie's death was a suicide.

Since the remains were found near the Perry, Pulaski, and Saline County line, confusion existed during the investigation among law enforcement over jurisdiction. Calls to the sheriff's office and the State Police proved no documentation remained.

The Sherwood Police kept the file opened after the remains were found, according to Patrick Haynie. Lt. Mike Payne with the Sherwood Police said what probably occurred was that the death was ruled undetermined at the time, and since no physical evidence existed to move the investigation forward, the case became inactive. This may explain why law enforcement agencies could not provide reports going back to the event 21 years ago.

An arrest was never made in the vandalism of Michael Wayne Haynie's car, and the specks of blood on the windshield were never identified. According to Patrick Haynie, it's possible the blood belonged to the perpetrator(s) who stripped it.

Interviews with several family members demonstrated frustration and disagreement with the events and investigation behind Michael Wayne Haynie's death. The death remains a mystery.

If you have information about the death of Michael Wayne Haynie, contact the Criminal Investigation Division of the Sherwood Police Department at 835-1425 or the *Sherwood Voice* at 835-4875 (editor@sherwoodvoice.com).

Six Feet And Below

Introduction

After repeated failed attempts to find a home for this story in either a contest or publication, I now retire it to my anthology. It's interesting to see what stories will place or get accepted to a magazine. Often you'll be surprised, so you writers don't give up.

This current narrative is one of my favorite mysteries I've written, and has received rave reviews from my critique groups and award-winning writers. Unfortunately, judges for the many contests and publications I've submitted it to have not agreed. One nationally multi-award winning author told me the story was better than many she had read in *Ellery Queen* mystery magazine, and to send it to them. I did, and received a rejection letter.

Originally, it had been accepted into an anthology with other authors' work, provided I would rewrite the plot from a single point of view. Time constraints prevented this effort. Also, since I consider this a plot-driven tale, I felt the rewrite would take away from the flow in the different scenes and how I wanted to present the story. So, what is the moral here for you writers? If I wanted to see it published I should have made the changes! Most likely the point of view issue kept *Six Feet And Below* out of contention from ever winning an award.

I will probably one day rewrite this tale from one character's point of view. Perhaps you'll read it in a few years in my third anthology.

Six Feet And Below

Sheriff Ronnie Andrews glanced up from the disinterment as a figure strode to him. He nodded when he recognized the Faulkner County Coroner. "Mr. Hawkins … how're you doin'?"

"Not sure, yet. I see you're digging up Kathy Mason's body."

Sheriff Andrews stepped back as the backhoe shook, removing another scoop of soil. He took a notepad from his shirt pocket. "Yeah," he said. "Got a court order at the Medical Examiner's request." He motioned at a white Chevy Trailblazer parked on the gravel road behind his vehicle. "They sent it with an investigator."

"Why wasn't I notified?"

The sheriff shrugged.

"But I own the cemetery," Hawkins huffed.

"It's a court order … I'm just doing my job."

"What's going on here, Sheriff?"

"Don't get me to lyin'. You'll have to ask the expert over there."

Hawkins turned and walked past several tombstones to the Trailblazer. Underneath his lumberjack shirt, left untucked and unfastened, he wore a cheap T-shirt. Looking in the vehicle's window, he saw a woman keying text into a laptop. The coroner tapped on the glass to get her attention.

She lowered the lightly tinted window, balancing the computer on her knees. "Can I help you?"

"Yeah. Why are you disinterring Kathy Mason? I'm the coroner, no one notified me."

"You need to call Dr. Gary Austin. He's my boss—he's the one who got the court order."

"Gary who?"

"Gary Austin—at the State Crime Lab. If you'll excuse me…." She pointed to the casket being loaded onto a flatbed truck. "I need to go assist them."

Hawkins stormed over to his four-wheel drive. As he drove down the gravel road leading from the cemetery, he picked up the phone and called his friend Richard Copeland at the crime lab. "What's Austin doing getting a court order to dig up one of *my* graves? I want to know what's going on!"

Copeland held the phone away from his ear until the coroner ended his tirade. He was not the state's senior medical examiner, but for some reason Hawkins always requested him instead of one of the other M.E.s.

"You know I'm not at liberty to discuss an ongoing investigation," Copeland said. "If Gary Austin asked to have the body disinterred, I'm sure he had a good reason."

"I'm the coroner in this county and I have a right to know details! For Christ's sake, I own the cemetery."

"Mr. Hawkins, Gary just walked in. I'll let you talk with him." Copeland smiled at the Chief Medical Examiner and handed him the phone.

Mouthing the words 'Thanks a lot,' Gary Austin took the receiver. "What's your beef, Hawkins?" The chief was not known for his phone etiquette.

"You're the medical examiner—you tell me. Why are you autopsying Kathy Mason?"

Austin sat and debated what to say. Oh, what the heck, he thought. Perhaps the coroner should know, despite the fact that it was his funeral home that buried the subject.

"Well?" Hawkins asked impatiently.

"Hold on."

This coroner system pisses me off, Austin thought. Anyone could be elected coroner with no training. Of the seventy-five coroners throughout Arkansas, only three held medical degrees. Most were funeral directors.

But then again, he couldn't blame them; it wasn't their fault. Various counties and the state itself allocated virtually nix funds to pay coroners. No physician wanted the thankless job of being forced to get up at all hours to go view gruesome scenes for a few thousand dollars annually. The system often resulted in sloppy investigations. Employees in the M.E.'s office often joked about whose county it would be best to murder someone in—hypothetically, of course. Many coroners never took time to view a body and usually finalized their inquiry over the phone.

"I'm waiting," Hawkins said.

Austin finally said, "Okay, Hawkins. I'll tell you why we need to see the subject's body. But I better not read about this in the newspaper."

"Of course not."

"A lady at the State Health Department sent us a letter from the doctor who signed the death certificate. He said the signature was a forgery. Definitely not his."

"...So?"

Austin noticed the uncomfortable pause before Hawkins responded.

"You *were* called, weren't you?" Austin asked. "Kathy died at home, the death certificate shows that you had been notified."

"Yeah, I was. But I didn't have to go see the body. I was led to believe she died of natural causes."

"That's what I plan to verify. The physician's irate. He's demanding answers from us and threatening to call the governor."

"Why did the Health Department get involved?"

"The death certificate lists cause of death as 'Cardiac Arrest'. The Health Department queries physicians and other certifiers if some vague cause of death is the *only* thing listed. They want to know what led up to the cardiac arrest."

"Well, I'm pissed as hell that no one told me about this."

"Listen, calm down," Austin replied. "I'm sure everything's okay. Because of the forged signature, we have to investigate. I'll keep you updated."

Copeland smiled after Austin put down the phone. "You'd think as coroner he would be concerned."

"He complains instead. Maybe it's his ego, maybe something else. I've asked the State Police to interview the family and co-workers of the deceased."

Photo by Lance Waters

Gary Austin stepped into the room where the casket lay upon a table. Popping several latches, he motioned to an employee to help him lift the top and remove the body to a table.

Adjusting a mike attached by a wire to the ceiling, Austin next stretched his fingers into rubber gloves and put on a mask and plastic protective glasses. "The body is well preserved," he recorded. "It's been interred for exactly eight weeks today—kudos to the embalmer."

He slowly undressed the cadaver while dictating into the recorder. As he was about to lower his scalpel to her chest, he noticed a heavy mixture of skin-tone paste applied to her forehead. Before making the incision, he took a sanitized cloth and began removing the make-up.

Why is it so thick? Especially in her temple area.

Austin found a contusion. Looking at his assistant, he said, "I want an X-ray of her head."

Stepping into an adjacent room, he watched through an inside window as his orders were carried out.

"What've we got?" Copeland asked, walking in with a cup of coffee.

"A hematoma along the temple and the skull appears fractured."

X-rays confirmed his suspicion. Slicing the skin in a circle around the head, Austin took a miniature saw and opened the skull until it lifted like a lid off a sugar bowl. Fractured bones protruded into the left lobe severely damaging the woman's brain. Hemorrhaging after a blunt blow to the head appeared to be the cause of death. It would be impossible to complete blood toxicology screening now since the body had been embalmed.

* * *

Lt. David Bowden with State Police met Sheriff Andrews outside Hawkins Funeral Home in Greenbriar. "Your wife had that child yet?" Lt. Bowden asked Andrews.

"Any day now."

"Give her my best wishes."

The two entered the establishment and found a receptionist just inside the door. She had been questioned the day before.

"Bill is waiting for you in his office," she said, pointing to a room down the hallway.

The Faulkner County Coroner sat behind a large oak desk that took up most of the floor space in his office. A book cabinet on the left contained many publications related to mortuary science.

"Come on in, guys." He pointed to two seats in front of his desk.

"Thank you," Lt. Bowden replied.

Both officers tried to appear authoritative, but it was difficult, having known the coroner for years and working many accident scenes together.

"Mr. Hawkins," Lt. Bowden began. "We have some discrepancies in our investigation."

"So I understand—but I can't get the medical examiner to tell me what."

"First of all, that body they dug up wasn't Kathy Mason at all."

When the coroner remained quiet, Bowden continued. "Miss Mason's sister lives in Oregon. We e-mailed a photo of the corpse to authorities out there and they said you should have seen her jaw drop when she saw it. We're trying to locate other family members, but we're having trouble finding any."

Bowden noticed Hawkins fidget as he tried to listen. The coroner's eyes kept switching from them to an invisible spot in an upper corner of the room.

Lt. Bowden continued, "You did the embalming, right?"

"Right," Hawkins said. "I just assumed it was her. My secretary takes care of filing the death certificates."

"Interesting…," Bowden glanced down at his notepad. "As coroner, you were notified of Kathy's death, right?"

"As I told the M.E.'s office, I only took the phone call. I figured the doctor would sign his patient's death certificate. No reason for me to get involved, it sounded like a natural event."

"But the doctor said it wasn't his signature. Who called you?"

Hawkins sat back in his seat and crossed his arms. "What the hell is going on here?"

"We have a body you embalmed who is not who she's supposed to be, and I guess now we have a missing person. Don't you think we have a right to ask questions? Your secretary said she never filed this death certificate with the Health Department."

As Sheriff Andrews listened, the facts of the case began to register with him. He hadn't considered all the implications, and now as the county coroner and owner of the local funeral home grew combative, the sheriff was feeling his own temper flare.

"Look!" Andrews glared. "If you don't want to answer our questions, then tell us."

"Give me your best shot," Hawkins responded.

"Yesterday when we interviewed your receptionist, she said you personally picked up Kathy Mason's body and embalmed it. Said you did it late at night, something she'd never seen you do before."

"I've had enough!" Hawkins shouted and stood. "If you're accusing me of murder then I want my attorney."

"Kathy Mason's sister said you insisted it be a closed-casket service—did you not?" Sheriff Andrews asked.

"What the hell does that have to do with anything?"

Lt. Bowden lowered his voice and relaxed in the seat. "You know the rumor mill in a small town," he said. "Eyewitnesses have placed you and Kathy together on several occasions. Were you two having a relationship?"

Hawkins' sudden lapse into silence shocked the officers. He always had a sound-bite ready at a whim. Andrews continued, "Where is Kathy Mason, Mr. Hawkins? Did you really think you could keep this quiet once we disinterred the body from the grave?"

A fire truck siren sounded outside, Hawkins turned and watched from his window as the vehicle disappeared down a long stretch of highway leading into town. Lt. Bowden felt a shiver work its way through his chest. He recalled the sudden death of Hawkins' wife a decade earlier, and how it shocked the community. Those familiar with the case were skeptical that a fall from a stepladder could produce the severe trauma she had on the back of her skull.

Then there were the events surrounding several prominent elected officials who sided against Hawkins when he was sheriff twenty years ago. Two died in what was ruled a homicide and suicide episode, and a third died from carbon monoxide when he fell asleep in his garage. Hawkins was deputy coroner as well as sheriff and had worked all three deaths. We'll never know, Bowden thought.

"I need a cigarette break," Andrews said.

Lt. Bowden stood and took a can of Copenhagen from his shirt pocket. "I'll join you—we'll be back, Mr. Hawkins. We have more questions."

The funeral director, who had been a confrontational coroner for many years, remained silent and seemed focused on a cow pasture visible out the window.

Outside, under an awning near a hearse, Lt. Bowden placed a pinch of snuff between his bottom lip and gums. "What'd you think?"

Andrews lit a cigarette and returned the lighter to his pocket. "I think the bastard's killed more than once. I've never trusted him. He has a habit of working death scenes before letting my department know. My deputies always complain."

The radio sounded and Lt. Bowden grabbed the mike strapped across his shoulder.

"The judge okayed the search warrant," the dispatcher said.

"Thank you," Bowden responded.

As Andrews flicked his butt to the ground and began to smash his boot on top of it, a blast startled the two and they hurried inside.

The receptionist was already running to her boss's office.

They all arrived together and pushed the door open. Hawkins sat at his desk with his head slumped on top. His fingers held a chrome pistol and his hand had twisted causing the barrel to point toward the ceiling. Blood trickled from a small hole in his temple.

* * *

Lt. Bowden and Sheriff Andrews turned into the gravel driveway at Hawkins' residence several miles outside Greenbriar. A dog tied to a tree barked and pulled at his chain.

"I didn't realize Hawkins owned all those rental properties," Andrews said.

"We've got our day's work cut out for us. Gotta search them all."

Behind them, another county sheriff's vehicle pulled in. Deputy Sheriff Jim Bell stood and placed a piece of gum in his mouth. "Did Hawkins really kill himself?" he asked.

"Sure did," Andrews replied.

Andrews tried each key from a set he had taken from the funeral home. When none worked, the three men checked the back door and found it boarded up. All of the windows had bars on them.

"Start kicking," Bowden said.

All three took turns pounding in the front door till it caved in.

The stench overwhelmed them and Bowden placed a cloth over his nose. Bell and Andrews used their hands. Filth of decayed food and discarded cans lined shelves and countertops. A form of fungus grew on piled dishes in the sink. Upon the floor, below a pantry door, lay rotting skeletal remains of what appeared to be a small dog.

A basement entrance gapped open near the hall leading to the back rooms. Bowden descended the steps as the other two searched upstairs.

Sounds of dripping water reminded Bowden of a horror flick he'd once seen. He pointed the flashlight quickly into dark corners as his skin crawled. In a murky recess he saw the shadow of a figure lying on a bed. Finding the light switch, his heart skipped when he found Kathy Mason strapped nude, each limb cuffed to a bedpost.

Her face was bruised with purple circles around both eyes. A device had been taped to her mouth that allowed the injection of material but prevented her from biting down. Tears rolled from her cheeks when she saw Lt. Bowden.

"Down here!" he yelled to his partners upstairs. He ran to her and had to use a screwdriver lying on the floor to undo the bedpost and free her arms.

She tried to mumble through the tiny cylinder within her mouth. Bowden removed it.

A scream of agony and relief sounded as she wrapped her arms around him.

"It's all right now," Bowden said.

Andrews and Bell appeared in the doorway, amazement and disgust evident on their faces.

Grabbing a blanket to cover her, Deputy Bell asked, "Why would Hawkins do this … and who was in the casket?"

"I'm still working on that," Andrews said. "Hawkins was Coroner … had access to a lot of bodies. Hell, he was the embalmer and funeral director also. There may be lots of empty caskets out there in the ground. Who knows what that bastard was up to all these years?"

The room grew quiet except for water drips in a sink near a workbench.

Deputy Bell assisted Kathy toward the door. At the threshold, she turned and said, "He seemed so nice at first—I trusted him. I don't think he was crazy. I think he knew exactly what he was doing. He said he would never be taken alive."

"He kept his word there," Andrews replied.

She pointed to a projector in the corner, set up near a white sheet hung to the wall. With tears, she said, "He videotaped us … said he liked to watch how he raped and killed women. Kept whispering in my ear that I was next."

Humor

Modernity

Introduction

Modernity won 1st Place in the 2004 White County Creative Writers'
Conference Crime & PUNishment contest.   Notice the capitalization of
"PUN" in punishment. The competition's requirements stated, "Story must
include a crime and at least one bad pun."

This piece could have been included in another genre section such as mystery.
But with the focus on puns, the story does not lend itself for submission into
other categories. I've yet to find another contest that felt right for the piece,
so I retire the tale here in this current anthology with a perfect contest record
of 1 for 1.

Modernity

The dark van slowed for the speed bump and then continued down the residential street. Multiple-story Victorian homes with immaculate lawns lined both sides of the road.

"Here! Stop here," Dos said.

The teenager punched at his keyboard and stared at the monitor sitting in his lap. Cut-off camouflaged shorts allowed full view of his hairy, skinny legs. A torn T-shirt displayed a picture of a marijuana leaf. Below it read, "Kansas, Land Of Grass".

Leo pulled the vehicle to the curb behind other parked cars along the street. "How's this?" he asked.

Dos adjusted the equipment and replied, "Fine. The computer card is working great!"

The two watched the monitor.

"She's inside, surfing the Internet," Dos said. "Looks like she's paying bills."

The screen on Dos' laptop displayed a banking site. He cracked his knuckles and stretched his arms as the moving cursor uncovered letters by the woman typing inside the home.

About to sneeze, Dos covered his nose and mouth. He then showed his friend the trickle of mucus on his fingers. "That's *snot* funny," Dos said with a laugh.

Leo shook his head. "Great—very humorous. Has she entered her password?"

"She's about to—write this down. 'J-O-N-E-S'. Ha! She used her last name for a password. How original."

The teenagers watched the outside of the home for several minutes. A man walking his dog waved at them and they waved back, smiling.

"Okay … she logged off," Dos said. "Me and Mrs. Jones got a thing going on."

Leo leaned back over, and after watching his friend log into the woman's banking account, said, "Don't take too much."

"We have one chance and I'm getting everything I can. Our clients can deal with it then."

His fingers tapped the keys with a blur, a result from years of playing computer games and high school training. His father, being a high-tech geek, also had its advantages.

"Done." Dos smiled. "She won't suspect a thing until she reads her e-mail. By then I'll have deleted all traces of the 'business account' I set up."

"What if she checks her statement online?"

"Relax, dude. I'll take care of it. Some *daze* you just can't seem to focus."

Dos next explored her e-mail account until he found her address. He sent the following threat:

> *We know what you've done. If you tell the police we'll turn over the evidence.*

Leo moved the van back onto the street and the pair exited the subdivision and disappeared onto I-30 toward Benton. Halfway between Little Rock and their next targeted neighborhood, they pulled into a Sonic.

"Check your account," Leo demanded. "Make sure it went through."

"It won't show until tomorrow," Dos replied.

"It should show it's been posted, right?"

A teenage blonde on roller skates took their order. Leo winked, and then said, "Number 4 with a large Coke. And give me *your* number ... we can pound the pavement at Burns Park—they have a cool place to skate. It'll give us a chance to roll up our sleeves."

She smiled and said, "I have a boyfriend."

The waitress took Dos' order and skated away.

"Bingo!" Dos yelled.

"What's up?"

"$80,000 will be posted to the account tomorrow."

"Cool!"

"No more cheap-ass weed. Hawaiian red bud from now on."

Leo opened the console between the seats. "Speaking of which...."

Pretending it was a tobacco cigarette, the two smoked the joint and blew the smoke out the window toward the red neon tubes outlining the fast food place. They had been careful to park away from other customers in the mostly deserted parking lot.

The waitress skated back with two sacks of food. She hooked a tray to the window and said, "That'll be $8.69."

Leo had a crooked nose and mouth, but tried to keep a straight face. "Sixty-nine, huh?" He then smiled, handed her two fives and said, "Hey ... do you know what winks and makes love like a tiger?"

She glanced at his red glossy eyes and answered, "No."

The two boys began winking their right eyes at her. "Very funny," she said.

The smacking of lips drowned out the Led Zeppelin CD. After an additional order of two banana splits with extra toppings, the teenagers pulled back onto the freeway toward an exclusive area surrounded by a high fence and a security post.

The front gate remained open and the check-in building was closed. Leo drove carefully over the cobblestone pavement while Dos fingered his laptop.

"Hey," Leo said.

Dos looked over.

"Did you hear the joke about the vacuum cleaner?"

"I'm busy. Be quiet ... please."

"Oh, never mind," Leo said. "It sucked anyway. And I'd tell you the joke about the roof but it's over your head."

Leo gave up when Dos didn't respond.

The newer subdivision had been built in an old cow pasture with few trees. Two- and three-story homes were covered with wooden shingles. Expensive automobiles lined the driveways.

"Are you really gonna do it?" Leo asked. He replaced the marijuana joint in the ashtray and tapped his fingers on the leather-covered steering wheel. "*Baby ... baby, baby, I'm gonna leave you,*" he sang. "*I say, baby, baby, I'm gonna leave you.*"

"Hush!" Dos looked up. "I need to concentrate. I know he lives around here somewhere."

An old woman with beehive hair walking a cocker spaniel watched them drive by in their black van with a dented bumper.

"Dude, better hurry up. That old bag's gonna call the cops. I could see it in her eyes."

The streets were designed like a grid. When they turned the last corner, about a half-mile ahead, they saw a mansion. "I bet that's it," Dos said. "She said we couldn't miss it."

"These houses are big, but that's huge!"

"I've got your 'huge'," Dos said, grabbing his crotch.

A maroon-painted driveway began where the cobblestone road ended. Leo parked near a towering oak; an iron fence had been bolted to the tree and encircled the estate.

Dos worked his magic on the computer. "There we go! Just like she said. People are so stupid about wireless Internet."

While Dos flicked his fingers across the keyboard, Leo tapped his nails on the steering wheel to the tunes reverberating from the two large speakers in the back. "I just love Zeppelin," Leo said.

"Turn it down," Dos replied, looking up. "I'm in!"

Leo reached for the volume control as his eyes darted toward the laptop lying on his friend's legs. The screen faded in and they saw the inside of an immaculate study. Mahogany bookshelves surrounded the room.

"Is that inside there?" Leo pointed toward the home.

"Yep. That rich bastard has a remote control camera attached to his computer."

Dos rubbed his index finger across the mousepad built within his laptop and the view on the screen shifted. With each stroke of his fingertip the camera would turn to a different perspective.

"So his wife—"

"Ex-wife," Dos corrected.

"Whatever. You sure she'll split the money? If he pays?"

"He's a top executive—he'll pay."

Dos clicked several keys and a view of a bedroom faded in. "Here we go."

He gently rubbed his finger across the mousepad and the view on the screen focused on a man lying in bed.

"He's naked as a nudist!" Leo remarked.

"And he likes to watch porn … or so I'm told."

Dos zoomed in and caught the man lying atop the covers with his hand wrapped around his manhood. Pushing a record key on his laptop, Dos slowly panned out and then sent a command for the camera on the computer near the bed to revolve left toward the TV.

A large television set ten feet from the foot of the bed illuminated the otherwise dark room. On the screen a tattoo-covered actor performed sexual acts on a beautiful blonde.

The two boys stared at the computer screen as Dos zoomed in even more.

"Okay, move back," Dos shouldered his friend away. Leo had continued to edge further toward the screen until he rested his arm upon Dos' side. "We're not here to watch porn movies, dude. We need to videotape the guy."

Commanding the camera to fade back, Dos rotated it toward their victim satisfying himself in bed.

"When I e-mail him this video-clip, the dude will pay," Dos said. "Wait a minute—I have an idea."

He keyed in several commands and the screen on his laptop popped into two smaller images. One continued to monitor the man pleasuring himself while the other clicked on the Internet function of the executive's computer.

"I bet he told his computer to remember his password," Dos said.

He clicked the 'favorite' key at the top of the man's Internet Home Page, and several banking institutions and credit card companies popped down.

After bringing up one of the sites, Dos moved the cursor into one of the two blank boxes and typed the man's first letter to his given name along with his surname.

Instantly the encrypted password box flashed in and the screen changed to the man's banking statement.

"Damn! I got it on the first try. What a loser."

Dos repeated the same sequence of events he had done earlier to victimize Mrs. Jones, and transferred $100,000 into his default account.

He then explored the man's e-mail file and found his address. After recording a clip of the man's activity in bed, he e-mailed him the attachment along with a message:

> *If you notify the authorities of the money transferred, the attached movie clip will be downloaded onto the Internet. By the way, we also know of your other illegal practices.*

For good measure, Dos created a new file in the man's computer and downloaded a folder of illegal pornography into it.

"That should do it," he said, taking the joint from Leo.

"Do what?"

"If the dude is more resourceful than we give him credit for, then I'll send an anonymous e-mail to the police that he likes to watch this crap made overseas."

"You're cruel, man."

The two exited the subdivision and took a highway home to Little Rock.

* * *

The third floor of the library contained the historical society along with adjoining rooms filled with children's books.

In a small space used for microfilm, Dos and Leo watched for several minutes through a window as patrons exit the elevator across the hall.

"There they are," Dos said.

Opening the door he motioned toward them, "Mr. Jones ... Mrs.

Carmichael. Over here."

The teenagers sat in small plastic seats they had removed from the children's area as the older man and woman made themselves comfortable in leather chairs provided by the library for those scanning microfilmed documents.

"Is it done?" Mr. Jones asked.

Pulling his laptop from the table, Dos said, "Just as you requested."

He plugged a telephone line into the wall socket and flickered his fingers across the keyboard. "I transferred the account several times, but I'm now ready to send it to you once you give me your account info—minus our ten percent."

Mr. Jones handed him a slip of paper with several numbers. "You sure this is safe?"

Dos smiled. "Kind-of-like, sort-of, in-a-way, but not-really." He then turned serious and continued, "You're safe—guaranteed. I'm just glad you believed me when I told you about the affair."

Mrs. Carmichael glanced through the window toward the elevators as a crowd exited. She seemed to be scanning each face. Looking back to the boys, she replied, "The pictures you sent of the 'affair' were quite persuasive."

Mr. Jones nodded. "My wife still doesn't know that I found out. It was very difficult to act—especially with the children around." He then smiled. "Perhaps my acting experiences in college prepared me for this most unfortunate role I now find myself in."

Dos closed his computer. "It is done. You should find the money in your account within a few days. Once there, you won't have any trouble splitting it."

The two adults nodded and then held hands—a gesture that Dos and Leo noticed.

Mrs. Carmichael seemed to have witnessed the boys' awareness and said, "We've bonded a relationship out of all this. Once everything settles we plan to divorce our spouses and get married."

"Good luck," Dos responded.

"I have a question," Mr. Jones said. "How did you know about them—our spouse's cheating on us, that is?"

Dos stood and wrapped the telephone cord around his hand and placed the laptop in a leather case. "Watch what you say on those chat lists, dude. Sometimes it's better to be quiet. Especially if they're wireless. The pictures were easy."

Leo reached for the door first when Dos stopped him. "And I have a question for you," he turned and looked at the man and woman. "How did you find out they were embezzling from your company?"

Mr. Jones looked at Mrs. Carmichael and then back to the boys. "They weren't."

"What!" Dos exclaimed. "You said—"

"Please forgive us," Mrs. Carmichael interrupted. "But you said you wouldn't help us if they hadn't really committed a crime."

"Oh, man," Leo said, rubbing his fingers through his hair.

"We're sorry," Mr. Jones said. "We were both devastated when we learned of our spouses' cheating. No wonder they spent so much time on 'business trips'. In retrospect, I wish we hadn't lied to you."

Anger flashed across Dos' face. "I e-mailed them a threat thinking it would keep them from going to the police when they found out their accounts had been robbed. I never wanted to hurt people that did nothing wrong. Think Robin Hood, dude."

"My husband lied to me!" Mrs. Carmichael responded. Then showing remorse, she continued, "But you're right, we should not have used you."

"I never want to see you again," Dos replied. "Let's go, Leo."

The two returned to their van. "Wait here, Leo," Dos said. "Don't drive off."

He pushed a computer card into the laptop and linked the wireless Internet with his home computer. Scrolling through his files he found the old accounts from which he had stolen the money. With a push of a button he transferred their percentage back into Mrs. Jones and Mr. Carmichael's accounts.

"Take me home," he demanded.

"So that's it?" Leo asked.

"That's it."

A few moments later Dos smiled. Reconnecting his laptop, his fingers rushed across the keyboard.

"What are you doing?" Leo asked.

"If we don't get ours, then they don't get theirs."

"Yeah, give their spouses their money back … that'll teach them."

"Okay, smartass—very funny. Now, drive. Let's make like a baby and head out."

Shake, Shake, Shake

Introduction

This somewhat autobiographical sketch of a family event was written for the Dorothy Truex Award at the 2006 Arkansas Writers' Conference. It won 2nd Honorable Mention. The requirement stated, "Humorous prose, subject 'dancing.'"

Paula Martin Morell, editor of the anthology *Tales from the South* for Temenos Publishing, then accepted the story in 2007 for publication in Volume II. She stated in the acceptance letter, "Great story." The criteria asked for a mom or dad related event in celebration of the upcoming Mother's Day and Father's Day.

A benefit of being included in this collection of stories by Arkansas writers is the author gets to read his tale on KUAR FM89. For more information into future events, see one of these websites:

www.kuar.org or www.awaywithwords.org.

Shake, Shake, Shake

"Okay, girls! Gather around."

My wife, Mary, clicked the TV off and grabbed the radio remote. Three daughters ran to her and waited.

"I love this song. Let's dance."

They all twirled to an Eagles' song. First they held hands in a circle, then the oldest daughter let go and began jumping like a monkey, biting her tongue at times. The smaller siblings—twins—imitated her until Mary retrieved her video camera to record the scene.

I sat in the background at my computer working on my next short story.

"Join us," Mary said to me.

Turning in my seat to watch, I shook my head. "I need to finish this."

"Oh, you fuddy duddy. Come on, girls. Let's hold hands again and dance."

When the song ended, the sisters followed Mary into the bathroom to get their bath.

I heard them play as my wife soaped and shampooed. Writing was not difficult—for me anyway—just time consuming. With a day job, I was forced to write at odd times.

"What're you doin'?" Mary asked as she entered the room. She used a towel to dry splashed water from her arms.

"Creating a western story for Dusty's contest at the writing conference this year."

"Have fun."

She kissed my neck and returned to the bathroom. I heard her try to tone down the children's increasing horseplay.

"Hey!" Mary shouted. "Keep the water in the tub."

I smiled from my computer at the silliness I heard, but tried to stay focused on my task.

Without an office at home, I worked from the family's only computer atop a desk in the open dining room. A twelve hundred square foot home didn't allow me much privacy.

Minutes later I heard my wife towel off the kids. I would need to help diaper toddlers once they ran into the front room near me.

An explosion of horseplay grabbed my attention; I turned to see my oldest daughter Skylar scamper from the bathroom. Her open terrycloth robe dropped like a cape from her head. She ran nude around the coffee table, followed closely by scurrying naked sisters.

They chased each other in circles before stopping. Skylar orchestrated the next event, arranging her siblings in a line.

"Okay, Sydney and Mackenzie, follow me … okay? Okay?"

The two-year-olds indicated they understood, although I doubted it.

Skylar began to dance, snapping her behind back and forth. "Sing with me," she said. "Okay? Okay? Shake, shake, shake … shake, shake, shake … shake your booty, shake your booty."

Mary walked out from the bathroom drying herself with a damp towel. We eyed one another from across the room, and then smiled.

Skylar again ran around the table singing as the twins followed. "Shake your booty!"

The young siblings tried to stay in tune with their older sister, but their underdeveloped voices wobbled like musical saws.

Once more they lined up, this time in front of me, and wiggled their behinds back and forth. "Shake, shake, shake…."

I again eyed my wife. "This would be a great video except we might get arrested for child pornography."

Mary laughed. "But wouldn't it be fun to blackmail them in the future when they get out of line, or embarrass them in front of their boyfriends?"

"Yes, it would."

Once more Skylar ran in circles with her sisters not far behind. This Kodak moment went undeveloped.

Lining up with her daughters, my wife joined the trio and began to shake her booty. "Come on, Daddy," she said. "Dance with your children."

Hitting the save button on my computer, I stood and began to bump my rear with my wife's. The family now danced as one.

Step, Step, Step ... One, Two, Three

Introduction

Step, Step, Step ... One, Two, Three won 2nd Honorable Mention at the 2005 Arkansas Writers' Conference, Dorothy Truex Award. The contest requirement stated, "Prose piece, humorous, around the subject of 'dancing.'"

Can you tell from these last two stories that dancing is popular in my home?

Step, Step, Step … One, Two, Three

Pulling a sweatshirt over his tank top, Phil stepped from the van and approached the School of Dance. He had just completed a grueling workout and wondered if others would notice the sweaty odor.

A BMW raced past and parked near the front, blocking other vehicles. Some woman jumped out and raced through the front door.

Why don't you park between the lines like the rest of us? Phil thought.

As he reached for the glass door, he noticed a sign taped to the front that read: *Please bring your child to Robinson Auditorium this Friday at 6:00 for rehearsals. The recital will begin at 3:00 Sunday afternoon. Have your child there by 2:00.*

Oh, yeah. That's this weekend.

After grabbing a sip of water from the fountain by the hallway, Phil stood near a corner and waited. Class would be over at any time. Small, plastic, elementary school like chairs lined a lobby near where he lingered, occupied by moms who chatted to one another, many with infants in tow.

The owner of the BMW impatiently moved about glancing at her watch.

A door opened from down the hallway and the voices of children filled the building. Phil ducked behind the corner and pretended to hide.

As he peeked he saw his daughter Skylar and her best friend Spencer following the group of girls to the front. They paused as they approached the area where Phil hid, seeming to sense something.

Suddenly, Phil jumped and the girls both screamed. Moms looked up.

"Sh, sh, sh," he motioned with his finger to his mouth.

Sheila, the dance instructor, yelled, "Don't forget, folks, to be on time this weekend. And don't forget to bring their costumes."

"Are you ready?" Phil asked the girls.

"Yeah!" they both said.

The arrangement was that Spencer's mom brought the girls and Phil picked them up. Normally, he was the only guy in the building, but playing Mr. Mom sat well with him.

"So, how were swim lessons?" he asked.

"We had dance lessons!" Skylar said.

"Oh, scuba-diving lessons?"

"Noooooo!" they both laughed.

"Your dad's funny," Spencer yelled.

The three held hands and followed one another to the van. He noticed the BMW had not moved and several parents waited patiently in their legally parked cars for the woman to move her vehicle.

Is she that unperceptive? Phil thought. *She parks her expensive car there every week.*

"Is this what you learned today?" he continued outside. Swinging his arms and jumping like a monkey, he said, "Look at me dancing!"

"Nooooo!"

"We danced like this…." Both placed their hands above their heads and did circles like a ballerina.

"Like this?" Phil imitated their movements and acted like a dork. From his peripheral view he saw moms laughing.

"That's goofy," Spencer said.

* * *

At two O' clock Sunday afternoon, Phil and his family pulled into the parking deck next to Robinson Auditorium. Skylar jumped from the van dressed like Raggedy Ann as Phil and his wife Mary unbuckled the sixteen-month-old twins.

Waiting patiently in the large auditorium were several hundred family members of the dancers. "Is she ready?" Phil asked his wife as she returned from backstage.

"Yeah … did you bring the rose to give her afterward?"

"It's in the twin's diaper bag."

Several groups of dancers from different ages performed before Skylar and Spencer's class strolled single file onto the stage.

The night before Phil had watched a videotape of the rehearsal. There had been no spectators and the girls performed flawlessly. *How will they do with hundreds of onlookers?*

The music started and the dancers began to twirl and sing, "Flop, flop, flop … one, two, three…." Skylar's class was nervous and their voices sounded weak compared to the powerful yells in rehearsal. Only Skylar's intonations could be heard throughout the cavernous room, and Phil smiled.

A grandparent had been holding one of the twins, and an uncle held the other. When Phil glanced to check, he noticed Uncle Stan with empty arms.

"Where's Sydney?" he asked Stan.

"I thought Mom was watching her."

Filled with panic, Phil stood but did not see his daughter. He maneuvered through the crowded seats to the aisle.

In the back of his mind he could hear Skylar on stage yelling out the song lyrics. But finding his twin daughter had turned to a crisis.

With his eyes, he followed the abstract-designed carpeted hallway up to steps leading onto the stage, where he saw his sixteen month old begin to climb.

Oh, no!

Trotting, trying to hide in the shadow against the wall, Phil hurried to the front. Sydney looked up and saw him coming for her. She dashed up the steps and onto stage. In his peripheral vision, Phil saw several video cameras pan toward him.

"Sydney, come here," he whispered, holding out his arms.

Too late. The music drowned out his voice, and she was already wobbling toward the dancers. Skylar looked over and saw her sister. Her eyes grew twice as large.

Do I go on stage? Phil thought.

Skylar tried to grab Sydney's hand, but the twin zigzagged around the dancers. She then stopped abruptly and began to sway to the music. When Phil looked toward his wife, he noticed the room filled with laughter. There was nothing to do but let nature take its course.

As Skylar and her class exited, a teacher escorted Sydney toward Phil. When he turned, he received a thunderous applause.

Not sure how to respond, he held Sydney up, over his head. After all, she had stolen the show. *Let's hope there's no encore.*

Listen to Me, Honey

Introduction

The story won Special Honorable Mention (4th place) in the September 2005 issue of *ByLine* magazine for its Short-Short Story contest. There were 137 entries nationwide, and the top three winners lived in Pennsylvania, California, and New Mexico. *ByLine's* editor wrote in the magazine about the contest, "Our judge was overwhelmed by so many solid stories and the number of writers with strong writing skills."

I first penned this tale for a contest at a local conference. The requirements stated the title must be *"Listen to Me, Honey."* The theme required, "Mary Crafton, matriarch of a large southern family, has worries about the new generation in the family." Although unsuccessful in this competition, I liked the character so much I had confidence the story could be published. I submitted it to another national magazine I subscribe to and it was reluctantly rejected. The editor stated, "Although a good story, I was afraid it would offend someone and didn't want to take the chance."

I don't blame the editor. The point of view for my main character is that of an elderly African-American woman. There are strong opinions that authors should not project themselves into roles dissimilar from their lives. For example, a man should not write from a female perspective, or someone of one race should not write from another racial perspective. I respectfully disagree. There are thousands of examples of successful books where the protagonist is a different race, color, gender, or sexual orientation from the writer. If a reader likes it, then it works. The main character in *Listen to Me, Honey* is the hero and strong person of the plot. Before submitting the story, I asked an African-American writing friend to proof the story. She liked it.

I praise my parents for raising me to respect diverse cultures. I have many friends of different races, and my children do as well. I can't imagine a reader feeling I intended to show bias toward African-Americans. But I anticipated this so I want to be clear this was not my intent. I encourage you to read my novel *Department of Corrections*, or my story *The Café* in my first anthology, for examples of the conflict I have with race relations.

With that said, *Listen to Me, Honey* will also be published this year in *Well Versed – 2008* by The Columbia Chapter of the Missouri Writers' Guild.

Listen to Me, Honey

Oh! She's a crazy woman ... let me tell you now.

That Mary Crafton's done been in charge since her husband, 'Colonel, Sir', we called him, died back in '72. I's worked for their family pert near sixty years, now.

Why I put up with her crap all these years, you ask? Well, life on the 'other side of the tracks' was not peaches and cream, if you know what I mean.

Colonel Crafton agreed to hire me 'part-time' years ago when he retired and they moves into that big mansion down there in Nashville.

No, that's Nashville, Arkansas, in Howard County.

I done think Mrs. Crafton gone crazy these past several years. Other day she says to me, "Melba, where did I go wrong? My family's abandoned me and the kids these days are why our country's going to hell in a hand-basket."

"I don't know, ma'am," I tells her. "Life's been pretty good to me—with your kind generosity, of course. But my goodness, I remember when all we had was a radio, no TV, and I had to draw the water from the well before you and Mr. Colonel had running water put in. Seems to me life is easier, nowdays."

"Oh, hush, you young Miss Pollyanna. You always see the bright side. Young Jim, Jr. and Sara sure seem a disappointment. My children never call or come see me."

Now, I knows that was a big, fat lie. The old bag talked to them at least once a week.

Did I call her 'old bag'? you ask. Hon, we've been together for sixty years! I have many names for Mrs. Crafton. Don't you go tellin' her ... I don't always tell them to her face.

You stop laughing!

Anyway, the other day she asks me, "Melba, what's gonna happen to this beautiful home when I'm gone?"

Now, I never gave it much thought since I've been well taken care of. My home over near the local junior college was paid off years ago. But it was a good question because I suspected her children would sell it right off.

"Ma'am," I says, "you should tell your lawyer what you want done with your home. You always gave me good advice, so I'm telling you the same thing you told me."

"Oh, my kids. They don't care!"

"That's not true, they loves you very much. Jim, Jr. sees that the place is mowed and kept up, and Sara still meets you at church."

"Just on Sunday."

"Now, listen to you. She's a busy woman bringing up your three grandbabies."

"They're not babies anymore. They'd rather fish in our pond out back than talk with their grandmother."

I've heard the same complaints over and over, year after year. Back in the '40s when she first hired me, I listen' to her complain about her husband not home enough. "Probably drinking and smoking cigars," she would say each Saturday night.

Photo by David Knight of Barbara D. Mills in the production *Crowns*

"What's wrong with these kids nowadays," I heard her say maybe a thousand times. "Don't their mamas and papas teach them right?"

Well, I wants to tell her to spank her kids sometimes when they get out of line. Lord knows the Colonel did. But she wouldn't hear of it. In my house my mama would spank me and my brothers for breathing wrong. But not Mrs. Crafton. She talked a mean game, but she was a pussycat deep down.

When Elvis hit, Lord help us. "What you kids looking at?" she screamed at them one day. She walked into the living room and there he was, jiggling those hips on national TV.

"Turn that off!" she yelled. "That's Satan there tryin' to influence you. Do you hear?"

Lord knows the preacher done got her thinking about the devil and the Second Coming! "Junior," I heards her say to her young boy. Well, he's a man now. Anyway, she says, "You need to teach your kids respect. Prepare them for the Lord."

Jim just looks at her and says what he knows she wants to hear.

The other day we were driving back from the Dollar General…. If 'driving' whats you want to call it. She drives so slow the young people honk and yell at her when they pass. Sometimes they pass us on a double yellow line!

Anyways … we passed the road leading to Okay. The town done closed down and a gate won't let you in. But years ago it was a thriving community and Mrs. Crafton lived there. Likes to talk about it a lot. "Look at the homes over there," she pointed. "Just like my family place growing up in Okay. Now they're run down and falling apart. Don't no one want to keep it up anymore. Kids moving to Little Rock and leaving their parents behind. What happened Melba?" she asks me.

"Times a changin'," I says. No reason telling her none of my family ever benefited from that oasis there at Okay. I still wasn't allowed in many stores there in Nashville at the time, or on a bus, much less in the planned beautiful community of Okay. The good-ole days? Yeah, right. Go tell it to the mountain!

"I'm ready to pass on and be with the Colonel," she says.

"Ma'am, I likes having you around," I says. "You should hear those grandbabies of yours brag about their grandma. They loves you very much."

"It's no use. This country's changing … and not for the better. I fear for my children and grandchildren. My generation tried to prepare them for a better life, but look what we get."

What's the use in me arguing with her? I gave up decades ago. "Yes, ma'am," is all I say and leave it at that.

But you know, at night when I see her stretched back in that big, cushy chair with her remote controls, and me heating her up dinners in a microwave, it's hard for me to feel sorry for her. Doctor done told her she survived that breast cancer because of some new technology. Would be dead had we been back in the '50s! All she said was that the Lord will take her when He's ready.

Dern woman can't put two and two together. Life's so much better these days … but she'd complained her entire life, so why should I expect her to change in her glory years?

I remember my grandmother, back before the war, tell me how to act when I'm away from my people. That woman saw hardship, I know.

Well, nowdays I just be myself. No need faking that 'Yes, sir, Mister, Mister' mumble-jumbo. I don't know about Mrs. Crafton, but my life certainly better.

When I see Jim, Jr. and Sara smile and play with their kids it brings joy to my heart. Despite all of Mrs. Crafton's complaints, she did a good job.

Our kids are good friends. You wouldn't see that back in the 'good-ole days.' No, sir. Times a changin', sometimes for the worse, but many times for the better. I know Mrs. Crafton knows it deep in her soul, where it counts.

I do.

You shush, stop your laughing and listen to me, honey. Mrs. Crafton's a good woman.

Pooh & Jesus

Introduction

I first penned this tale a few years ago based upon a true event I experienced with my daughter Skylar. Although unsuccessful in one or two contests, the story was accepted by Regina Williams, editor for *The Storyteller* magazine. She wrote, "Cute Story!" in my acceptance letter. It was published in the January/February/March 2006 issue.

Pooh & Jesus also appeared in SouthLit Magazine, an online magazine edited by Robert Hall.

Later, you'll see similarities with this story and the ending to my essay, *Voltaire and 9/11.*

Pooh & Jesus

Standing, Steve said to his wife, "Pause the movie. Emergency restroom break."

He strolled toward the bathroom and noticed the closed door. The smell of popcorn still filled the air from where his wife had microwaved a bag earlier. Gently knocking, he asked, "Who's in there? I need to pee."

"It's me," his four-year-old daughter responded.

"What're you doing?"

"Using the potty."

"Can you hurry? I really have to go."

"I'll be awhile."

"Why?"

"I'm poopin' and readin' about Jesus."

"…? Okay, I'll wait."

"That was fast," his wife said when Steve returned.

"Skylar's in there … said she's poopin' and readin' about Jesus."

"See. Those Bible stories you read to her are paying off."

After a few moments of laughter, Steve continued. "Start the movie, I'll have to wait."

"There's only twenty minutes left. Guess we need a bigger house with *two* bathrooms."

When the show ended, Steve returned and saw the open restroom door. He could hear Skylar playing in her bedroom—she was supposed to be asleep.

They had played in the pool most the afternoon, and then circled firework sparklers in the air out back in preparation for the 4th of July event the next day in an open field by the airport.

Last year she had sat motionless in his lap in the foldout chair while watching the display light up the night. Steve spent more time watching her expressions at the bright colors blasting outward than he did of the extravaganza itself. She had worn a glow-in-the-dark necklace purchased that night, and would keep it under her pillow for weeks after the radiant chemicals lost its powers of luminosity.

Flicking the bathroom light on, he walked through the saloon-style doors separating the sink from the commode, and raised the toilet lid. The sounds of his daughter whispered down the hallway.

"Skylar! You're supposed to be asleep."

"I'm not sleepy."

"Well, try. Close your eyes."

"But there are monsters that will get me."

"No, there're not. Go to sleep."

Steve looked down; on the rug laid a book. Thinking it the Bible because of what Skylar had said earlier, he reached to pick it up.

Bet she was reading this, he thought.

Glancing at the cover, it read: *The House at Pooh Corner*.

Poopin' and readin' about Jesus … what a little stinker.

Blue Dog by Skylar Whisnant and Liz Morris

Synchronicity

Introduction

It was a pleasant surprise when I received the e-mail from multi award-winning writer and publisher Lou Turner that *Synchronicity* won 3rd Place in the Ozarks Writers League's 2006 Dan Saults Memorial Award. There were approximately 100 entries from around the country. The contest's requirement states, "Entries may be in any form—fiction, non-fiction, essay, or poem."

The story was published in the October/November/December 2006 issue of *The Storyteller* magazine.

Synchronicity

Professor Gustav stared at the students. *What a bunch of weasels*, he thought. "Today we will continue our discussion on knowledge."

Everyone remained still. "I suggest you write this down."

Several pulled out pens and notebooks.

"Who would like to start?"

No one raised a hand.

Gustav continued. "We are discussing how we, as humans, can test the validity of what we know. What did Plato tell us Socrates said in *Apology*?"

Santana raised her hand; it was impossible not to notice the bush of hair under her arm. Today she wore extra piercings in her eyebrow and nose. "I'm sorry."

The professor repeated, "What did Socrates say in—"

"He said 'I'm sorry' in his *Apology*."

Classmates laughed; the joke appeared to go over the professor's head.

"He stated," Gustav continued, "that 'I am wiser in that what I do not know I don't think I do.' In other words, the more I know, the more I realize I don't know."

Santana laughed. "Sounds like the lyrics from a Don Henley song."

"Don who?"

"The Eagles, dude."

The professor shook his head. "Let's stay focused—we're discussing *knowledge*."

He walked to the blackboard and scratched out the words, 'Collective Unconscious.'

"I'm assuming everyone read the assignment. We were comparing instinctive knowledge with empirical. What did Jung say about archetypes?"

Norville adjusted his tie and read from a book. "He remarked, 'The unconscious, in its totality, is the deposit of all human experience right back to its remotest beginning. Simply, archetypes are the forms which the instincts assume.'"

"At least someone read his assignment," Gustav replied. "Now, what did he say about synchronicity?"

Santana spoke first. "The do, do, do, the da, da, da."

"Excuse me."

"Your logic ties me up and rapes me."

"What the hell are you talking about?"

"*Synchronicity.* It's the name of an album by *The Police.*"

Gustav put his hands on his hips and smirked. "Can we stay focused and stop talking about music?"

He turned and wrote on the blackboard, 'Causality.'

"This is the way we explain the link between two successive events. Synchronicity designates the parallelism of time and meaning between psychic and psychophysical events, which scientific knowledge so far has been unable to reduce to a common principle. The term synchronicity explains nothing, it simply formulates the occurrence of meaningful coincidences, which, in themselves, are chance happenings."

"Say, what?" someone yelled.

"It's on page 505 of your assigned reading."

Johan had sat quietly until now, dressed in a green army coat with the German flag embroidered on the right sleeve. "Vas you say ist das our universe like tiny atom in fingernail of giant human?"

"Humorous, Mr. Mann. From the movie *Animal House*, right?"

He replaced the marker on the ledge, underneath the blackboard, and faced the class. "Actually, there is a sound philosophy behind those lines in the movie. Some scholars throughout the centuries postulated that reality, as we know it, like when you feel the five senses and assume they are real, is an illusion, a.k.a.—Solipsism. The Hindus use the term 'Maya'. A dream can tell us much about our unconscious ways."

Johan blew a kiss toward Santana, then said, "Das ist vas rips the stamps."

"Please explain."

He smiled at Santana. "You know das experiment—put row of stamps around penis and find them torn in the morning. Es ist your dreams and fantasies."

"Why would anyone put…." Gustav nodded. Were they all idiots? Did they ever stop and think before reacting?

He had many intelligent acquaintances who pondered the world's existence. Smart people who made wise decisions. Was it due to the immaturity of his students that they didn't care?

That night in his one bedroom apartment, he turned on NPR and enjoyed Bach as background noise, while reading *Journal on Philosophy*. The news caught his attention.

"…a bus bomb killed thirteen and injured twenty-eight today in Tel Aviv, and two soldiers were killed by a landmine outside Baghdad…."

The silliness and innocence of his students, and his stern reaction to those qualities, began to weigh upon him. Here was the relativity and ephemera of life thrown in his face, and he's upset over such trivial issues. Why should his students care in a world of chaos?

Where had his funny-bone gone? Which was worse, the herd's apathy, or his endless evaluation of life's circumstances? Might there be a balanced medium?

The next class Gustav wore a 60s hippy attire with a bushy wig. Strands of beads with Yin & Yang symbols dangled around his neck.

"Peace," he said to Santana. He held his index and middle fingers up.

She furrowed her forehead in contemplation.

Pulling the TV-VCR on a cart to the front of the class, Gustav pushed the play button. "Who knows what this is?"

"Woodstock," someone answered. "I watched it on MTV years ago … with my mom."

"With your mom? Groovy. What was the meaning?"

"A new generation coming together," Santana said. "They were protesting the hypocrisy of the day."

Gustav gestured as if he had taken a hit off a marijuana joint. Everyone smiled. "I was there. All we did was get wasted and pretend we knew about life. I see the same crap today."

Jimi Hendrix thrummed his guitar while topless women danced in mud and drank wine.

"Were these your parents?" he continued. "Are they now you? Anyone want to hazard a guess why I'm showing you this?"

"Because you're cool, dude."

"No. Well, yes, I'm cool. Anyone else?"

Norville spoke. "You wish to demonstrate how the more things change, the more they remain the same."

"Bingo! I don't expect you to remember verbatim the deep philosophical tangents we go over. Hell, most of it is bickered over by the great minds of history. How can you derive a conclusion if they can't? Keep an open mind."

Santana said, "My daddy named me after his favorite group, and they played at Woodstock."

"No shit? That's, how does your generation say it, 'gnarly.'"

A Little Light

Introduction

In December 2004, *A Little Light* won 3rd Place in the flash fiction, on the spot Fiction Writers of Central Arkansas Christmas Contest Writers' Award. Participants had fifteen minutes to write on the theme: "A light, I see a light straight ahead. But it's so small. Could that possibly be...?"

We did not know the theme until right before the fifteen minutes to write began. The story is rough; I tried to leave it close to its original form so the reader can see why some editing is always good. I did make a few grammar changes from my original hand-written piece of paper.

A Little Light

"Martha's in her backyard again … drunk! I bet it is."

"I think you're right," Sally replied. "Christmas Eve and too much eggnog. I thought you hid her flashlight?"

"I had, why does she wander in her backyard like that—thru the trees, could get an eye poked out."

"It's a mystery," Sally said. "Who knows? Last year she scared the little girls next door. They were up late watchin' for Santa. Had to call the police when the dogs ran her down."

"I remember the picture in the newspaper! She was dressed as that abominable snowman character from the Rudolph the Red-Nose Reindeer show. Boy, was she drunk that night!"

"Let's go see if it's her," Sally said.

The two women, who had roomed together for fifty years, put on their slippers and housecoat and walked outside.

The light zigzagged through Martha's backyard like a firefly. The closer they got, the more it seemed to sink into the woods behind Martha's house.

"Are you sure it's Martha?"

Suddenly, the light beamed toward them. A large flash sent the two women screaming randomly throughout their neighbor's backyard.

A porch light was flicked on and Martha ran outside.

Dressed as elves holding Jack Daniel bottles stood Sally and her roommate—drunk as a skunk.

Ballroom Blitz

Introduction

Yet another story on dancing!

Ballroom Blitz won 2nd Place in the 2007 Arkansas Writers' Conference's Dorothy Truex Award. The contest's requirement stated, "Humorous prose, subject 'ballroom dancing'."

Quick background: My family is a member of the Central Arkansas Mothers of Multiples (MOM). They sponsored a night of dance lessons; only 3 couples showed, including yours truly. I took the events of that evening, embellished them (just a little), and below is the result.

Ballroom Blitz

An arrow, on a hand-painted sign staked in the churchyard, pointed toward the parking lot. It read, "Mat & Kelli's Ballroom Dance Academy."

"There it is," Rachel said. "Right off of R Street and University—just like the map said."

Her husband Troy whipped the 4-Runner into the side road behind New Age Church. Two other couples stood outside their vehicles conversing.

Rachel rolled down her window. "Hi, guys. Is the dance instructor here yet?"

"The doors are locked," Eddie replied.

His wife Krissie added, "I'm not sure we're in the right place. This looks like the basement, not a dance studio."

"The sign says to pull in here," Rachel said.

Troy leaned over and smiled toward Eddie. "Well, we tried. I guess we should go."

"Not so fast, guys," Krissie challenged. "You're not getting off that easy. We *are* going to dance, even if it's here on this asphalt."

Eddie laughed. "Great, I brought a cardboard box to break-dance on."

Someone walked outside the church carrying a garbage sack. "Excuse me," Eddie said. "Is this the dance studio?"

"Yes, I'll open the door. Mat and Kelli should be here anytime."

The couples walked into a large room below the cathedral. Smooth linoleum floors reflected bright overhead lights. A mirror dance-globe hung from a beam.

"The teachers are late," Krissie said. "Our appointment was for five-thirty so we can make our dinner reservation at seven."

The three women were members of a local mom's club. Their husbands were acquaintances without much social history together, but after a few minutes everyone found common interests to carry on conversations.

"I wonder where the teachers are?" Krissie said again.

Fifteen minutes late, Mat and Kelli entered the glass-door. Introductions were made. "Are we ready to dance?" Mat asked.

He wore an ancient dark suit and his palms were funeral director soft. Perhaps in his late fifties, his graying hair was tied into a mullet that fell several inches down his back. Kelli, his wife, appeared normal dressed in a black skirt and hair that looked modern and not from the sixties.

"Three steps … that's all you need to know to learn ballroom dancing," Mat said. "And that's all we have time to teach in our one-hour here today. I hope you sign up for our weekly lessons."

Mat's voice sounded soft, yet sure of his skills; he held his arms in rhythm to rocking blues music Kelli had turned on. "Watch my feet."

The men eyed one another, secretly they had hoped the instructors would not keep the appointment—their excuse to skip dance lessons. Mat continued, "Short, baby steps. Men, put your left foot just behind your right. Ladies, you do the opposite."

After a moment of practice, Mat said, "Now we dance. From these three simple steps you can learn many forms of ballroom dance like the waltz, salsa or even the hustle."

The instructors put their hands together. "Watch us," Mat continued. They danced in place taking steps back and then forward toward each other. "Now you."

Each couple replicated the teachers. Mat and Kelli strolled back and forth watching their students. "Here, let me show you what you're doing wrong," Mat said to Troy. The two put hands together and danced. Troy's awkwardness at dancing with a dude seemed apparent.

"Small steps, remember," Mat said. Each couple had their chance to practice with an instructor.

Troy and Rachel rehearsed steps as the other two couples worked one on one with Mat or Kelli. Unexpectedly Troy shuffled his feet and imitated Michael Jackson's Moon Walk.

"Stop that," Rachel whispered, trying to suppress a smile.

They continued their awkward dance-in-place movement, rotating hips as they stepped back and up, back and up. Troy looked over and saw the other men, each dancing with an instructor. The husbands made eye contact and seemed to share a moment, as if to say just fifteen minutes left … just fifteen minutes.

Mat's low monotone instructions, with that dangling gray mullet outside his shirt collar, reminded several students of flamboyant TV stars that now made the dance zeitgeist of the time feel palatable. Someone normal guiding the steps might give off impressions that the teachers were impostors.

"Now we'll try spins with the ladies," Mat continued. "Watch me and my beautiful wife."

Kelli turned up the music and then held her husband's hands. They did three steps this way, and three steps that way, then she swirled under Mat's arm and threw her fingers skyward as if encore. Then she circled back under his arm and they continued the same movement again.

The men seemed thrilled more by the moving clock than their teachers.

"We dance, fellows," Mat said. "Now you follow us."

The three couples paired up and replicated the same steps—grace and swan-like-movement was not in the air this night.

Mat and Kelli stood motionless for a while, watching. They seemed to enjoy such scenes—or sensed the hopelessness and chaos in showing couples proper, refined, dancing steps.

Krissie finally said, "It's 6:30, guys. We have to leave to make our dinner reservation."

A relief sigh seemed to fill the air, like someone opened a door and tension escaped into an outside vacuum.

In the parking lot everyone huddled beside a vehicle. "I'm ready for *Dancing With The Stars,*" Troy joked.

"Was Mat drunk?" someone asked.

"I think that's just his personality … he was nice enough."

"I'm starving," Troy said. "If we don't leave now, I'm going to start dancing out here in the lot."

"No!" his wife shouted.

Everyone hurried to his and her vehicle. "Meet you at Cajun's," Krissie said. "And no more dancing!"

Rachel climbed into the 4-Runner and found Troy staring. Unexpectedly, he sang. "Dance with me, I want to be your partner, can't you see…."

She cranked up Guns & Roses' *Welcome to the Jungle* on the radio to drown him out. "No dancing or singing; I want to enjoy my dinner tonight."

Horror

Certification of Death

Introduction

Certification of Death won Honorable Mention in the February 2006 issue of *ByLine* magazine for the New-Talent Short Story contest. It's unknown how many entries there were, but the top three winners lived in Massachusetts (two winners), and South Carolina, with other honorable mentions throughout the country. The judge wrote, "The honorable mentions ranked extraordinarily high."

The story is also published on *Amazon.com Shorts*.

As I've mentioned before, in my day job I am the Field Representative for Vital Records within the Arkansas Department of Health. We are responsible for filing approximately 100 new Arkansas death certificates daily, and 150 new birth certificates. I supervise the Death Registry section within the division. We review the death certificates as they arrive to fix mistakes before permanently filing the forms. I wondered what would happen if, while reviewing the forms, you came across your own death certificate?

Certification of Death

God, I'm getting burned out in my job. Perhaps I'll retire this time.

Seated alone, in a room off a murky hallway, Malcolm scanned through the stacks of documents cluttering his desk.

The mail was always slid across the floor from the corridor in a white plastic container. It happened so fast, he couldn't tell who delivered it.

There were numerous envelopes—white and manila—in all sizes. It took a full hour just to open the daily mail. Death certificates arrived from all over Arkansas signed by doctors, coroners, medical examiners, and hospice nurses. Malcolm saw it all.

For twenty-eight years, he had given his life to the state Health Department—the past fifteen as Document Examiner within the Division of Vital Records. He'd seen tens of thousands of death certificates.

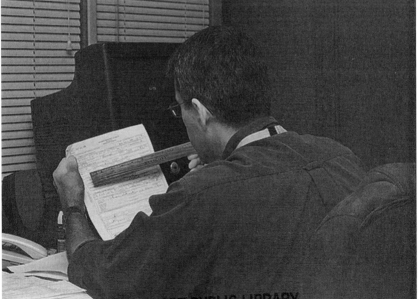

Photo by Stewart Matthews

His job was to review the forms and correct mistakes before Data Entry keyed them in. *Can't these people ever fill the forms out right?*

With a 12-inch ruler, moving it up and down to keep his eyes focused, he scanned the certificates for consistency. Age and date of birth must match. County of residence and state had to be cross-referenced. Someone who died from a shotgun blast could NOT have a natural manner of death! It had to be Accident, Suicide, or Homicide—or maybe Could Not Be Determined. But NOT Natural!

And this is what he did, everyday, for eternity it seemed. The third death certificate had a blank social security number. "Dadgummit!"

He picked up the phone to call the funeral director for the information, only to find no dial tone.

Can't the State pay its bill? Phone's been out all morning.

Setting the document to the side to verify later, Malcolm continued his review. *Old people, it's always old people.*

Laughing at his frustration, he remembered he was now in his sixties. Those pains that used to heal quickly, now took days to go away.

Thirty minutes into his work he stumbled across a certificate of a seven-year-old boy hit by a truck. "Multiple Head Wounds" the cause of death read.

A long, suppressed flashback reared its ugly head. He remembered running from the living room, past the screen door, with his former wife. The squeal of tires and loud bang had been followed by screams.

"Oh, my God! Oh, my God! What have I done?"

When they arrived at the end of the driveway, they saw him. Their son entwined within his bike under the truck; blood covered the pavement. The driver stood outside the open cab squeezing her cheeks with her hands.

It had been a closed-casket service.

Standing, Malcolm walked to the doorway leading to the endless hallway. He looked up and down and saw no one. Only laughter could be heard echoing from somewhere—*probably the break room*, he thought.

At least someone is having fun around here.

The phone rang. When he answered, he heard the gibberish of a child. "You've got the wrong number," he said, and hung up.

He sat and began to review the certificates again. An hour had passed when another box of mail was slid across the floor. "Come on! Does it ever end?"

Several certificates later, he came across a familiar name. "Janice! Good, grief."

The form showed she had remarried and her surviving spouse was named

"Walter."

The heat clicked on and he undid the top button on his shirt.

It was difficult to take his eyes off his ex-wife's death certificate. She had been a social worker at the local children's hospital, the occupation block read. Breast cancer claimed her soul; a nurse had signed the certificate.

She was in hospice. How awful to know you will die within weeks.

Again, he stood, and walked toward a file cabinet. For fifteen years he had worked in a room with no windows. *Is it raining outside? The weather report said it would rain today.*

Memories of his only marriage invaded his mind. Now she was dead—not that they had talked in over twenty years. Malcolm saw the death certificate of everyone who died in his state. And, as he aged, he recognized more and more of the names, former friends and relatives.

Sometimes, he would search the computer to see old certificates of people who had died before he took the job. All the documents were scanned and indexed. His mother and father, and a brother who committed suicide, he learned. He had always been told it was an accident.

Time was passing and he needed to complete his review of the newest certificates. Data Entry people would complain if he failed to meet deadlines. Again, he sat and placed the ruler on top of the next form.

"Malcolm Robinson," the decedent's name read.

Ha, he thought. *We have the same name.*

Malcolm moved the ruler down the document and found they shared the same date of birth. Then he read the parents' names and gasped.

That's my mom and dad…!

Quickly, he glanced at the occupation block, which read, "Document Examiner." The space for industry read, "State Employee."

"Is this a joke?" he yelled toward the hallway. "It's not funny!"

Marching into the corridor, he noticed many burned out overhead florescent lights. *Can't maintenance keep anything fixed?*

He headed for his supervisor's office at the end of the hall. As he continued, a weight began to press against his body. "What the hell?"

Confusion blinded him and he wondered if he was having a heart attack. But, as he took a few steps back, the pressure eased.

Again he walked forward and the pain returned until he stopped and went back to his office. Thirst now invaded his senses and he headed to the mini refrigerator located under a countertop.

"Empty? What the fuc…!" His hand shot to his mouth and he looked around, realizing he had almost screamed the four-letter-word.

A light in the hall flickered; he neither saw, nor heard, anyone. *I just filled it up. Someone's stealing my drinks again.*

On the opposite end of the hallway from his supervisor's room, was a water fountain. When he tried to approach it, the searing pain brought him to his knees and he was forced to crawl back to his desk. The agony again subsided.

"Hey! Is anyone out there?"

Am I in purgatory?

He smiled. Raised Catholic, he now considered himself a closet atheist. For several years he had attended a non-denominational church with his wife. But after the split, he never resumed.

Returning to his chair, he sat and glanced at the death certificate again. The cause of death read, "Gunshot Wound To Head."

"Very funny, guys!" He assumed his colleagues were watching by some hidden means.

Flashes of past events formed within his mind. Feeling his head, he found an unusual indentation near the temple.

Opening his desk drawer, he took out a small mirror. The reflection outlined a tiny hole, but no blood.

When he felt around the circumference, then explored the inside with his index digit, his finger disappeared into his skull.

"What the...?"

Several thumps outside brought him back to the present; for a moment he imagined he had fallen asleep.

Then he pulled his finger from his head.

He jumped up and rushed for the door, stopping just outside in the hallway. He had forgotten about the pain in his chest from a few minutes earlier.

When he turned to step back into his office, he tripped over several new white boxes of mail.

"Dammit!"

Kicking them to the side, he returned and sat at his desk. The death certificate—his certificate—remained on top. Below the cause of death read the manner of death: Pending.

"Pending?" The coroner had signed the certificate.

He couldn't determine.... It was an accident, right? I didn't mean to....

Leaning back in the creaky chair, defeated, Malcolm reevaluated the events. The illusion, or hallucination, seemed to go on and on.

I would never kill myself.

He thought about the coroner for each of the seventy-five counties in his state. Most had no training in crime investigation. *Perhaps I was murdered!*

"Pending?" *Why would the coroner need to investigate? I talked with him all the time about other peoples' death certificates. He didn't make many mistakes.*

With a smirk, Malcolm thought about the crime scene investigation shows now popular. No coroner he knew had access to the expensive equipment portrayed on the dramas. How many death determinations were ruled erroneously? How many suicides should have been classified as accidents, or vice versa? Or even homicide? How many surviving family members got screwed out of insurance money from an inaccurate manner or cause of death?

Spinning his chair around, he stared at a cockroach scampering across the floor. Finally, after several moments of contemplation, he grabbed another box of mail. Something … anything … to focus his mind elsewhere.

These envelopes were post marked from outside his state. The first piece contained a death certificate from California. Malcolm threw it into the in-basket to deal with later. Maybe mail it to Vital Records out there.

The second envelope held a certificate from New Hampshire, and in the third he found a death certificate from Australia. The fourth came from Saudi Arabia, he assumed, from the swords under a palm tree symbol. The logo had been on letters his dad sent home years earlier when Malcolm was in grade school. His father spent many years in foreign countries.

"I only review death certificates from Arkansas!" he yelled, looking from side to side. His surroundings remained silent.

Although some forms were filled out in a foreign language, most were in English and he noticed a trend. "Another suicide!"

And on he went, never raising his head. Certificate by certificate, he inched his way through the baskets of mail, finishing them, only to find new replacement containers each time. The clock on the wall never advanced.

"Goddamit! What am I looking for?"

Then a familiar envelope materialized with a well-known address: the coroner from his home county. *The legal Supplemental! I bet he ruled on my manner of death. About time … how long has it been?*

Slicing it open with his index finger, Malcolm read the findings: "Accident."

Injury description read, "Accidental shooting with a .22 handgun."

Ha, Malcolm thought. *Fooled them!*

After uttering these words, his memories broke through the wall of repression.

The gun had lay hidden in the glove compartment of his 2002 Dodge Ram—he had parked in a grassy ditch off dusty County Road 72. A forest expanded along one side of the road and tall cornfields on the other.

Years of isolation and worsening health had worked its toll. No children, most friends and family now dead. Retirement had sucked. Why did he put it off and work all these years before announcing his decision to leave? *It was that new boss. Said my bad memories were affecting my job performance. He forced me to retire!*

Placing the barrel to his temple, his last recollection was blood splattered on the inside windshield … a brief flash before white light, then darkness.

How could it be ruled anything other than suic…? *The coroner must have done me one last favor.*

Something dripped on Malcolm's shoulder and he looked at shadows leaking from the ceiling, onto the floor.

Black drops congealed and formed patterns. Scooting his chair back, he noticed a single envelope in a color he had never seen before, laying atop the desk.

At first he refused to open it, his ability to decipher time processed in slow motion. Perhaps eternity passed before he reached for the envelope.

He slid the paper from its cover into his hand and unfolded it.

Now frightened, he was unable to speak. A new Supplemental corrected the original copy from the coroner. The manner of death now read: "Suicide." The certifier's signature was in an unfamiliar font and he could not make out the name.

Malcolm turned to stand, but the shadows began to rain heavy upon him. The void rose, now ankle deep; he tried to think. Something had to be done.

Perhaps it was all a nightmare.

Kicking at the black ooze, he screamed, "Help!"

A burst of thunder sent the surroundings into darkness. An unknown sensation played on his skin as the shadows rained down upon his body.

He closed his eyes. Please…, God. I always wanted to have faith. You know that.

Skittering

Introduction

Many of us, especially homeowners, have experienced a sensation that an animal is in our attic. Will it gnaw through wires, causing a fire, or damage the roof causing a leak? Maybe nest and raise babies! It's an uncomfortable feeling to think wild critters are loose in your house. This was the motivation for *Skittering*.

It first won 3rd Place at the 2007 White County Creative Writers' Conference, Storyteller Award. The theme stated, "Ghost story, fiction or non-fiction. Setting must play an important role." It next won 1st Place at the 51st Grand Prairie Festival of Arts' fiction writing contest in Stuttgart, Arkansas. This was cool when Stuttgart mayor Marianne Maynard called to congratulate me.

The narrative then received Honorable Mention in the October 2007 issue of *ByLine* magazine for Spooky Story contest. The theme was, "Short story of 2,000 words or less with a Halloween or haunted plot." The number of entries here is unknown, but 1st Place winner lived in Oklahoma, 2nd Place in Tennessee, and 3rd Place lived in Grilly, France. Can I call this an international win? The original title of the piece when entered to *ByLine's* contest was *Scampering*. My mother-in-law read the tale and felt that "skittering" better represented the sounds I described. I agreed, thus the name change.

Finally, it is with great joy that I retire the creepy story to publication by the Ozark Writers League's (OWL) anthology, *Echoes of the Ozarks Volume IV*. Next time you think you hear something in your attic, I hope you remember my tale here.

Skittering

With a last paint stroke, Carlos stepped back to admire his finished work. The bathroom had been his pride and joy.

One final touch-up along the floorboard completed his task. Kids in the neighbor's backyard ended his gloat; he leaned over the tub to peer out the tiled window. Children jumped on their trampoline, each of the three kids trying to touch overhead oak branches.

Damn kids!

His old home was a fixer-upper in a once posh sub-division; Carlos moved to the area for quiet in retirement years.

He stepped back to the bathroom's middle to inspect his work again. Asian rugs lay atop newly polished wood floors, tile covered the area around the bathtub and separate walk-in shower. Gold plated faucets were installed on sinks, the new tub served as a Jacuzzi. He could sit on the fold-down seat molded inside the shower. This would help his aging, arthritic body.

Setting oil based paint cans on drop-rags in the hallway, he stepped into the bathroom's large closet. A fresh coat of burgundy hid markings from the former homeowner's children.

New shelves would arrive tomorrow from Home Depot; he tried to decide on which side he wanted them, when something skittered across the attic floor.

Dammit! Don't tell me I have squirrels.

The post-World War II home had been designed with little crawl space above the ceiling. Taking down his stepladder in the garage, Carlos climbed and pushed aside a square panel to reveal darkness.

The flashlight failed; he shook it and a weak beam wavered forth. It exposed long support beams stuffed with insulation. Tacked behind a crossbeam he found a black and white photo of an old woman standing outside the home glaring at the camera. She reminded him of some tongue-speaking, religious-freak mother who forced her kids to church every night.

Carlos' eyes fixed upon the woman's form, robed in plain dark dress that buttoned up to the neck, her hair tied in a knot. Those piercing pupils entranced him until he thought he heard a child's laughter deep in the musty attic.

"Who's there?"

Turning an ear toward the sound, he realized the noise originated from the kids next door. His mind focused back upon the claws he heard in the bathroom.

With a whistle, he called, "Come here. Come here little squirrel."

It's too dark and hot up here; no animal would make a nest in this heat.

Once he climbed down and replaced the stepladder on a wall-hook, he glanced toward his Cadillac sedan. It was nice to have a garage for the first time as a homeowner. He would tell the insurance man; maybe rates would be reduced.

Returning to the bathroom, he lifted the commode lid and relieved himself. New cabinets around the sinks, and hanging light fixtures, all added ambiance. Kids next door must have gone inside and he enjoyed the quiet.

Then he heard claws scamper again above his ceiling.

"Dammit!"

The kitchen was a work in progress; he would soon continue renovations. A directory lay atop the shelf under his phone. After looking up the number, he called animal control.

"When can you come out? It's disturbing to have animals in my attic."

After listening to the speaker, Carlos continued. "Today would be great. Thank you."

With a cup of cinnamon tea in hand, he exited the front door and walked around the home, inspecting any possible entrance to the garret. Several air vents were spaced along the side and he examined each one. Wire mesh already firmly installed should prevent any critter from entering.

He heard a vehicle pull into the driveway and returned to the front. "'Bout time you got here."

"It's been less than an hour … I was in the area when they radioed me."

"The thing's in the attic." Carlos reached into his pocket and pulled out the key chain. Pushing a button, the garage door began to rise.

"You can get up there this way," he continued.

Below the square entrance through the ceiling the two stopped. "Not much room up there," Carlos said. "Good thing you wore shorts on this hot day."

The city worker rolled his eyes and reached for the stepladder. Once he climbed up, he commented, "Definitely will have to crawl up here."

Without a reply, Carlos stepped out into the driveway and enjoyed a warm breeze that rolled down from nearby Ozark Mountains. Fort Smith had a rich history and he liked his 40's-style home surrounded by nearby

Victorians. He was glad the previous owner had closed in the carport and installed a garage door opener.

Modernizing the house would keep him occupied during retirement. Now the lavatory was complete; after the kitchen, he would work outside at bleaching away putrid green algae, or mold, or whatever it was, from the dark crimson brick around the sides.

Thick holly bushes with red berries lined the front of the one story structure. Perhaps he would hire a landscape expert for yard work, which he disliked. Something flapped in the breeze, hooked to a branch, caught his attention. He reached for it, scratching his arm on the prickly shrub.

Another snapshot of the old fundamentalist lady in dark dress stared at him from a different pose; her eyes like black marbles and cheeks with fissured skin. She stood in the front yard beside a magnolia tree that no longer existed. Some kid in the house at the back of her peeked at the photographer from behind curtains.

Carlos glanced up at the window and noticed drapes move. Hurrying to the front door, he stormed through the home. "Who's in here?"

A side door to the garage creaked open and Carlos stopped. The animal control expert looked in. "Mr. Sanders…."

"Yes," Carlos snapped.

"I found nothing in your attic. There's just no way anything could get up there, let alone survive in that heat. All possible openings around the house are secured."

"I know what I heard!"

"I'm sorry. If you hear it again, call me. Here's my card with my cell number."

Carlos watched the small truck pull out, camper mounted atop the bed and city advertisement decal fixed to driver's side door.

* * *

The evening sun began its decline; Carlos pulled his sedan into the garage. Rubbing his stomach, he realized he had eaten too much at Ryan's restaurant.

Bright solar rays disappeared as the automatic entrance lowered. He had taped aluminum foil over the door's three windows; the room was dark except for an overhead light that popped on each time he opened the electronic access.

Bones and muscles ached from a long day of painting and tiling around the tub and shower. Grout was probably not dry, but he'd be careful not to splash when he took a warm bath.

With closed eyes, he enjoyed hot rising water against his naked body. His back rested along the built-in deep, lumbar support. Loose, wrinkled skin dangled from his bony frame.

Once water covered the whirlpool jets, he turned them on using a thirty-minute timer. Retirement would be sweet.

Sleep descended and dreams invaded his mind. Memories of his deceased spouse and their routine days surfaced. His refusal to have children caused a bitter tension that exacerbated over the years. She died an unhappy woman with a weakened heart made worse by his stern disposition.

Carlos' brain wandered further back in time; she had been pretty but let herself go. Her last ten years she lived in a spare bedroom, at the end of the hall.

His eyes twitched under closed lids; an outside noise brought him out of sleep. Sitting up, he noticed the timer had stopped and water had cooled. It was dark outside and he saw the moon through the window.

After letting some water out, and reheating the tub, he rested his head once again. With closed eyes he thought about amiable retirement, alone, without the roommate he stopped loving years ago.

Then nails scampered across the attic floor, several animals he guessed. They stopped a moment, then scurried again, claws scratching wood planks atop support beams above the bathroom.

A snort that sounded like it was inside his room caused his heart to race and he sat up. His eyes focused on a blurry image reflected off white tiles in front of him, above the faucet.

He rubbed his eyes and looked again. The old woman from the photos, with black pupils, glared his direction. Splashing water in his face, he used fingers to stretch his tired eyelids. When he looked again he saw only bright overhead lights that played patterns off his newly tiled bathroom.

An illusion, ha.

Then clawed feet again skittered above his ceiling.

"Dammit!"

Toweling off, he threw on a robe and walked to the phone in the kitchen. He had thrown the animal control expert's business card into the drawer.

When he opened it, a picture stared at him. The woman in her dark dress and shadowy eyes peered at the photographer. Behind her, in a basket, stood some breed of animal that looked a cross of an armadillo and possum. Yet the creature contained traits of a predator-stalking prey.

Carlos threw the print in nearby trash and called animal control. After leaving a voicemail, he sat at the kitchen table, atop a metal chair with plastic wrapped seat.

Furniture covering was his idea, which his former spouse abhorred. Her siblings stopped visiting with nieces and nephews. Too many rules around his red-glass, 1800's antiques.

The hot bath had made him thirsty, so he fixed himself a glass of tea and stepped toward the front room. Opened drapes revealed the driveway.

"I closed those curtains!"

Adjusting his unfastened robe to cover his chest, he stormed to the window and pulled the string to shut the drapes. Once again he walked through the house, peeking in closets and behind hundred-year-old furniture.

The feeling that he was not alone would not abate.

He walked by a polished brown table in the hallway, a wall mirror hung behind it decorated with adjoining framed pictures of his spouse black and whites. Wooden floors squeaked under his bare feet. A metal heating grate within the foundation echoed a growl from deep within.

Then a flash in the mirror stopped him and he backed up to peek.

Nothing at first seemed unusual, until he saw the old woman in the looking glass, gazing at him through his window.

Quickly turning, he glanced toward the front room windowpane. The drapes remained closed.

Petrified, his eyes crisscrossed the view before him. An eerie calm returned, then he heard claws tap across the attic floor.

Pulse pounded in his temple and he raced to the bedroom to retrieve clothes and his billfold.

Once dressed, he sat in his sedan and tried to open the garage.

The electronic switch failed; he kept pushing the button when he noticed the side door to the kitchen creep open and shadows crawl out along the floor.

Slamming the gearshift into reverse, he crashed through the metal barrier and backed into the street, before gunning the vehicle forward.

At the hotel overlooking Garrison Avenue, in downtown Fort Smith, he threw keys atop the table and sat on the bed's edge. Running fingers through tangled gray hair, he tried to make sense of events.

His neck ached and he rubbed muscles, then raised his head toward the mirror fixed to the wall opposite the bed. The woman glared at him in black and white; death orbs would not release his trance. Her dark soul radiated from behind empty eye sockets.

Claws skittered above the ceiling.

Essays
and
Nonfiction

Voltaire and 9/11

Introduction

Without a doubt, this is one of my most successful pieces. I've won other essay contests on the same theme, and may one day write a nonfiction book on the subject. It's difficult to be an optimist in a world of chaos. But when you put our lives in historic perspective, it gives us reason to pause and count our blessings.

Voltaire and 9/11 initially won 1st Place at the 2005 Arkansas Writers' Conference in the Grand Conference Award. This is considered the top prize for the conference. Local author and judge, Vic Fleming, sponsors the contest. His crossword puzzles are published in national magazines. His guidance has assisted many writers, and I thank him for that. The award's theme stated, "An essay that addresses the extent to which your view of the human race has changed since September 11, 2001."

The essay next won 2nd Honorable Mention at the 2005 White County Creative Writers' Conference, A Lesson Learned from Life contest. The theme required, "Personal essay: real-life experience that has provided a philosophical basis for your life."

Voltaire and 9/11 then won Special Honorable Mention (4th Place) in the November 2005 issue of *ByLine* magazine for its Creative Nonfiction contest. The judge wrote, "The winners of this contest were savvy folk. Reading them, I applauded their strong writing skills, distinct attitude, strong sense of place, with maybe a million or so written words behind them. Practice tells." There were 90 entries; the top three winners lived in Ohio, Texas, and Idaho.

In 2006, at the Arkansas Writers' Conference, the piece won 3rd Place in White County Creative Writers Award. The requirement stated, "1500-word essay, 'A Humorous Look at the World Today.'" Unlike the *ByLine* competition above, with 90 entries, this contest had three submissions. Now you know the rest of the story.

Don't be fooled to think the story won every contest I entered. It didn't. But I did get some nice, and not so nice, rejections. I entered *Voltaire and 9/11* in The Society of Southwestern Authors 2006 Personal Essay/Memoir writing contest. One judge wrote on the comment sheets sent back, "Nice irony. Needs editing." Another judge wrote, "For a memoir, I think it's important to focus on a situation, which is instructive. The same with the child could be more developed to show the beauty of life in the present." And the third judge said, "Good writing and valid points, but too much like a sermon." I had a rating of around 50 from all three judges, which led me to believe I placed well among the 336 entries from around the globe.

Finally, *Voltaire and 9/11* will be retired to publication both in this current anthology, and in late 2008 when Temenos Publishing will include the essay in *Tales From the South: Volume III*. I read the piece in public on KUAR FM89 at The Starving Artist, a restaurant owned by Paula Martin Morell (editor) and her husband. An incredible place to eat. I strongly recommend it.

Voltaire and 9/11

During a conversation with a friend, she explained, "…peace in the Middle East, the tsunami in Asia, and 9/11—it's all there in the Bible. I believe the world's coming to an end."

I smiled and contemplated a reply. This woman was serious; she thought the apocalypse was near. Of course, as a man of science, I knew men much smarter than I had theories to believe why the sun would go nova in a few billion years, taking mankind with it. And we're always under threat of another meteor that may cause mass extinction. A nuclear war would not surprise me either, seeing how human nature has warred throughout history.

"There have been many prophecies from most religions about the end of the world," I said. "I'm now reading a collection of history by the Durants called *The Story of Civilization*. It amazes me how often some cultic leader screams to his followers that the end of the world is upon us … a few denominations actually had a date, such as the Jehovah's Witnesses. Or what about the presumed Y2K computer glitch at the beginning of the millennium? Nuclear weapons were supposed to be launched when the date went from 1999 to 2000. I'm sorry, but my view of the human race has not changed."

"How can you say that? People have lost faith. I think God was telling those unbelievers in Asia something when He sent the wave."

Remaining quiet, I tried to avoid an argument. The pastor at a church I once visited made a similar juxtaposition a few Sundays after the tsunami's death toll passed 250,000. I wondered what he would say about the millions who died in floods in China before Christ? What of the Christians among the dead? Was it okay to make such generalizations to his 'sheep'? Every time I heard him refer to us as his flock I wanted to lean over to my wife and say, "Baaaaa."

"Look," I replied. "What happened on 9/11 was awful and I'm glad we did something about it. Send a message not to screw with us Americans. Heaven knows we need a strong military to avoid the city-state chaos of ancient Greece. But millions have died in wars. Death and suffering is what writes history. My God! The Bible is nothing but blood and guts. 9/11 was bad, but there's not another era in human history, or another country than America, that I would want to live in. We lazy bastards have it made and don't know it. Give us an inch and we want the entire damn mile! Larger homes, nicer automobiles, phones, cable, computers, medical care—it's never enough. We want Utopia and it doesn't exist! At least not in my experience."

"Okay … okay," she whispered. "Calm down."

"I'm sorry. I'm just tired of everyone complaining about the awful conditions of our modern world. Suffering is part of our existence. I'm so thankful for those remarkable individuals who shaped our lives. The 'Founding Fathers' may be an abstraction, but these men were incredibly insightful for the times they lived in and the ideas they advocated. For the laws and morals to evolve and curb the negative aspect of human nature are among the most fantastic ideas in history. It allowed our social structure and checks and balances to come into being."

I had rambled long enough evidenced from my friend's response.

"That's why He gave us the Ten Commandments."

Oh, my God, I thought. She's a Christian living under Jewish law. Faith alone, yet look at all the stipulations our Protestant friends have forced upon us.

"Look," I said. "Our consciousness is a miracle and it amazes me. I see, or try to see, goodness in the human race. Yet, having studied history, I'm very skeptical. The past replicates itself because the next generation lacks the experience of the previous one. So we make our mistakes, only to watch our children repeat them. That's my view of the human race. We had 9/11 and what the meaning of 'is' is, my father had Vietnam and Watergate, my grandfather had World War II and The Great Depression, and my great-grandfather had World War I and Prohibition. Not enough? My great-great-grandfather had slavery, the Civil War, and then Reconstruction. Read up on European history. It's nothing but conflict. Voltaire lost faith after the Lisbon earthquake so he built a garden. Hell, the entire world is nothing but conflict—always has been. Family members kill loved ones faster than the terrorists kill strangers. Damn you, Cain! Nope, my views didn't change. With all the evil, I somehow find more goodness. I guess I'm just a bowl full of irony."

I could see that far away look in her eyes—a response I was familiar with whenever I gave my 'great-time-to-be-alive-despite-the-chaos' speech. Speaking in a softer manner, I said, "Okay, so I choose to look on the bright side. Nevertheless, we are all going to die. It's just that your chance of dying suddenly from a brain aneurysm is higher than from a terrorist attack. There, do you feel better?"

She had been in deep thought and I don't think heard a word I said. "What about the United Nations uniting all the countries? It's a sign."

Oh my God!

We said our goodbyes and she left. I proceeded to the back of the house and could hear my four-year-old in the bathroom, singing.

"What're you doing?" I asked from the other side of the closed door.

"Poopin' and learning about Jesus."

Oh, I love God. What a beautiful sense of humor He has.

Later, when I went to the bathroom, I found the book my daughter had been 'reading' on the floor by the commode. Reaching over, I picked it up. The title said, *The House at Pooh Corner.*

What a wonderful life I have, such a shame I will one day die. Just hope the end is painless. At least I have my faith.

Sybil

Introduction

I have written two versions of *Sybil* that I believe are different enough to be considered separate stories. The first attempt at this nonfiction piece developed in the late 90s as I first tried to learn the techniques for writers. The University of Arkansas at Little Rock's *Quills & Pixels* published that essay in 1999.

Since then I have joined local writing groups, attended conferences, and attached myself to several mentors such as Jim Bell and Dusty Richards. I've learned much, and with Paula Martin Morell's help, I rewrote *Sybil* into the version that was published in 2006 by Temenos Publishing in its first anthology, *Tales from the South*. In Paula's acceptance letter she wrote, "I really like this piece, and there are a lot of very interesting things to work with."

Sybil won its first contest when it took 3rd Place at the 2004 White County Creative Writers' Conference, The Mary Ann Trulock Award. The contest theme stated, "Essay about a friend, mentor, or guide who has influenced your life."

Next, the essay won Special Honorable Mention (4th Place) in the February 2005 issue of *ByLine* magazine for the Personal Experience Article contest. The number of entries was not stated, but the top three winners lived in California and Wisconsin (two from Wisconsin). Special Honorable Mentions and Honorable Mentions came from over a dozen states.

The Storyteller magazine editor, Regina Williams, accepted *Sybil* in its 2005 January/February/March issue. The essay went on to win 2nd Place in the magazine's People's Choice Award. Among my most cherished accomplishment, several hundred readers from around the U.S. vote this acknowledgment.

The title *Sybil* is derived from the 1976 movie staring Sally Field and Joanne Woodward.

I would like to thank Jeannine Coiner and the other Independent Living Program coordinators at the Arkansas Department of Human Services. What you do is so important.

Dedicated to Priscilla, I pray your adult life has brought you peace.

"Priscilla's and Brian's Song"

I walked into the courtroom
and what did I see?

My Mom, a looking at me.

You see the judge sitting in her chair,
you see my Mom playin' with her hair.

You see my Dad didn't show up for court.
Now they are going to have to throw him in jail, of course.

I looked to my left,
I looked to my right,
And tell myself everything's going to be all right.

Priscilla

Sybil

"If I join up, can I kill somebody? I wanna kill someone."
The armed forces recruiter ignored the boy. The other kids snickered.
Somehow I got *stuck* as a volunteer with the Department of Human Services. The whiny kids—fourteen to eighteen year olds—disrupted the speaker every month.
Another spokesperson, a woman from the bus company, arrived to explain how to read the schedule. She left in tears. Other presenters did their best. None of the kids cared about how to create a resume or balance a checkbook. They just didn't give a damn.
They'll all go to prison when they leave this Independent Living Program, I often thought. *The State won't house them forever.*
Months into the program an event occurred that gave me a new outlook

on life. My only participation up to that time had been to assist the program coordinator with errands and provide moral support. Not bad for two hours a month. The volunteer experience might look good on my resume—always looking out for myself.

On that particular date, I met the class on the seventh floor of a downtown building. The teenage foster adolescents paraded outside the meeting room doing everything but what they were supposed to do.

It was a Tuesday night and I was already yearning to go home. Anything would have been better than being there. Like smoking a joint and watchin' *The Simpsons.*

"We're going as a group to McDonald's down the street," the coordinator said, once she got everyone seated. "Then our speaker will talk about what you need to know once you become independent of the State and are on your own."

Great, I thought. Now I have to walk.

I followed behind the kids to ensure no one snuck off. As always happened, Sybil trailed my every step. Sure, I knew she had a crush on me—I guess. But she listened to my advice, words of wisdom if you will, so I used the relationship under the impression I might set someone in distress on the right path.

The line stretched twenty yards as we all made our way across busy streets toward our fast food treat. Sybil and I were alone in back.

Our conversation consisted of small talk. She then said, "I had a Norplant put in my arm last week."

What? I thought. *Was she hitting on me?*

I knew that a Norplant was a birth control device—but why would she tell me this?

Struggling for the right response, I decided on the safe option and remained quiet.

The girl frustrated the heck out of me. She was cute, but her attire seemed like a purchase from Goodwill. With long brunette hair and cheeks that highlighted her face, she could be a knockout at her high school with the right attitude. Only I suspected she hung in corners and shied away from crowds. Perhaps *Carrie* in Stephen Kings' novel is a good illustration.

She never looked me in the eyes for more than a second. This irritated me to no end. *Look at me, dadgumit!* Only her eyes always focused down.

You had a Norplant put in your arm last week? I wanted to ask, to make sure I heard her right. *Why are you telling me this?*

But I said nothing for several long moments.

At least the dinner is paid for by the State. I can't wait to get home.

We walked a block in silence, although it felt like a mile. I had to respond but did not know how. If I said the wrong thing it might be perceived as a 'come-on'.

Two boys in front of us got a driver mad when they gave him the middle finger. He blew his horn and flipped the boys in turn.

"Stop that," I told them.

"Yes, sir," they both replied.

Discipline was not my forte and I hoped they would listen. The program coordinator was not far ahead; so I dropped behind the crowd further ... *let her deal with them.*

My mind drifted back to Sybil. Her disclosure of using birth control needed a retort. It had to be an adult reply. But who was I to step up to the plate, a spoiled college graduate who sat at home on weekends in a marijuana induced stupor feeling sorry for myself because I didn't have a date? I would grow old alone and the thought gave me angst.

I think I said, "You need to be very careful."

"It's not what *I* do," she said staring down. "It's because of something my dad and brother did to me."

By this time we had reached McDonald's and the group ran around seating themselves. I stood speechless for a moment before finally sitting next to the program coordinator; Sybil slid in beside me. The guest speaker said she would probably mention Pell Grants for college and my young admirer seemed interested.

For the next twenty minutes, I told her everything she would need to know for school: how to enroll, get an advisor, balance the easy courses with the hard ones, etc. But our earlier conversation always remained in the back of my mind.

I looked over at a youth in a heavy coat laying his head on the table. A pick was lodged into his Afro. Three other boys began to blow spit-wads through straws.

Sybil and I listened to the program coordinator tell us how she got her job. *I hope I get a job that pays more than you probably make*, I remember thinking. *And who wants to work with these punks?*

But Sybil ... what of her? I considered myself someone who could handle most situations. Maybe she would become a veterinarian or lawyer to help others, as she told me she wanted to do. I doubted she understood the hard work involved to get a college degree in these fields.

That evening I discussed the conversation alone with the program coordinator as we walked out to our vehicles.

"Sybil had a horrific childhood," she said. "Both parents were drug users and her father and brother raped her repeatedly. She sees a psychiatrist several times a month. Her father beat her once because he said she looked at him wrong."

There it was, out in the open. No more guessing on my part. I looked at the teenagers around me who had formed small groups while waiting for their foster parents to pick them up. Something awful must have happened to each of them to be taken from their natural homes.

And what did I do that evening? Went home and smoked a joint—that's what. As the smoke curled around my head, I tried to ignore the events of the night and pain of those children.

I retrieved the remote and turned up the volume to a comedy sitcom. But deep thoughts kept invading my mind and the actors' jokes flew over my head. I clicked the TV off and lay back on the couch. Blurry subconscious images began to focus and I couldn't hold back any longer.

For the first time in my life I realized how I projected my ideas of life onto others. It dawned on me how a friend's father's violent temper and alcoholism had affected him growing up. And an old girlfriend from college, I had helped her pick her drunken mom off the floor that night—the first time I met her.

Cool, her mom likes to party. Perhaps I was wrong?

Over the next year I tried to live up to mentor-status with Sybil. She eventually married a man she met through a personal ad, and dropped out of college after her first semester using a Pell grant.

The last time I saw her was five years later during lunch at Ryan's restaurant. She was my waitress and we talked on and off during the meal. Her hidden smile remained and she still avoided eye contact.

She was separated or divorced—I don't remember which. Eschewed from her family and now independent from the State, I wonder to this day how she turned out. Will she ever know how much more she taught me about life while I was her mentor?

Perhaps one day after I become a wealthy writer, and I'm signing books at a local event, Sybil will come up to me. I'll hug her and make everyone in line wait, and then ask her to sit by me as I continue to autograph my novel. Maybe I can offer her hope if she's down on her luck.

"It's so good to see you Sybil. How have you been?"

Her response.

"Tell me about what's going on in your life? Where do you work? Are you married? Do you have kids? Did you ever go back to school? Is there anything I can do to help?"

Her response.

"Let's stay in touch, okay? I would like for you to meet my wife and kids."

Her response?

Monkey Ranch Creek

Introduction

Monkey Ranch Creek took 2nd Place at the 2004 White County Creative Writers' Conference, Children's Story contest.

The story next won 1st Place in the December 2005 Arkansas Only Short Story Contest. *Arkansas Only* is an online magazine. The theme stated, "We are looking for short fiction. Make it touching. Make it funny. Make it a thriller or make it a coming of age. The subject is up to you." In the notification letter, editor Lisa Ahne wrote, "Of all the entries, yours was by far the finest. It was a delight to read."

By winning 1st Place, Lisa Ahne published the essay on her online magazine in January 2006.

This nonfiction piece took place at my maternal grandparents' cabin on Greers Ferry Lake, near the now submerged former town of Shiloh, Arkansas, in Cleburne County. The cabin was sold in the late 80s after my grandfather's death. As I write this introduction, my grandmother suffers the ending stages of Alzheimers and occupies a bed in the Salem Place Nursing and Rehabilitation Center, Conway, Arkansas.

I dedicate this piece to Pampa Eddie and Mamma Rhea

Monkey Ranch Creek

Finally, it was ready!

Steve glanced toward his grandparents sipping coffee on the porch. "Come and see!" he yelled.

Pampa Eddie and Mamma Rhea looked through the woods and found him standing at the base of a cluster of pines and oaks. Several two by fours were nailed like a ladder up the trunk of a tall tree. It had taken much of the week to build and seemed the only source of entertainment for their grandson. Steve was used to morning cartoons and boxes of toys to choose from. With no cable, he would have to find other sources of fun.

As they made their way, Steve noticed the sunlight reflecting off the waves in the lake down the dirt road leading from the cabin. The caw of crows could be heard in the distance and a granddaddy long legs spider climbed over the decaying pine needles littered along the ground.

"Oh, that looks nice," Mamma said. "You and your grandfather did a good job building it."

Steve climbed until he reached the pallet nailed to several boards anchoring the tree house. "It's my spaceship!" he said.

"Spaceship?" Pampa smiled. "You need to name it."

Oh, yeah, he thought. He looked around for ideas.

Ten feet away, a trickle of water flowed down a normally dried creek bed. It had rained briefly yesterday when an afternoon thunderstorm passed over the lake.

The mud dam held where Steve had constructed it last evening. The mini reservoir spilled around the structure and flooded over the pine needles pushed to the side until it drained back into the creek below the dam.

"Monkey Ranch Creek," he said down to his grandparents.

That was the name he and a friend had given to the brook last year. How they decided upon it was long forgotten.

"Watch out for robbers!" Steve suddenly stood and pulled two pistols from his holster.

Pointing them toward the surrounding woods, he yelled "Pow, pow, pow," as the popping noise echoed from the red-capped paper fed into the guns.

"You don't let them get us," Mamma said.

Shasta, a black collie, danced around along the ground and whined as if she wanted up with Steve.

"It's a monster!" Steve yelled, pointing a pistol at the dog and pulling the trigger.

"Poor Shasta," Mamma said, reaching down to pet the animal. "Steve got you. Play dead."

On command, the dog lay down and pretended to be asleep.

He laughed. "That's funny." Snatching several pinecones from a nearby limb, he yelled, "Grenades!"

Ignoring the explosion noises her grandson screamed, she said, "I need to get breakfast ready. Why don't you two check the trot-line?"

Steve scurried down and followed his grandfather back to the cabin.

After grabbing a bucket and his tackle gear, Pampa said, "Let's go."

Through a rollout window in the cottage, Steve saw his grandmother slicing potatoes for morning hash browns. She smiled at him.

Monkey Ranch Creek zigzagged across the muddy road leading to the lake. The downhill flow was no stronger than the wash-off on the curbs back at his parents' home. That's where he would float pop-sickle sticks over the mini rapids he would create.

His grandfather reached into his green jumpsuit. "Here … would you like a mint?"

Steve popped it in his mouth and pulled his squeezed-money-pouch from his pocket like his Pampa had just done, and removed a small pocketknife.

"Don't open that," Pampa said. "We'll need it to cut the fish from the line."

Near the shore, several yards into the water, was a submerged thicket of gray leafless trees. Jumping into the Johnson boat, the two pushed off with paddles and maneuvered themselves to the trotline that made a tiny indention along the water surface.

Steve held the boat steady against a decaying limb as his grandfather pulled the boat from hook to hook. "Here we go," he said.

A bream with red along its gills thrashed as he unhooked it and strung a stringer through its mouth and tied it to the boat. He then flipped it back in the water.

Easing over the side, Steve watched the fish. Next week he started second grade and would have something exciting to share with his schoolmates.

He then reached into his holster and pulled out a pistol and squeezed the trigger. Several pops echoed along the shoreline. "Got you!" he yelled.

Pampa looked over his shoulder and smiled.

This is fun, Steve thought.

He then wondered what his grandparents did for excitement. TV was not allowed at the cabin, and they had told him that they never had television growing up. Fortunately, there were many outdoor things to do.

That evening, as the sun lowered behind a mountain on the other side of the lake, Steve grabbed a second helping of Pound Cake covered with strawberries and climbed into the tree house overlooking Monkey Ranch Creek.

Sitting on a lawn chair his grandfather had earlier helped to lift, Steve swiped his foot along the plank and swept a pile of pine needles to the ground. Through the loose canopy of pine and oak he saw Pampa start a campfire in front of the cabin. A bag of marshmallows lay on one of the several chairs nearby.

Below, on the ground, he saw that the creek bed was now dry. Its name would remain with him for all times.

"Let me help," he yelled, climbing down, and running the short expanse to the cabin. He held the straightened metal hanger over the flames. After several roasted marshmallows, the three campers sat in silence and looked to the sky. Stars filled the heavens like the bumpy ceiling on his room back at home. In the distance a thunderstorm echoed and the wind began to blow through trees. Tomorrow the creek would flow again and he could repair the dam.

Steve listened to the crickets against the approaching storm. What a wonderful life. He and his grandparents would do this forever—*every* summer. He would never forget these moments. That was a promise.

Little Rock and Home

Introduction

This short essay won 3rd Place in the 2004 Arkansas Writers' Conference, Kohler/Spratt Award contest. The theme required, "Essay about your memories of Little Rock, 750 word limit."

Photo courtesy of Arkansas Department of Parks and Tourism

Little Rock and Home

My first memories as a child of Little Rock was crossing Levy Bridge on Interstate 40 and looking south at three skyscrapers that then dominated the skyline. All those lights mesmerized me as I rubbed my young eyes after waking from a nap in the backseat of my parents' Dodge Charger. The trip from Mountain Home had taken three hours and the curvy Ozark roads had left me carsick.

Since it was the holidays, there was one tall middle building with windows lit up to look like a thirty-story Christmas tree.

Wow, I remember thinking. How did they do that? The capitol looked so beautiful and gave me a peaceful feeling as a symbol that life would be okay as long as it stood.

Of course I learned later that Little Rock was relatively small for a city, about the 99th largest in the United States. But I recalled once driving through Houston and being terrified. It was too much. Little Rock was a right-sized city with small town atmosphere.

Twenty years later I moved back, permanently. Several years in Texas, Kansas, and Germany left me with great admiration for home. Both sets of grandparents lived north of Little Rock, and with relatives and childhood friends scattered all over central Arkansas, I knew that one day I would live in Little Rock—or close by.

With amazement I listened to my grandmother tell me about construction of I-30 bridge over the Arkansas River, and how she endured long traffic jams making her way down Main Street to Southwestern Bell where she had retired as an operator.

I still wait for the mighty river to freeze again the way my grandfather described it occurring back in the 20s. I remember watching Steve Little kick a sixty-yard field goal for the Razorbacks in War Memorial Stadium. Then there was the time my father and I fired our shotguns at floating lilies in the swamp near Maumelle as I-430 was being constructed.

The best memory of all was in 1981 when my family and I landed at the airport after living two years in Germany. A picture I have expresses it best.

The look on my face said, "Ah, home at last."

There is no doubt that there are many amazing skylines worldwide. My favorite, however, is coming in from Pine Bluff and seeing Little Rock suddenly appear on the horizon. The I-40 vista from Levy Bridge is most nostalgic, and the highest point on Highway 67 at Jacksonville has a pretty cool view. The most peaceful scene is from Fort Roots' armed forces hospital across the river. I wonder what visitors and veterans from throughout the decades thought of our city?

No tour of the area would be complete—whether you like him or not—without a discussion of Bill Clinton. The transformation of the river area in downtown, with his presidential library anchoring the periphery, has changed River Market from a high crime area to a fun location for family. 'No coolers allowed' ordinances, and three dollar bottles of water announce to visitors that our city is now in the big times!

Sarcasm aside, my fair city has the feel of a large, bustling metropolis with that small Mayberry town attitude. We have our problems, no doubt—public school complaints, crime, vagrants, high cost of living—but I've yet to hear of a large city anywhere worldwide without criticism. It is a symbiotic condition of growing pains.

A good friend and former independent bookstore owner wrote a history of Little Rock because so many customers kept requesting it and one had never been written. As I read his work I saw the wonderful and colorful past of the city come alive. From events back in the French explorer La Harpe's days, to Civil War era up through the 20's, 30's, and World War II, Little Rock has much to be proud of—and others to learn from.

My father-in-law moved to Memphis in the 50's as a result of the Central High School race crisis. An unfortunate affair? Sure. But look how much we learned from it and how far we have come. Utopia is not upon us yet, but we are one step closer. At least we are striving toward a goal, and gained knowledge from past mistakes.

Even today, I cannot pass over I-40 bridge at Levi without glancing over to see Little Rock. It always brings back the pleasant childhood memories of when my family visited my grandparents.

I remember darkness at night, and then suddenly streetlamps lit the surroundings with an orange glow. I would pop up from my nap and look at the tall building across the river.

We were almost home.

Utopian Dreams

Introduction

The reader will notice a similar theme with this essay and *Voltaire and 9/11*. The ideas expressed in the two pieces have given me a better outlook on my future, and I hope it will the reader as well. You might guess one of my favorite comedy skits was the grumpy old men on *Saturday Night Live*. "In my day we didn't have running water and we liked it! Yeah, we stunk and everyone else did, too. If our innards fell down into our ball sack, we liked it. We'd lie on our back and kick until our stomachs went back up. And we liked it!"

Utopian Dreams won 1st Place in the 2006 Essay Contest sponsored by The Spring River Branch of The National League of American Pen Women. The essay topic stated, "My dream for the new year." The number of entries was not stated, but other winners lived in New York, Georgia, Arizona, and Arkansas.

It next took Honorable Mention in the April 2007 issue of *ByLine* magazine for the Personal Essay contest. There were 98 entries with the top two winners from California and the third from Wisconsin.

Finally, the essay won 3rd Place in the 1st Annual Columbia Chapter of the Missouri Writers' Guild Prose and Poetry Contests.

By placing in the contest above, *Utopian Dreams* was considered for publication by The Columbia Chapter of the Missouri Writers' Guild anthology, *Well Versed - 2008*. I'm happy to say it was accepted.

Utopian Dreams

The time is near—New Year's resolutions. Our hopes and dreams for the future, both personally and collectively. What will it be: more money, lose weight, bigger car, a love interest ... a better love interest? Perhaps world peace! Yeah, that's it. World peace.

I've given up on the global harmony issue—I'm too old and wise to waste energy. No, sir—or ma'am. As a student of history, I've learned that man has warred since the dawn of civilization, and hold little expectation he will ever stop. The reader may suspect I'm a bah, humbug personality.

So where can one with my mentality find a sliver of hope, some reason to dream vigorously? Do I focus on beautiful sunsets and colorful flowers, or climbing murder rates and parents struggling with spoiled, me-generation kids?

My optimism may surprise the herd followers, but I figure Cain killed Abel, so what's new? The prophets complained of their generations, too! Class struggle, religious wars, battle of the sexes ... our forebears have been there and done that. But ah! Here's the starting point to my secret.

If we become aware of the past, the harshness of those societies, and compare it to modern times, might there be reason to celebrate? The horror witnessed on daily news is not original, but technology brings it instantly to a worldwide audience. Genocide, suppression, maiming, corrupt governments, child abuse, and other revulsions are historical facts.

Watching it on my flat-screen television, in my heated home, with a microwaved dinner upon my lap while reclined in a La-Z-Boy, is comforting. At forty-three years of age, I would be considered an old person had I lived during the Civil War, the American Revolution, or some other ancient society, like the Roman Empire.

How nice it is to drive my automobile to the store on paved roads. The Apian Way was no picnic in the park for weary travelers.

My hernia surgery, and cancer operations family and friends have endured, are modern marvels. It scares me to know George Washington was actually bled by leeches! Voltaire decried the doctors in his day. Such was the medical community of the time. Nope, I have no desire to live in those epochs.

Years ago, while at a work-related conference in Florida, I met a group after hours at a sports bar. A gentleman in the group kept complaining about the state of affairs in modern life.

A few beers into the conversation, I asked, "So tell me, in what era and country would you have preferred to live?"

After a few seconds of contemplation, (and it was only a few), he replied, "Athens, during the golden time of Socrates, Plato, and Aristotle."

"Let's contemplate your choice," I said. "You can't take your modern conveniences back in time with you. They had no air conditioning or electricity, no cable or satellite; most men and women were considered slaves; a simple broken bone could be a lifelong problem, and they were always under threat of war by neighboring countries. The dictatorship of Pericles would not sit well in America of today."

He gulped his beer. "But that's when men knew how to be men."

The individual had been engrossed in several sporting events broadcast through wall mounted TVs. A philosophical exchange of ideas seemed pointless, so I changed the subject.

Had the athletic-minded gentleman an inkling of erudition, I might have reminded him of the hard times so many of our famous writers, leaders, and heroes suffered throughout the ages: Consumption (that's tuberculosis to you and me), syphilis, gonorrhea, smallpox, malaria, yellow fever, scurvy, and so much more. Of course the big 'C'—he's got the cancer!

I pictured this middle-aged man, beyond his prime, living in the past. I projected him into different roles, existing as a tribesman in some ancient civilization, to perhaps a chimneysweeper in London during the Industrial Revolution. Perhaps on the wrong end of a spear during Alexander's march to greatness.

The BMW he drives, nice tailored suit, and gold Rolex watch would have to go. Father Time wouldn't allow such anachronisms. Instead of football, baseball, and hockey, it would be jousting, wrestling, or the Mayan form of basketball where the losers were executed. Maybe a marathon in the nude! And we get upset over a little *accidental* halftime nipple exposure.

Now don't get me wrong, I'm not squandering sleep over such idiosyncrasies. That would go against my confessed optimism.

But I do have dreams and wishes—I am human.

I *would* like to see our media less tied to global corporations. But then I've read about the harsh treatment journalists and antagonists of yesteryear gave to the leaders of the time. Those pamphlets and flyers during the Reformation and Counter Reformation, or during the era of our Founding Fathers, were not written with kid gloves. The cartoonists and caricaturists were just as talented and stinging as our modern artists. Propaganda can be traced back to the dawn of humankind.

Corrupt politicians? Give me a break. Machiavelli wrote the book in the 1500s. History is full of evil dictators and materialistic officials. Even King David sent Uriah off to war for less than admirable reasons.

Less child abuse? Of course I never want to see a boy or girl raised in an awful environment. But think of life before the X-ray. Broken bones went undiagnosed. "Spare the rod, spoil the child," was the motto. Plutarch, St. Augustine, and so many other teachers and philosophers spoke of the strict discipline forced upon young students. The Code of Hammurabi outlined penalties for certain abuses, and Tiberius created edicts against sacrificing children in the fires to Moloch. So glad I wasn't a toddler at the time.

Scarifications, female genital mutilation, pederasty, throwing unwanted infants over mountainsides ... such acts were legal and even encouraged in ancient societies. "I brought you into this world, and I can take you out."

Greek and Roman boys were taken from their homes and prepared for war. Education went to the opulent class—everyone else, the Untouchables if you will, worked in fields or sweatshops of the day.

And why the complaints of how our schools have failed? Compared to what? Literacy is up, more books are read, and students are forced to learn more and more about every discipline, from anthropology to zoology. The "4 Rs" only scratch the surface of what is forced upon the current generation. My four-year-old manipulates the computer, which was unavailable in my childhood.

Grumpy old men bicker. "In my day, schools were segregated and women learned how to cook so they could stay home to raise babies." The good old days? Those in power taught that the Earth was flat, and if you disagreed you would be excommunicated.

Specific theological tenets were forced into textbooks, and if one asked for separation of church and state in our land of free speech, the usurper was ostracized. After all, the original settlers traveled to America to escape the same coercion in the Old World (only to renew the strategy under their denominational reign). The Quakers, Puritans, and Catholics, oh, my! Lutherans, Calvinists, Presbyterians, oh yeah. Poor native pantheists had no chance.

Fortunately, our checks and balances in present United States have found a nice balance—subjectively speaking, of course. All those sects are living peacefully throughout America.

I'm often bewildered when conversing with someone of my grandparent's generation who agrees he or she would not want to go back and live in the days of his childhood. Followed soon by complaints about the problems of modern life.

I smile and think about the Roman orators, Levy and Cicero, who also complained about the young people of their days. Popes, tribal councils, mayors, scholars and so many others spread such despair of immorality, as if it were an invention only of their particular era.

So what is my dream for the New Year? I would like our population to become aware of the past … to realize we are blessed here in this modern age. Yes, we will die—some in a lot of anguish. So what's new? At least we have pain medication. The image from John Wayne's movie comes to mind, where the Civil War soldier is told to bite a stick as the doctor saws off his leg.

My diatribe here doesn't mean I don't want people to stand up for their rights. Hypocrisy should be shown for what it is. But wouldn't it be nice if we could put events of our day in historical perspective? Wouldn't it be nice to thank our lucky stars that we live today, in our secure country, in what may one day be called the Golden Age? Wouldn't it?

Parents, in what generation would you have preferred your children to be raised? Think it out carefully. I may quiz you on it.

Dusty

Introduction

I will bet you money there is no author in America that does more to help struggling writers than Dusty Richards of Springdale, Arkansas. The following short bio should support my claim.

Dusty won 3rd Place at the 2006 White County Creative Writers' Conference, Personality Profile. The contest required, "Must be suitable for newspaper publication."

Thank you, Dusty!

Photo courtesy National Cowboy
Symposium & Celebration

Dusty

Who would have known, that at the age of seven, when he attended his first roundup and sat on a real horse in Washington state, that Dusty Richards would go on to pen over 60 novels and win many of the top writing contests for his genre in the nation?

From a young age, Dusty read every western on the library shelves. At Mrs. Winter's ranch, within the cabin of the famous western writer Zane Grey, Dusty promised the author's ghost that his books would join Grey's some day on the bookrack. Years later, in 2005, Dusty was allowed to sit for a photo op in the very same chair where Zane Grey created many of his masterpieces, a rare feat since the museum curator strictly forbids such an event.

Dusty said that his English teachers never read westerns, so he wrote book reports like *Guns on the Brazos* by J.P. Jones: a story of a Texas Ranger who saves the town and the girl. Already displaying his entrepreneur skills, Dusty sold the stories for a dollar.

At the age of 13, Dusty's family moved to Arizona where he eventually graduated from Arizona State University in 1960. Soon after, he moved to northwest Arkansas where he has ranched, auctioneered, announced rodeos, anchored TV news, and worked for Tyson Food in management for 32 years.

In the midst of this hectic schedule, somehow Dusty found time to create 65 novels (and counting), dozens of short stories, and hundreds of articles and columns.

His first novel, *Noble's Way*, was published in 1992. In 2003 and 2004, his books *The Natural* and *The Abilene Trail* won back-to-back Fiction Book of the Year Awards at the Oklahoma Writer's Federation conference. No small achievement!

It's safe to say that there is not another author who has helped his fellow writers more than Dusty Richards. He serves on the board for the Ozark Creative Writers Conference, held annually in Eureka Springs. His *Nuts & Bolts* to writing seminar (A.K.A., *Writing 101*) is the most detailed step-by-step course any novelist will ever attend. Many up and coming authors have benefited from Dusty's advice and gone on to win awards and published books.

Award-winning author Velda Brotherton said, "Fellow western writer Dusty Richards has influenced my career more than anyone. He never let me give up, and there were times I wanted to. He always told me, 'The road to success is littered with quitters,' and I've never forgotten that."

For several years now at the conference, Dusty challenged the participants (well over a hundred attend each year) to submit a brand new novel to him to review. "If I like it I'll see that my editor and agent look at it," Dusty said.

His "How To" columns have appeared in many national magazines, including *ByLine Magazine* and *The Storyteller*. He volunteers enthusiastically for several writing groups around the country, including his acceptance of e-mail queries from on-line forums asking for tips. Members of his writing group in Northwest Arkansas have gone on to win many prestigious awards. Dusty is also an active member and serves on the board for Ozarks Writers League, one of the premiere writing organizations in the country.

Although no longer an active board member of the Western Writers of America, don't be fooled thinking he's not a participant. He was there at this year's annual conference in Cody, Wyoming with all the other best western authors of the world.

Arkansans like to claim Dusty for themselves. In 2004 he was inducted into the Arkansas Writers Hall of Fame, an honor that includes Dee Brown and Charles Porter. In 2006 Dusty was voted an honorary member of Fiction Writers of Central Arkansas.

And what is Dusty's biggest award? In 2005, at The National Cowboy Symposium and Gathering in Lubbock, Texas, Dusty was presented with their lifetime achievement award (National Cowboy Culture Award for Western Writing) for his writing and generous efforts to help others in their endeavors to write. Past recipients include Max Evans and Elmer Kelton.

Dusty and his wife, Pat, reside next to Beaver Lake, east of Springdale, Arkansas (when they aren't traveling to writing events). They have two "wonderful" daughters, Ann and Rhonda, and four super grandkids from ages 12 to 20.

If you're a new writer with a desire to learn what it takes to become successful, visit Dusty. His website is: www.dustyrichards.com. Catch him at his book-signing table after the crowds have thinned out. He'll talk with you, and afterward, your motivation level will dramatically increase as that fuzzy road to publication begins to clear.

(Editor's Note: In 2007 Dusty Richards won two Spur Awards for his novel and a short story. This is the most prestigious western award; no other writer has ever won more than one award in the same year.)

Christian

Road to Damascus

Introduction

Road to Damascus has been entered unsuccessfully in several contests. It's a story close to my heart, and although I tried to make the tale worthy of inclusion in this anthology by bragging of a win or publication, it didn't happen.

I did submit the piece to *Rock & Sling* magazine, a Christian theme journal. They sent me a nice rejection letter that said, "Don't lose your head. We are sorry that your submission to *Rock & Sling* did not meet our current needs. Getting writing/artwork published is often a matter of the right editor reading your work at the right time. What one refuses another may publish. Be encouraged, the next editor you try may be the one."

Members of my wonderful church at Calvary often ask me if I plan to write Christian-theme stories. I penned this tale many years ago when I first began to write. So I retire *Road to Damascus* here and let's see what happens. Thank you, Brother Ed, for all you do!

Road to Damascus

"Sam!" Pauline shouted. She gripped the armrest and her knuckles turned reddish purple. "Pay attention to the road—you're driving too fast. You know this is the bridge where I saw the accident."

"What is it with you today?" Samuel's eyebrows twitched and his heart raced.

"It's nothing."

"Nothing? I wish you'd tell me." He slowed from 55 to 45 as they approached the tiny town of Damascus along Arkansas Highway 65.

"We can talk about it later."

They drove past a front yard where children played near a pine wrapped in Christmas lights. A woman inside the home watched from a picture window.

"No, you're not goin' to do that to me again," he said. "We're on our way to see your grandfather … I don't want to put this off."

"We probably should wait … oh, be sure to drive the speed limit through this town."

"I know about the speed-trap. What's wrong?"

"Well … uh … this morning when you tried to make an excuse about not going to church tomorrow…."

"Is this about religion again?"

"I want to know you're saved." Tears welled up in Pauline's eyes. "And that you've accepted Jesus as your savior … this is important to me … and to you."

"Look…" he began, and then paused. It would be prudent to analyze every word he was about to utter. The wrong statement could end their relationship. "I've told you I believe I'm saved."

"But do you believe Jesus Christ died and went to Heaven for your sins?"

"What does it matter? That's a religious question that has nothing to do with my faith," Samuel heard himself snap. Immediately, he wished he had kept quiet.

The two stared out their windows, avoiding eye contact. Another brightly lit house, this one with icicle lights hanging from the edge of the roof, and a miniature homemade barn with a nativity scene in the yard, appeared in Samuel's line of sight. He noticed a Christmas tree inside the patio window and a small plume of smoke ascending from the chimney.

"But it *does* matter!" Pauline broke the silence. "I want to know you're saved."

"Look—in His omniscience, God knows everything we're thinking before we think it, right?"

"Of course."

"God knows what I'm thinking and that I'm sincere when I tell you these things, because I could lie to you and tell you what you want to hear. The fact is I can't prove that Jesus died for our sins and actually went to Heaven."

"I want our children to be grounded in a strong belief. I'm not sure you can provide that anymore."

"If I'm wrong about not confessing I believe one hundred percent that Jesus died for our sins, then God will forgive me—and I'm convinced of it. That is, if He knows what we're going to do billions of years before we even do it. What if I knew what God knew about what I was about to do, then did something else? Is it allowed?"

"What's your point?"

"I have faith that transcends your religious questions. I'm not a fundamentalist, but I'm also not agnostic—"

"You *are* agnostic." Pauline wiped a tear before it fell from her cheek. "You believe you can't prove God exists."

"What proof? Like *x* equals *y* and whammo, God exists in a mathematical formula. You act like it's black or white, either you're an atheist, an agnostic, or a fundamentalist. It's not that simple. Like when you tell me you're not a fundamentalist, and you don't interpret the Bible literally word for word. Are you so special that you can pick and choose what you believe from the Bible?"

"Where are you going with this?"

"I think of religious beliefs along a continuum, where atheists are at one extreme and fundamentalists are at the other with agnostics falling in the middle. I bet you and I are closer in belief than you give us credit for. I'm excited that Jesus died for our sins and went to Heaven, but I can't prove it as fact. History distorts the truth, and I'm skeptical of human interpretation."

"Okay, okay," Pauline said. "What about the theologians who have gone back to the original New Testament manuscripts and corrected the mistakes from translations over the centuries?"

"But the originals were still written by men, so we're back where we started.

They even tell us to beware of false prophets. How do we know they aren't themselves false prophets? Kind of ironic, isn't it?"

"All your worries would wash away if you'd give yourself over to Christ."

"You know I've given it a lot of thought."

"I know you have." Pauline focused her eyes on her feet in the floorboard.

"Pauline, think about it. Origen was one of the first church fathers in the early part of the third century … over two hundred years *after* the death of Jesus. He felt all people would be saved and was skeptical of an eternal hell. Then, years later, St. Augustine and other church fathers tell us that this was a mistake. Who do you believe?"

"You believe in Jesus."

Samuel sighed. "I've always kept an open mind. Who am I to say that two billion Hindus and Muslims will burn in hell? And which Christian group or sect should I accept as being correct … Catholics … Baptists … or perhaps the Latter Day Saints? Maybe I should stick with the Old Testament and become Jewish. So sure, I hope that Jesus died for my sins as we are conditioned to believe. But don't force me to throw my hands in the air and begin to speak in tongues yelling for Jesus, because I can't tell you one hundred percent that it's true as the New Testament says."

"I need to know that the man I marry is saved," Pauline whispered, barely audible.

Samuel did not respond. His excitement of spending the day with his fiancée evaporated, his entire future now seemed to hinge on the next few hours.

* * *

Several miles up Highway 65, past Damascus, Samuel pulled into a nursing home parking lot inside the county seat of Clinton. Pauline's grandfather had been a resident for ten months.

Samuel looked cautiously toward her. "I love you."

"I love you, too," she responded, not making eye contact.

After they exited the vehicle, Pauline started for the front door without waiting.

Samuel stretched and looked around. Greers Ferry Lake sat within twenty miles. The couple had camped at a few of the many parks that dotted the shoreline. The entire Ozark region contained wonderful memories that were overridden by current circumstance.

He locked doors and rushed to catch up. Samuel trailed her down one of the long hallways that extended out from a central area where receptionists sat, then followed Pauline into her grandfather's room.

The elderly man perked up as he lay on a raised bed with protective bars. "How're you two kids doing?"

"Merry Christmas, Pampa," she said. "We're fine. You're looking well."

Samuel forced a smile. "Yes, you do look good, J.C."

Pampa patted Pauline's hand. "Well, thank you. I wish I felt better. Some days are better than others."

Samuel asked, "Would either of you like something to drink?"

"Sure," Pauline said with a certain demure, still not looking directly at him.

"No, thank you," Pampa responded.

Samuel walked back through the long hall toward the receptionist. Inside each room lay a bedridden figure, many alone, staring at a TV or out a window. Directly in front of him a woman in a wheelchair was bent over, trying to pull herself along by grabbing the handrail.

As they passed, he noticed her arthritic hands and stooped back. One arm hung useless by her side, leaving only the other to pull herself forward.

He stopped and looked back, debating whether to help. She inched ahead, mumbling something to herself. Samuel continued on when he saw a nurse arrive to assist.

Around the corner sat other residents in wheelchairs lined against the wall, staring out a large glass window. Cars on Highway 65 raced past, going north and south. As he walked by, Samuel observed the silence between them.

The cafeteria was now in sight. Between him and his destination stood several nurses helping a woman rise from the floor. Her walker had tipped over sideways. Samuel squeezed past and paced toward the soda fountain.

With two drinks in hand, he procrastinated his return and decided to explore the compound. The earlier conversation played hard inside his head. Turning another bend in the labyrinth of halls, he stumbled upon a lounge with a large TV hanging in the corner.

Several older men and women, a few in wheelchairs, sat in front of the television watching a basketball game.

"Is this seat taken?" Samuel asked a woman sitting on a hard green plastic chair. A gray metal walker stood next to her, orange tennis balls were impaled on the two back legs. She seemed oblivious to the game as her tiny fingers frantically worked knitting needles. Brown spots covered her frail forearms.

She gestured toward the seat. "No, you're welcome to sit … my name's Bonnie." Thick hairspray held her gray hair in bondage. A wool jacket covered both shoulders, and underneath she wore a light pink dress, a style his grandmother sported years ago before she passed away.

"I'm Samuel … or Sam. How are the Razorbacks doing?"

"Just started," a gentleman in the corner answered.

Samuel looked over and said, "Should be a good game."

The resident stood using a cane, and strolled slowly over to sit next to him. "I'm Elmer," he said. He wore green slacks fastened high on his waist, pleats rose an inch above his black shoes, and a short sleeved buttoned-up shirt with vertical stripes and tiny flower patterns. "A Razorback fan, uh?"

"Yes, sir."

"Me too, me too." Elmer patted his hand on Samuel's knee. "You sure are young, must be in good shape. My, goodness! Feel those muscles in that leg … do you run a lot?"

"Some," Samuel said, feeling uncomfortable. "My fiancée and I play softball in the summer."

"Yeah … yeah," Elmer sighed. "I'm eighty-five years old, you know. I remember being fit when I was your age. You should have seen me during WW II."

Samuel opened his mouth to say Elmer didn't look in that bad of shape, but decided not to.

Elmer reached his hand up and grabbed Samuel gently by a tricep. "Strong arms, too."

"I try to work out."

"I don't feel good anymore," Elmer continued. "I thought I had a heart attack last week; false alarm. Not much left to look forward to."

How do I respond? Samuel thought. Elmer's healthy years are over. He finally said, "Oklahoma is undefeated and in the top ten. And Arkansas is also undefeated—should be a good game."

"Yeah, I like the Razorbacks," Elmer replied. He struggled to stand. Grabbing his cane, he moved forward inch by inch, having to lean over from the painful arch in his back.

"I remember when Elmer was so energetic," Bonnie said, after he had disappeared down the hall. "He had a quick mind … he's really gone down hill this past year since the fall. I've never seen a man get religious so quick."

"Uh-huh," Samuel muttered, nodding his head. A chill crept into his bones and he looked away from Bonnie.

"You get a lot of that in here," someone spouted from a recliner several yards away.

Samuel had not noticed him until the outburst. He also carried the features of a resident, only his mobility appeared less hampered. His stubby face folded over layers of wrinkles. Standing, he approached Samuel.

"They go their whole lives paying no attention to religion," he continued. "Then they get old and think of death and have second thoughts. I'd say they're hypocrites."

"Now, Niccoli, this gentleman isn't interested," Bonnie said.

"Oh, I don't mind," Samuel replied, shifting nervously in his seat. "My girlfriend and I had a similar conversation on the way up here."

"Oh, yeah?" Niccoli roared. "Well, look around here. Do you think God is concerned with us? Walk down that hall over there and look inside each room—see for yourself. This is what you have to look forward to. No wonder people commit suicide. If I only had the nerve, and I'll admit it, I don't. I've watched everyone important to me suffer long deaths. Is this God's plan?"

"Boo hoo, boo hoo." Bonnie stopped knitting and glared at Niccoli. "My first husband died in World War Two, and my daughter died fifteen years ago in a car wreck, but you don't see me crying, feeling sorry for myself."

Samuel's eyes shifted back and forth at the man and woman, it soon became obvious that they tolerated each other. Samuel smiled. Maybe they even dated.

"So what did you and your girlfriend talk about?" Niccoli asked.

"Well…." Samuel stopped. Perhaps his conversation with Pauline was a private matter.

"Oh, give me a break," Niccoli said. "Who are we gonna tell? And who cares, anyway?"

Taking a deep breath, Samuel continued, "She's worried that I'm not 'saved' because I won't admit I believe one hundred percent that Jesus died and went to Heaven for my sins. I told her it's possible, but I can't prove it. My faith comes from a respect for the unknown … I want to believe that there's something out there after this life, but who can really know?"

"Aren't you worried about an eternity in hell?" Bonnie asked.

"I don't believe in an eternal hell. I don't believe God, or a Creator—or whatever you want to call a higher power—would do that to His creation."

"I remember thinking that way when I was your age," Niccoli said.

"Leave the boy alone!" Bonnie snapped.

Samuel tried to end the conversation and quietly stared at the basketball game.

"Don't be fooled!" Niccoli unexpectedly shouted. "There aren't as many people with *real* faith as you might think. Most are afraid to admit they don't believe. Religion is nothing more than society trying to keep people in line … morality my ass. Live your life to its fullest, because you only have one chance. When you die, it's over."

"Quiet!" Bonnie said. "Sam, don't you listen to this old fart. No wonder he never married, with that foul mouth of his. You *should* let Jesus into your heart. Don't become an old grump like Niccoli. Enjoy life, but believe in the Lord and the hope He offers."

Thanking them, Samuel held up his drinks. "I need to get back; they're waiting on me."

A mixture of emotions circulated through his head. Why did he have this conversation now? His mind was already in an unsteady state from his earlier discussion with Pauline.

How beautiful life seemed, Samuel remembered, while staring out a window at traffic on Highway 65. The afternoon sun hung low over the Ozark Mountains. Sunrays bounced off low clouds and sent light and dark lines across the atmosphere.

In his youth he spent days at a time with his grandparents at their cabin by Shiloh on nearby Greers Ferry Lake. And then Pauline and him, in recent years, camping at US Army Corps of Engineer's parks along the lake's shorelines.

Focusing his attention away from these memories, Samuel again started his return to Pauline and her grandfather. Hiding emotions was always difficult.

Through a glass door, at the end of the hallway, Samuel saw a car pull into the parking lot. A young boy climbed out, followed by what appeared to be his grandfather. A woman in the driver seat also exited and grabbed a walker from the trunk. The boy was excited and jumped and yelled while hugging the old man's leg.

Feelings overwhelmed Samuel, tears rolled down his face. Last memories of his grandfather had been at a nursing home. *He never woke so I could say goodbye. It was always cancer—cancer, cancer, cancer. Why, God?*

Orange flickering finger-like sunrays intensified through the glass door as Samuel leaned against the wall fighting back emotions.

"Sam!" Pauline said. She stood halfway between him and her grandfather's room. "Are you okay?"

"Sure. I love you, you know?"

"Of course. Are you sure you're okay?"

"Yes. How's your grandfather?"

"Fine. He's asking about you."

"Does he feel like getting out of here for a while … taking a drive around the lake perhaps?"

"Probably, but my father's coming up this evening."

"Good, that's good." Samuel gazed at the polished floor, finding it difficult to meet Pauline's fixed stare.

"Come on. Pampa has the Razorback game on."

* * *

Dusk had arrived, the two kissed Pauline's grandfather goodbye and walked to the car. The uncomfortable mood still hung in the air. Their relationship teetered on the edge of no return, and Samuel had a sense of helplessness. What could he say to bring balance to his chaotic world?

"Pauline, I…." The words caught in his throat.

"What is it, Samuel?"

Her eyes said it all; their future would soon end. How many times had they discussed honeymoon plans, where they would live, even kids?

He kept quiet and she never pushed forward, managing only an occasional glance. Music from the car stereo could not hide a silence building between them.

The asphalt road leading south into Damascus appeared dark in the dying light. Highway 65 felt deserted as families living along the way retreated to their homes for the evening. Even Christmas lights looked cold and distant.

A straight stretch of highway led into Damascus. Solar remnants of the sun blinded Samuel's face as the couple passed a used bookstore on the left.

His eyes strained into brightness praying for a sign, anything that would direct him down the correct path. All his life he had tried to make sense of existence, and now he desperately needed guidance.

The fiery circle on the horizon appeared to him to pulsate as they passed a road sign, Highway 285 to Wooster. Samuel continued to stare ahead believing truth would be revealed … it had to be discovered. He didn't want to lose Pauline! But he knew he could never lie to her.

Out of the corner of his eye he caught two children playing basketball in a driveway. The white house behind them had been brightly decorated for Christmas with strings of lights dangling along the gutter, a plastic Santa arranged atop the chimney.

In the front yard, under a miniature wooden roof, sat a manger with baby Jesus and His parents' replicas. The Three Wise Men stood to one side. A series of spotlights lit the scene.

"Pauline…." he tried once more. Words were lost.

"I can't read your mind, Samuel."

An eerie silence again filled their car; life around him felt blurred. The sun's tip was all that could be seen on Highway 65's horizon where it curved downward, away from Damascus. Pauline had been the best thing in his life. She had brought him out of darkness from his isolated cell. Before her, he had accepted he would die old, alone.

"Pauline, I don't want anything to come between us."

"We've had this conversation … you know how I feel."

"We're engaged, damn it!" Samuel suddenly said. "Now you're telling me we'll never get married if I don't fall to the ground and accept Jesus into my life?"

She raised her voice, "I never said it like that. You've always known how I felt."

"Then why did you say 'yes' when I proposed?"

"Perhaps I was wrong."

Again the silence fell between them. If there had been doubt, Samuel now understood the seriousness of the situation.

At the top of a ridge passed the valley outside Damascus, the road rose above distant landscape and the sun appeared again, only to blind him. He shielded his eyes with a hand. A fuzzy orange and blueness colored the sky. "Pauline, I don't want to lose you."

"The decision is yours. I'm struggling too, you know?"

"I believe in Jesus, I'm just skeptical sometimes."

"But you can't unconditionally let Him into your life."

"But I *have* faith. I truly believe there's a higher power behind everything we see. I'm just cynical of men thousands of years ago telling us what to believe."

"I want my children raised by a father with a strong faith."

"I just told you that I have faith."

She turned her head and stared out the window.

Samuel reached and turned up the radio. Glancing at the rearview mirror, he saw Damascus disappear behind him. His choices were obvious, but could he compromise? Could Pauline? Could he take that leap of faith when so much skepticism rushed through his blood?

Descending another hill, bright lights suddenly hit him in the face.

"There's a wreck on the bridge!" Pauline gasped.

Motorists used their vehicles to block the lane, and a bystander directed traffic around the scene. Emergency crews had not yet arrived.

Samuel drove carefully past the calamity. It appeared that a truck had crossed into the opposite lane and hit a van head on. That's when he saw a blanket-covered body along the side, a woman in the ditch leaned into someone's shoulder and wept.

"Oh, my God," Samuel said.

"Keep driving," Pauline directed.

Speeding over the hill toward them rushed an ambulance and two police cars. Their dazzling flashers and sirens caused his heart to throb. His brain fell into a myriad of thoughts as he reflected upon the awful scene and his own crisis.

"Pauline," he said, pulling the car to the shoulder. "You and I were meant to be together. I think it's important that our children be raised in a strong Christian environment, they should understand the choice about bringing

Jesus into their lives. I'm committed to it and always have been. I do believe in Jesus, but I also feel that I have the right to philosophize occasionally regarding theological questions. God is in my heart, Pauline, and I promise you He always will be."

She reached over and grabbed his hand, a smile widening across her face. "I need time, Samuel, I trust you. My grandfather talked to me about our situation. He said I shouldn't be 'unequally yoked' with an unbeliever ... but he also said I should win you over by my conduct if you're worth fighting for. You better not make me regret this."

Samuel smiled, and pulled back onto Highway 65 as a second ambulance passed. Hope is all he sought, and now perhaps....

Literary

(And Other Stuff)

I write eclectically over most genres, usually for a specific contest. Sometimes it's difficult to pigeonhole a story for a certain category of style. The tales in this section may or may not fit literary fiction. I've heard several debates over the definition for this type. A quick Google search defined it this way: "A general category for nonformulaic, intelligent, and serious fiction," and "Literary fiction is a term that has come into common usage since around 1970, principally to distinguish 'serious' fiction (that is, work with claims to literary merit) from the many types of genre fiction and popular fiction."

I suppose some really smart scholarly professor would conclude a few of these tales are not literary. Thus the subtitle: And Other Stuff.

Just Sitting

Introduction

Just Sitting won 1st Honorable Mention at the 2006 Arkansas Writers' Conference, Margaret Ponder Thompson Award. The theme requirement stated, "Prose with an Arkansas setting, 1500-word limit."

AWOC.COM Publishing then accepted the story for publication in the Ozarks Writers League's third anthology, *Echoes of the Ozarks: Volume III.*

Just Sitting

The red cooler contained drinks and sandwiches, along with chips. Harold loaded it into the passenger side floorboard of his Mazda pickup. Before departing, he glanced in the back and made sure the folded lawn chair and backpack were tied down.

Apartment's locked up, and I have my sketchpad, he thought. *Time to go.*

The warm Arkansas morning sun would only get hotter as the day progressed, so he had worn jean shorts and a T-shirt with "Children's Hospital" printed on front. The forecast for Sunday was perfect weather.

Only the birds welcomed him as he climbed into his vehicle and turned the key. Neighbors most likely had slept in.

He listened to the radio hoping for something classical from the local NPR station, but heard only news that didn't interest him. Changing stations, he found a morning jazz broadcast. The soothing sounds relaxed his nervous disposition.

Before departure, he opened his map where he had outlined the route he'd take. I-40 to Conway, then Highway 65 North past Marshall, would be most direct.

The freeway felt abandoned except for family sedans and semis. Morning church crowd and truckers trying to beat the end of the weekend traffic home, he thought.

His mind drifted to a family he'd helped yesterday at the hospital. The boy had fallen from a bike and needed stitches on the knee. He'd assisted the doctor, completing RN duties.

The youngster would be okay, but the bickering and disconnectedness displayed by the parents confronted him again. Harold's childhood seemed like a surreal fantasy that vanished into a void. Ever since *the* event. His father and that damn gun!

Shifting gears, he pushed the gas pedal to the floor to help his Mazda climb the hill on Highway 65, after he had exited the Freeway in Conway and turned right. Soon, the valley where Faulkner County seat existed faded from his rear-view mirror.

An hour later, on the other side of Clinton, he drove behind an RV that struggled against the Ozark Mountain inclines. Stickers on the travel trailer said, "Proud Parent of Child at Jefferson Elementary," and "Soccer Mom." Children's bikes and deflated inner-tubes were tied to the back.

Although he was in no hurry, he passed the RV before the town of Marshall materialized, when the road topped a hill and curved down into another breath-taking valley. The mid-morning sun began to heat away a light fog.

Once past the sleepy hamlet, Highway 65 descended further into the local hills, and snaked along the bottomlands occupied by grazing cattle. At Highway 74 he turned left toward Snowball.

Thick forest hugged the narrow road as the two-lane highway twisted into the countryside. Several miles up 74 he slowed to search dirt paths that suddenly appeared.

There it is!

A white painted metal sign, with aged, dark streaks camouflaging sections of words, pointed to "Wilson Cemetery."

Harold carefully turned onto the rutted path and drove fifty yards to the gravesite developed along a treeless side of a hill. The horizon showcased the crystal clear expanse of the mountainous region.

Scattered oaks around the cemetery were allowed to thrive. Parking alongside a rusted barbed wire fence by the grassy road, Harold pulled his lawn chair and other items from the truck and walked to the shade of a nearby tree.

He looked around and saw no one.

Relaxed in the chair, he consumed a sandwich and drink. *How beautiful this is.*

A breeze rustled the treetops and the distant caws of crows entertained his senses.

Several tombstones of marble and granite lined up before him. "Mr. And Mrs. Floyd Wilson," he read out loud. "Mr. Wilson … I see you were born in 1888 and died in 1945. So you got to see the end of the war, yes? Mrs. Wilson. You died a year later … heartbroken, perhaps?"

Harold stood and walked a few steps to read the next marker. A lamb had been designed atop the tiny rectangle shaped headstone placed flush with the ground.

"Oh, Mrs. Wilson. You had a toddler who died after a year. I'm so sorry to hear that."

Backfire of an engine caused Harold to glance toward a line of trees that separated the cemetery from the highway. He heard the vehicle disappear down into the valley.

"We're all alone, aren't we?"

Walking through rows of tombstones, he stopped to review the etchings in each stone. "So, Mr. Searcy. You were a loving father and caring husband, were you? Then why isn't your wife buried beside you? Did she remarry perhaps? Or maybe your children bickered over where to inter her ... or your epitaph is a lie."

Stop it, Harold. Why do I have such negative thoughts?

Climbing the landscape took a toll on his heavy body, so he sat and drank another Coke. Once rested, he took a spray bottle and nylon brush from the backpack and knelt before the selected tombstone.

He believed this gravesite to be oldest in the cemetery, and the marker would work well with his rubbing.

Careful not to kill lichen, he sprayed water onto the tombstone and wiped the dirt away. Next he used garden tools to clean around the bottom of the monument. He then took a piece of pellon paper and taped it to the stone.

Unwrapping a piece of chalk from aluminum foil, he took it and rubbed the paper diagonally from top to bottom. When finished, he laid the rubbing on the ground, removed tape, and sprayed Krylon onto the paper to set the chalk.

With his knees hurting, he returned to his seat and rested. After consuming another Coke, he picked up the paper and placed it in the sketchpad, one of several he had. This latest addition would go behind a similar piece from a cemetery he visited last week in Ouachita County.

On a printout of Arkansas cemeteries, downloaded from a website, he crossed through Wilson Cemetery. His next and last stop for this week was to a memorial park in Carroll County, where rumor had it family members from the Utah massacre laid buried.

Before departing, he took a plastic flower from his backpack and placed it on the grave.

Late that evening, as he made a second trip from his truck to carry in gear to the apartment, a neighbor approached.

"Hi, Harold. What're you up to?"

She smiled while waiting for a reply. Like him, she was big boned in the legs, and perhaps a little heavy in the waist. Yet her rosy cheeks and perky expressions made her attractive.

Harold slowed but never stopped. "Just had some work to do."

"Those sketchpads ... are you an artist?"

"Not really. Talk with you later."

With that, he sped up and turned the corner to his apartment.

Inside, he sat the rubbing equipment on a cluttered dining table and grabbed a Coke. After placing a frozen pizza in the oven, he sat and glanced through his images again. He also took photos, especially of the gravesites where outlining a picture with chalk was not possible.

Some tombstones were too fragile or too big. One picture in his album showed a tall obelisk dated to 1910. His photo of the Veteran Cemetery in Little Rock was taken from two angles. One showed the small, white cross markers lined diagonally. Another angle gave the perspective that the cemetery planners positioned them straight up and down.

All those symbols speckled the well-manicured green lawn along the rolling landscape. *How many soldiers had to die?*

Picking up a history book with photos, he again scanned through images.

Civil War era pictures of injured men after battles, in a field hospital behind the war zone, watched the photographer take the shot. Old black and whites of proud Native Americans glaring at the camera, anticipating some future person seeing them as they were in the 1800s.

All dead. All dead!

Swirling thoughts forced him to the restroom where he vomited. Those eyes from the long departed stared out through the ages. Flushing the toilet, he watched excrement disappear.

Why, Mom and Dad? A suicide pact! I was so young.

A buzzer sounded in the kitchen and he hurried to turn it off. Cutting the pizza into sections, he sat back at the table.

While eating, he opened a small sketchpad and took out a pencil. Gently filling in the details, he added additional tombstones in the background, under dogwood and willow trees.

The doorbell sounded and he went to look through the peephole. It was his female neighbor. He stood motionless for a minute until she left, then returned to the table and picked up the pencil.

Again he erased his epitaph and changed it. One day he would get it right.

Photo by Lance Waters

Soccer Mom

Introduction

Soccer Mom was published in the October/November/December 2005 issue of *The Storyteller* magazine.

Soccer Mom

A cool breeze from the nearby river eased over the field of young players kicking the ball. Under shade of cottonwood trees sat Mackenzie's mom with other parents.

"Come on Mac!" She jumped up in frustration. "Kick the ball into the net. Be aggressive!"

Her daughter forced her way past a defender but then missed an open shot after the goalie had fallen.

"Great!"

Debbie Mann turned from the fielders out of aggravation and noticed a woman sitting on a rock ledge overlooking the soccer complex.

That's the fourth week in a row she's been there, alone. The same person from last year. Strange … better keep Mackenzie away. Who knows with all the psychos these days?

Debbie returned her attention to the field. "Go get the ball! Do you hear me? Get it!"

"Calm down," her husband said. "It's just a game."

Just a game! Yeah, right. My daughter is not going to lounge around like that lazy teammate of hers. "Get aggressive, Mackenzie!"

At the end of the game, after the coach dismissed the team, Debbie walked with her husband and daughter back to the car, carrying a folding chair over her shoulder. "I can't believe you missed those three shots."

"But Mom … we won. And I scored two goals."

"You should never accept being mediocre; you're the best player on the field. Act like it."

Debbie saw her husband look away after flashing a nasty expression.

The woman on the ledge continued to watch a different game on another field as Debbie and her family approached.

"Follow me," she said, directing them away from the lady.

The unknown soccer fan glanced up; the two made eye contact. No words were spoken, but the women seemed to have an understanding.

Debbie leaned down and whispered to Mackenzie, "Stay away from her."

"Who?"

"Her," she pointed.

The mystery woman appeared to notice Debbie point. *What are you looking at, you hussy?* Debbie thought, sending daggerous stares her way. *I've seen you leave without a child or talking to other parents. Are you looking for someone to kidnap when no one's looking? I know your kind.*

Thrusting her nose in the air, Debbie turned and followed her husband up a slope toward their vehicle. Once in the Ford Explorer, as the family exited the soccer complex, she said, "Let's eat at the Macaroni Grill."

Mackenzie complained. "But my teammates are meeting at McDonald's. We want to have fun in the PlayLand."

"You're too big for that. Besides, McDonald's is for losers."

"Honey—" her husband said.

"Macaroni Grill!"

"Fine."

Photo by David Knight

"There's a thirty minute wait," the manager said.

"We'll wait outside," Debbie replied.

Mackenzie balanced herself on the curb along the parking lot as her parents sat quietly on a wooden bench next to the restaurant.

After a few silent moments, her husband said, "You're too hard on her."

"And you're not hard enough. Really, I worry about you sometimes. Do you want her to live in a trailer with a husband named Billy Bob who smokes pot and breeds pit bulls to fight? She'll have tattoos and nose piercings before high school."

"I need to use the restroom." He stood, and disappeared inside.

Debbie noticed a two-story building next door with a sign that read 'St. Patrick's Rehabilitation.' Several pedestrians entered the automatic doors; some looked like patients with walkers or canes.

At that moment a woman exited marching next to a child restrained in an electric wheelchair. She looked familiar in the bright, flowery dress.

She's the one at the soccer game!

Debbie stood and walked closer, hiding herself behind the candy apple red steel of a nearby truck.

It appeared that the child used a finger to maneuver the wheelchair forward. It was a hot day and the girl's bare arms were exposed to the sun.

She looks emaciated, Debbie thought.

Tubes to canisters on the back of the chair connected a tracheotomy. The woman, possibly the little girl's mom, pointed a set of keys toward a van. Side doors opened and a lift slowly descended to the ground.

After the girl inched her way safely inside and the door closed, the woman turned to step into the driver's seat. With the front door ajar, she glanced up, making eye contact with Debbie for a second time in the same day.

Oh, my, Debbie thought, her peripheral vision seemed to vanish. She wanted to look away, but the other woman held her gaze. Although it felt like eternity, in reality only seconds elapsed before the woman climbed into the van and backed away from the parking space.

Debbie returned to her seat and watched as the vehicle disappeared down a hill. Twice today they had glared at one another … with Debbie forming two very different impressions.

What have I done…? What have I done!

The sound of Mackenzie playing hopscotch drew Debbie's attention. Her daughter had experienced a perfect birth and normal childhood through her first seven years. Mackenzie laughed and played, and climbed and sang.

How fast she's growing up.

Debbie then stared at a cigarette butt lying on the ground. Repressed emotions were bubbling up and she tried to quell them. *What has that woman gone through? And that poor girl.*

The thought of a mother waking everyday to an unhealthy child sent an echoing wave of pity into her hollow stomach. To watch your child struggle in life…. To want to give up your own health so the child could experience normalcy…. *Even for a day. Even for a freakin' day!*

The wall crashed and tears washed from her eyes; Debbie's strong will crumbled. After a lifetime of promising herself this would never be allowed. It was so unexpected. But the stares, and the image of that girl being lifted into the van….

Damn it! What is wrong with me? I don't want to be like my parents.

"Mommy, are you okay?" Mackenzie touched her mom's knee. "Mommy?"

Lifting her eyelids open, Debbie leaned down and swept her daughter into her arms. "I love you so much."

"I love you too."

Wiping her eyes, Debbie continued. "Let's go find your father."

* * *

A cool breeze from the nearby river eased over the field of young players kicking the ball. Debbie kept glancing toward the rock ledge.

Her husband reached over and held her hand. "Still no sign of her?"

"No, and it's been three weeks. I really wanted to say something."

"You never know … that could make it worse."

At the end of the game the parents created a tunnel on the field by facing each other and holding their hands together in the air as the children ran under them. "Great game!" Debbie yelled to each player.

Back on the sidelines, as things were being packed up, Debbie asked Mackenzie, "McDonald's? Are we going to McDonald's today?"

"No, Mom. We're going to Pizza Hut. That new one in North Little Rock. They have a cool PlayLand."

The Tree of Life

Introduction

The Tree of Life was published in the July/August/September 2005 issue of *The Storyteller* magazine.

The image of the tree is based upon a real depiction I experienced in Searcy, Arkansas.

Photo by Stewart Matthews

The Tree Of Life

Jumping from the parked Mazda van, Seth followed his mom toward the glass doors. Atop the red brick building he noticed a tower of sorts, maybe an old chimney. Images of white doves had been attached in flying formation.

Inside, behind the receptionist station, stood an assortment of cubicles, many empty waiting for absent employees to return.

"This is where your aunt works," his mom said, sliding her fingers through his hair.

He pulled his head back in protest when he noticed an attractive female in a green vest walk around a corner. She glanced up from her clipboard, smiled at Seth, then entered a glass-enclosed office and sat behind a desk.

After tucking his shirt into his designer jeans, Seth adjusted his maroon windbreaker.

"There you two are!" Aunt Audrey smiled and walked toward her sister and nephew. "How are you, Seth?"

"Okay."

"How old are you now?"

"Almost fourteen."

"Fourteen! My, you sure have grown. How was your trip from St. Louis?"

"Fine."

Audrey seemed to wait for more, but the young man remained silent. "You'll like Arkansas—there's a lot to do here in Searcy."

When Seth did not respond, she continued. "Come on, now ... you and my daughter—your cousin—will have a lot of fun. You're only here for a few days."

"Okay," Seth replied.

"Y'all follow me back to our conference room so we can visit. We have donuts and Coke." Audrey looked at Seth and he smiled. "Sis," Audrey continued, "have you discussed the arrangements with Mom?"

"I was hoping you had."

"Well ... Jacob and I spoke with her last week at her home. But her memory's gone."

"I heard she can't remember our names."

"Some days are better than others."

Seth grabbed a donut and drink, then sat at the opposite end of the conference table from where his mom and aunt talked.

He could see their mouths moving and hear an occasional whisper. Now he could sulk in isolation, upset that he would miss his friends back in St. Louis and soccer games where he was the star player.

The sweetness of the donut led him to a second helping. Time seemed to go nowhere. He tried to invent new mind activities to take his thoughts off his boredom.

Looking around the room, he noticed a cool wallpapered border, although décor was not his cup of tea.

The long conference table was polished and mirrored the overhead florescent lights. Comfortable executive chairs lined the sides. A cabinet built against the wall contained a sink at one end and mini-refrigerator below the cupboard at the other. Bottles of assorted beverages were spread about on top.

Taking more interest, Seth noticed nicely framed paintings hung on the wall. In the corner on the other side of the room, he saw what looked like a tree drawn from floor to ceiling. Branches spread out in a crisscross patchwork of artistic design.

Photos, many of them Polaroids, were clipped on the limbs.

Glancing at his mom and aunt, he noticed they remained in deep conversation and seemed likely to continue. The boredom kept biting so he stood and wandered from painting to painting until he stood in front of the tree.

There must have been over a hundred pictures of people spaced out along the branches. Photo gazing was not his forte. It had always frustrated him when his mom pulled the albums out at Christmas. He shot a quick look outside the open doors to the conference room and down the hall to see if a pretty girl might be within eyesight.

When no one appeared, he decided to study the images.

Beginning at eye-level, he examined several Polaroids that ran along a thick appendage toward the trunk. *Bunch of old people*, he thought.

Then he noticed a little girl with black hair and school uniform sitting properly on a couch with her hands resting in her lap and staring at whoever was taking the picture. A man about Seth's father's age leaned into the frame and smiled as the photo was taken.

His face was leathery and eyes darkened like a raccoon. The curve of his lips looked forced.

Recently, Seth had half-listened to a teacher in junior high say something about eyes being windows to the soul. The little girl's stare hid something, but what, he did not know.

The other pictures on the branch looked like the photos of his grandparents, the type his mom forced him to *enjoy*.

Several images showed old people alone, smiling, and often with a pet animal of some kind in the frame.

Leaning down, he scanned a second branch protruding from the main trunk. A picture of an old black woman caught his attention. She looked like that lady on *The Jeffersons*, he thought. *Lurezzie or Lizzie? Maybe Whezzie? That's when Mom made me watch her show and wouldn't let me watch MTV.*

The woman's smile looked sincere, as if she was at peace. What Seth liked most was the bright tie-dye orange T-shirt she wore with abstract fractals that bloomed from the fabric. Behind her, on a cabinet, were what appeared to be family picture frames, and figurines on a glass-enclosed shelf below.

Using his finger, he quickly scanned the photos, moving from limb to limb.

His mom and aunt remained in intense conversation and again, time began to drag.

An image of two old people holding a baby reminded him of his infant pictures. His grandfather had died four years ago leaving an empty feeling he still suppressed.

The wonderful times he experienced with him and his grandmother at the cabin on nearby Greers Ferry Lake surfaced in his mind. *Wow, I had forgotten about that.*

Behind him at the table he overheard his mom say his Mamaw's name again. Turning, he heard her ask, "…has the doctor officially admitted her? I heard it has to be terminal."

"Six months," his aunt responded.

That summer after his grandfather's death, Seth had asked his mom when he could go to the cabin on the lake again.

"Mamaw had to sell the place," she answered. "She couldn't keep up with it after your Pampa went to the Lord."

Not understanding why, Seth projected his mind away from these thoughts and back on the photos. *There are a lot of old people here … and all these babies. Must be a grandparent tree.*

Boredom grew overwhelming and he thought about visiting the park he saw down the street when he first arrived. Then he heard a sound behind him.

"Hi, Mommy."

Aunt Audrey looked up. "Toni … there you are."

Both women stood to welcome the newcomer. Seth watched his mom give her a hug.

"Seth, don't you recognize your cousin?" his aunt asked.

It had been four years, and time had been nice to this girl not much older than him. With blonde hair in a ponytail and jeans with an untucked dress shirt, there was no doubt in his mind about her popularity in the local school.

"Seth?" his mom continued. "You were asked a question."

"Oh, yeah." He stumbled over his tongue at first, then recovered. "It's nice to see you again."

"Why don't you two go and have fun," his mom said. "Your aunt and I have important business to discuss."

A smile widened on Seth's face and his mom shook her head in reply.

"Hey," Toni said, walking toward him. "You found the Tree of Life."

"This? I guess so."

"My mom's still friends with many of the families. One of the ladies who work here calls the tree 'Gao-kerena'—hope I said it right. Somethin' to do with mythology and immortality."

The two stood side-by-side and pointed toward several photos.

"Oh, see that guy there?" she pointed.

Seth leaned closer and saw an old man in overalls with a John Deere cap. The bill had been bent in a deep curve over his face. He sat in a lawn chair on a gravel driveway surrounded by farmland. An oak tree behind him shaded the area.

"What about him?" Seth asked.

"I liked him—he was funny. Used to bring me candy. Good candy, not that nasty mint stuff. My mom said he had no family."

Seth saw nothing special in the man, but had no reason to doubt his cousin's testimony.

"See that man there," he pointed.

"Yeah."

"He reminds me of my grandfather. And that woman in that picture up there reminds me of my grandmother."

"Mimi?" she questioned. "I can see that."

"Well, I call her Mamaw."

"She's sick, did you know that?"

"That's why we're here."

"Hey, I'm supposed to meet some of my friends at the park. We may go play miniature golf. Want to go?"

"Sure!"

"Mom," Toni said. "Can Seth go with me to play miniature golf? Nancy and Lisa are going."

Audrey looked at Seth and then at his mom. Smiling, she said loud enough for Seth to hear, "Nancy and Lisa are cheerleaders, very pretty." Then looking to her nephew, she said, "You be a gentleman, okay?"

Seth's eyes grew wide when he realized whom his escorts were. "Okay." He then looked toward his mom who nodded her head and smiled.

"Let's go," Toni said.

They arrived at the front doors as several older women were entering. Remembering what his father told him, Seth hurried to open the glass entry out of respect.

"Oh, thank you young man," one of the women said.

He noticed 'RN' behind her name on a tag pinned to the green vest she wore.

When they were out of earshot, he asked Toni, "What does 'RN' mean?"

"Registered Nurse. That's what my mom is."

Seth looked back at the doves atop the building and noticed a sign below them. At first he thought it said hospital, then realized he had never heard the term before.

"What does that word mean?" he pointed.

"Which one," Toni responded. "Hospice?"

"Yeah. What does it mean?"

"Seth ... we need to talk."

Reflections

Introduction

While lost in thought, I came up with this story's idea sitting at a stoplight in Jonesboro, Arkansas. I entered it unsuccessfully in several flash fiction (short word count) contests, but always liked the piece. I therefore retire it to publication here in this anthology. If some big, fancy literary journal would like to republish it, give me a call and we can discuss it over latte.

Reflections

Samuel gazed at the passing vehicles from his chair on the second floor.
Everyone's in a hurry.
Adjusting himself in the seat, pain seared through his body again.
How long have I been in this hospital … if that's what they call it? When did Deloris call 911?
His wife found him in the bathroom where he had slipped and hit his head on the tub. The skull fracture was slow to heal.
In the weeks since, forced to share a room with a comatose elderly patient, he felt depressed. Family rarely visited; children out of state, and Deloris not able to drive.
I'm ready to go home!
When the RN first wheeled him outside for much needed fresh air a week into his stay, he noticed the other residents. So many on their last breath.
Does the town not have a nursing home—this is a hospital, for Pete's sakes!
Down the hall Samuel saw a furrowed old man in a wheelchair, tubes impaled in his arm. The patient's head tilted sideways; he was asleep.
Memories of his grandfather crept into his mind that time he saw him at the Manor Oaks Nursing Home. *The walking dead.* The RN changed the sheets where he had crapped on himself.
Getting old sucks!
And now he was trapped at the local hospital in his small town. No one gave him a straight answer when he asked about being discharged.
Damn it!
He had to get out but his skull hurt and body refused to respond to his mental commands.
Pushing his fingers on the armrest, he tried to rise from the seat but strength evaded him.
"Here, let me help, Mr. Strong."
A woman approached wearing a flowery scrub-shirt. "RN" was printed on her nametag.
She rolled his wheelchair down the hall; Samuel felt too weak to

converse.

At the end of the corridor, atop a counter, was an arrangement of flowers, several candles, and a Bible. Above it fixed in the ceiling was a half-ball mirror. He could see down the side hallway.

Then he noticed himself in the twisted reflection!

Glancing at his hands he found old deformed arthritic fingers with brown spots running up his arm. With difficulty he reached up and touched his face. It felt bony like a thin latex covered skull.

Yesterday he had watched his children graduate ... or was it a wedding? Or grandchildren? *What year is it?*

"Deloris?"

"I'm taking you to your room, Mr. Strong."

Realization made itself known—again—in that fleeting moment.

Toast to Innocence

Introduction

This slightly embellished nonfiction piece has never won an award, although I've tried. Like the lyrics allude to in The Eagles' song *Wasted Time,* I suppose we should be grateful for the learning experiences from our past. Perhaps without this knowledge we would not have become who we currently are. Of course, that can be good or bad, depending upon your circumstances (see my essay *Sybil*).

Toast to Innocence

Forty miles outside Memphis, on I-55 toward St. Louis, Phil read the sign, "Crossroads 20 Miles."

Good, I'm almost there, he thought, lost in contemplation of the upcoming holidays.

The Christmas song on the radio ended and an old tune by Dan Fogelberg began. "Met my old lover in the grocery store…."

"I hate this song!"

Clicking the button, he found another station.

Examining the landscape, he saw cotton fields that extended to the horizon in the Arkansas Mississippi Delta. How did Jordan Shockley manage to make her store one of the premier booksellers in the country? Famous authors, and even presidents and other statesmen considered it a "must do" place to sign their latest works.

He glanced at his watch as he exited the freeway. *Good, I'm thirty minutes early!*

Downtown Main Street seemed to have done well despite the drain from a local Wal-Mart. The Air Force base closure didn't help the local economy either.

That Bookstore in Crossroads was located on a corner; he found a space to park on the side street. Tiny Christmas lights peppered the bushes and railings along the avenue. At five-thirty in the evening, the sun was quickly disappearing. He hurried to take snapshots of the store's front for his Internet site.

Jordan stood behind the cash register as he entered; her employee, Nancy, walked out from back.

"You must be Phil?" Jordan asked.

"I am. Thank you for the opportunity."

"We're glad to have you." The two shook hands. "Let me show you where you'll be sitting."

Shelves of books surrounded the table. Atop the signing desk Phil noticed photos lacquered to the surface. *What a tradition. I'll be at the same table as all these famous authors!*

"Give me five books to log in," she said, "while you set up."

He did as requested, then reached inside the plastic container he had carried in on a dolly and removed an exhibit stand to balance an enlarged front cover of his paperback. He arranged a bowl of candy on the desk.

"Hope we have customers," she said, returning.

"I'm just excited to sign here. You know your store is *the place* to hold an event like this in Arkansas?"

"Thank you. Before I forget, please sign the author's chair."

All right! He had heard of the famous chair and worried the invitation to autograph it might not be extended.

Once Phil got his table prepared, Jordan Shockley sat nearby as Nancy manned the cashier counter. "I can tell you put a lot of work into your writing and promotion," she said. "You'd be surprised how many authors aren't willing to put in the extra effort."

"It is time consuming … but I love it. The promotion is almost as much fun as the writing."

A bell on the front door jingled and she looked up and smiled. Phil was seated at an angle where he could not view the potential customer.

The antique hardwood floor creaked as someone walked back; Jordan stood. "Welcome. Are you here to see our author?"

"We are." From behind a bookshelf appeared a woman with two children in tow. She looked at Phil and smiled, then walked toward him.

Something about her eyes reminded him of someone? As she approached, it seemed she expected he would recognize her.

Standing, he moved up in front of his signing table. His mind searched for some form of recognition. Five years … ten years … of past acquaintances and friends and no faces reminded him of whom she might be. All he saw were her eyes and lovely smile.

"Do you remember my mom?" the adolescent girl beside the woman asked. She smiled as if in on a joke.

He again looked into the stranger's eyes. He had a cousin who lived in Crossroads years ago, but last he heard she now lived in Texas.

"Do you need a hint?" the girl asked.

When he remained quiet, the girl whispered, "Shelli Shan…."

"Shelli Shannon!"

He shot forward and wrapped his arms around the mom. When he stepped back the memories hit him like a wall of water. Again their eyes locked; college recollections roamed throughout his head, mixing with all the things he had wanted to say to her those eighteen years ago but didn't know how.

I should tell her how nice she looks.

Before he could speak, Shelli said, "We saw your picture in the paper where you were signing your book. This is my daughter Nicole and that's my son Mike."

"Hi, Nicole and Mike."

"I had to show them an old picture of us before they believed we once dated. You being a *famous* writer and all."

He smiled again. Might as well keep the illusion alive. Maybe one day he would be up there with the John Grishams and Stephen Kings.

Pulling a photo from her purse, Shelli continued. "Do you remember this?"

"I'll be darned … there's Mark and Karen, and Scotty—isn't that Paula Skaggs? And Mike and Michelle. I kept all my pictures from college, even the party scenes. Won't show those to my mother."

The two smiled, followed by a few seconds of silence. "We want your book and for you to sign it," Shelli said, replacing the photo in her purse.

Sitting, he grabbed a pen and started to write, then stopped and contemplated what notes to scribe. So many emotions swirled inside his head. He noticed a small tremor in his hand. "Did you recognize me in the newspaper at first?"

"I thought you looked familiar, then saw your name."

With a nervous grin, he continued. "See—I don't feel so bad now not recognizing you. It's been twenty years."

Shelli patted her hair and seemed to blush. "Don't date me. It hasn't been quite twenty years."

Not sure whether he had insulted her, he refocused upon autographing the book. Nicole broke the brief silence.

"I like to write."

Setting his pen down, he looked at the daughter. "You do?"

"Yes, sir."

"I'll bet you'll be good at it." He glanced at Shelli who had taken the seat Jordan vacated to go help another customer.

He started to ask how life had treated her, but she spoke first. "Your children in the newspaper picture are beautiful. What's your wife's name?"

"How do you get published?" Nicole interrupted.

Phil answered Shelli's question, then addressed Nicole's. "First of all, listen to your English instructor very carefully and practice your writing. Enter contests and work with other local writers. Then, as you get better, you can think of getting an agent or publisher."

Shelli's watching me…. Can't believe I didn't recognize her; I feel like an ass.

Memories danced within his mind. How often had he sat alone, after they stopped dating, wanting to scream, 'What happened to us?'

"How long have you been married?" Shelli asked.

"Seven years...."

Jordan walked over and said, "Shelli's one of our best teachers."

He started to ask Shelli questions about her after-college years, so many queries he wanted to pose. What was her husband's name? Was she happy? How long had she lived in Crossroads? But the questions seemed inappropriate in present company. What if she was unhappy and had experienced a horrible divorce—or something worse?

As Shelli described her job, he tried to actively listen, while searching for non-embarrassing remarks to make. A photo of them at a forum in Shreveport popped into his head. He had taken several pictures that night during a drunken blackout—one of many during that era of his life. Her eyes projected daggerous stares toward the camera. Perhaps he had embarrassed her that night in front of friends. One binge had led to another, and suddenly their relationship went south.

Should he now explain how his ideas of relationships had been shattered by a previous romance with an active alcoholic a few years before Shelli and he had dated?

For years, even after college, he swore he would never let another woman get close to hurt him like that again.

There had been no closure between him and Shelli. No fight. No long good-bye. They simply just stopped calling one another. There had been no official break up.

It took many long nights—years—of self-imposed isolation and existential conditioning to learn how his past experiences had affected his personality and motivated his behavior. Slowly, cause and affect began to make sense. Like peeling layers from an onion, he realized how the alcoholic girlfriend before Shelli had been a codependent product of a chronically drunken mom. Through retrospect, he saw how his individuality had evolved. The science of psychology began to make sense.

Freund, Jung, Adler, and Roger; all those theorists he had studied in graduate school had started to speak to him. And his interest in philosophy—the existentialists—Viktor Frankl, and so many writers—Tolstoy, Dostoevsky, Ellison, Chopin, Durant, and on, and on, and on—opened so many cathartic doors. He had soaked it all up in seeking his place on earth.

A multitude of thoughts bombarded his mind in the here-and-now as Shelli and her daughter continued the conversation. Over and over he wanted to ask Shelli if her life had turned out as wonderful as his, despite the many bad decisions he had made.

Finally, he *had* found his soul mate and life was good. Surely Shelli had found the same peace and happiness … she deserved it. Her children were so well behaved. But he never asked. The opportunity never presented itself with so many distractions.

"Well, we need to go." Shelli stood and looked at her son Mike, who had gotten involved in a children's book. "Are you ready?"

"Can I get this?"

"We'll see … Santa Claus might bring it."

Phil glanced at his book and realized he still needed to autograph it. But a simple signature with 'Best wishes' didn't seem appropriate.

As Shelli helped Mike put the book back, he wrote, "What wonderful memories—it was really great to see you again. Hope you aren't embarrassed by my short stories and never claim to know me again (smile, smile). You have a beautiful family."

Rereading what he had written, he thought he misspelled 'embarrassed'. *Shit! Is it right? Let me see … e.m.b.a.r.r*—

"Okay, we're going," Shelli said.

He handed her the book; then followed across the creaking floor toward the cash register. A conversation started between mother and daughter.

Ask her something besides how's work going? Tell her your impression of what happened those many years ago.

Nicole looked up at him. "Thank you for your advice, sir. It was nice to meet you."

"It was nice to meet you, also. Please e-mail me if you have any questions about writing."

"Yes, sir."

Nicole ran up the aisle to meet her brother at the front door and wait for mom.

Putting his book in a paper bag, Jordan handed the item to Shelli. When Shelli turned, he reached out and gave her one last hug.

"It was great to see you again," he said. "Thanks for stopping by."

"Good luck with your writing. I'm excited for you."

Unexpectedly, he found himself saying, "Did you know I worked with a drug and alcohol abuse program for five years?"

After a quick laugh, she said, "You did?"

"Definitely learned a lot about myself there."

"We did party a lot. Well, I'm looking forward to reading your stories."

From near the cash register he watched her walk toward the front. When she reached the children, she looked back and smiled. Then she was gone.

Phil glanced over at the bookstore owner. "Could you tell we once dated?"

"I got that feeling."

"I wanted to ask her so many questions, but didn't know if it would be appropriate with her children around. Darn it, I don't think I left a good impression."

"You must have or she wouldn't have come in."

Sitting back at the book-signing table, he looked around at the empty store. Christmas decorations lined shelves and strings of lights flickered, draped along the wall.

I'll probably never see her again ... I should have brought closure to our chapter in life.

Jordan walked back. "I'm about to close. Do you need any help packing?"

"No, ma'am. I can do it. Just can't get Shelli out of my mind; wish we had the opportunity to talk about our past experiences."

"I'm sure she understands. It's difficult to carry on an adult conversation with children running about."

"Please don't get me wrong, I love my wife. I would never have married her if I didn't think she was *the one*. When I was single, I pledged never to settle out of desperation. But I cared for Shelli a lot back in college. I understand now, sort of, why our relationship didn't work. And I'm sure she's had many of the same cathartic experiences. But what if she hadn't? What if her life went downhill? Maybe something I could have said tonight might have helped. I was just afraid to ask with all the commotion and surprise of seeing her again after so long."

Jordan rubbed her lower spine. "I think she's doing well; perhaps you'll have the opportunity to discuss it another day. But right now, I need to get home to put a heating pad on my back. Let me write you a check for the books we sold."

With his gear loaded in the container atop the dolly, he rolled it toward the cash register. "You know, my wife's my soul mate. But how do we determine there aren't hundreds or thousands of soul mates for us around the world? Think about every action in a long line of human history that had to occur for you to meet your soul mate. One deviation by an ancient ancestor could have set your life on a different path. If you had met someone earlier or later in life then..., well...."

Jordan smiled. "Perhaps that's the definition of a 'soul mate'. The miraculous events that brought you together at the right time is what was meant to be ... or God's way of telling you this is the right path."

"Good point. It's been nice talking with you, and thanks again for the opportunity to sign books here."

"Hope to see you next year."

After loading the container into the trunk, Phil sat in the car for a moment and studied the decorations of downtown Crossroads. It was mostly deserted now, he assumed everyone was at home having dinner or watching an evening sitcom. When he started the vehicle, the tune on the radio was *Same Old Lang Syne*.

Shifting the car into gear, he pulled onto Main Street.

The Elevator

Introduction

Other than dry, official statistical reports, I hadn't started to write seriously until the mid 90s. My first attempt at fiction was work on my published novel *Department of Corrections*. At the time, to practice my craft, I wrote a few short stories. *The Existentialist*, published in my previous anthology, was my first attempt. *The Elevator* is my second.

This piece is long, which prevents me from entering it in many contests. I did try unsuccessfully to compete in two literary journal contests. With over 700 entries, I was not surprised *The Elevator* did not place. The neat idea of these competitions is that the $20 entry fee also gives you a year subscription to the magazine. I would advise any writer to try this, then read the journal. It gives you a concept of what types of story they accept.

The Elevator

Joe couldn't get the country lyrics out of his mind: *When people left town they never came back.*

Fox, Arkansas was a dot on the state map, a blemish in Stone County.

Shifting his BMW into low gear, he hugged Highway 263 as it snaked through the Ozarks toward the town's edge. How long had it been?

A few Ma & Pa stores remained open; pedestrians gawked when he entered the tiny hamlet. Many structures had witnessed former prosperous periods but now crumbled with passing of time.

Not much has changed.

A gas station in the town's center served as the area grocery store. He pulled into the parking lot and stopped by an old gas pump. A hand-written sign taped to the machine ordered patrons to pay inside, no outside credit card.

Backfire startled him and he glanced across the highway where a rusted-out 1970-something Ford pickup, with bed and no tailgate, pulled onto the road. A woman scolded her son as they exited the store and climbed into a 1982 Cutlass with only one whitewall tire and no front bumper. The trunk was tied down with a clothes hanger.

Opposite his gas pump, in a newer model Ford Explorer, sat a lovely redhead Joe's age. She smiled, and he immediately averted his eyes.

When he looked back she had put the vehicle in gear and started forward.

Hot summer months in the hills felt deadly still with no breeze forthcoming; most men and women wore tee shirts. Sweat began to stain Joe's button-up Ralph Lauren after being outside his vehicle for only a few moments.

He kept his arms from swaying as he walked inside to pay. An elderly man on a bench smiled; Joe successfully avoided him.

At the checkout line, an old woman in a flowery dress slowly pulled produce from a grocery cart. "Sure is hot," the customer told the cashier.

"Yes, ma'am, Mrs. Hammond. Heard tomorrow will be hotter."

"I understand we need to watch how much water we use since we ain't had no rain in a while."

"Yes, ma'am."

"Did your son ever get his Eagle's badge?"

"Yes, ma'am."

"He's a good boy. How's Chester doing?"

Oh, come on, bitch! Joe thought. *Will you hurry?*

The woman looked back at Joe and smiled. He stared downward.

When Joe squatted back into his vehicle, he pulled to the shoulder away from traffic, and wiped sweat from his brow. How the hell did he put up with eighteen years of this? Why couldn't he have been raised in Little Rock or Dallas? Anyplace but bumfuck Bugger Hollow.

The highway curved up into Fox and straightened until it disappeared around a bend at the opposite end of town. Joe stared at an imaginary dot in the side of a hill where the road twisted. His temples throbbed and he tried to practice breathing techniques he had learned back in Chicago.

Coming home was never easy.

* * *

He shook dirt from his boots and stepped up to a wooden deck that circled half of his home. "Joe," his mama called.

"Yes, ma'am?"

"You gotta letter there on the table. Some man in a big brown truck brought it."

He picked up the tan envelope and noticed a return label that read The University of Chicago. A bird or lion logo covered part of the sticker.

Opening the tri-fold, he scanned the note. When he read, "You have been accepted" he dropped the paper and stepped back until he bumped into the gun case. "I've been accepted … I've been accepted…."

"What is it, Joe?" his mama asked. She walked from the kitchen with an apron wrapped around her hips, stirring a wooden spoon in a bowl.

"I've been accepted to the University of Chicago!"

"Is that good?"

"Mama! It's very good. I hope to get into their Department of Economics one day."

"What does this mean, Joe? I didn't know you applied to one of them outta state schools. It doesn't mean you're leaving us, does it?"

Their eyes locked, but both remained silent.

From the porch, Joe eyed the dirt road twenty yards away. Rose bushes grew along the outside wall of the house, and a tall oak near a ditch contained a permanent dust layer from passing vehicles.

A song he often hummed spoke of someone being on his way, making it.

To the city, the big, big city. *Yeah, that's right. I'll make something of myself as soon as I can get away from this hellhole.*

"Hey, Joe." J.D. stepped onto the porch and let the screen door slam. The brothers got along as well as siblings could, often playing in the backwoods. "Mom said you got accepted into some school up north?"

"Chicago, J.D. I'm going to Chicago."

"I can see you goin' to Mountain View or Little Rock, but Chicago! You might get stabbed and kilt."

"Look around, J.D. Is this all you want out of life? A leaking house in the woods of Arkansas? Every time I see a car drive by I think how nice it would be to leave and never return."

"What the hell you talkin' about, Joe? You got it made here. Think of all them homeless people in the big town. Look at all the wide-open space here. Do you *really* want all those city dwellers and concrete buildings?"

"It's all I've ever dreamed about. Look at these filthy rags we wear; I'm tired of being poor. Why do you think Mama's brother never visits us anymore from Fayetteville? They're embarrassed for us."

"Well, ain't you just a peach."

"Why the hell do you think I studied so hard all these years? To work at the plastic factory or lumberyard my whole life? I'm going to make something of myself, J.D. You can stay here and rot if you like. But I'm leaving."

"Why Chicago and not somewhere close, like Russellville or Conway?"

"Arkansas is for losers, brother. The big cities are large for a reason. That's where you can be the best that you can be. And I want to make something of myself and be on top."

"You're speaking gibberish to me now, bro."

* * *

The memory of that acceptance letter replayed through Joe's mind in the here and now as he sat in his BMW at the service station.

Suddenly, two grease-smeared hands reached for his window and a face peered through tinted glass. "Joe Douglass! Is that you?"

Startled, Joe moved away from his door and tried to recognize the blood-shot orbs that peeked in at him. *Is that Jack Carson … a grease monkey, now? I'm not surprised.*

He gassed his sedan and squealed tires onto Highway 263. In Joe's mind, Jack had to be one of the dumbest hillbillies he knew. Stimulating conversation is what Joe needed now, not engine talk about what's under his BMW's hood and latest news of some dumb-ass drag race down a rural road.

At the end of town where the forest began, Joe saw Mildred Jones outside her home, pruning flowers along the wood-railed fence that separated her house from the road.

Pulling his vehicle to a stop in the gravel driveway, he admired how she kept up her place, despite its ancient, rock-framed appearance. One tall pine stood to the side with a birdfeeder tied to a limb, the birdbath underneath littered with pine needles and cones.

Her hand shielded her face from the sun; she eyed him stepping from the BMW.

"Mrs. Jones, do you remember me?"

Using the fence to balance herself, she groaned as she stood from the kneeling position. Joe noticed the stoop in her back as she rocked side-to-side, willing herself to the latched gate.

"I'm sorry, young fellow. Have we met?"

"Joe Douglass. I had you for several classes ten years ago."

"My memory's not what it used to be, but you do look familiar. Made excellent grades, if I recall."

"Straight A's. I still give you some credit for inspiring me."

"I'm glad I could help. What have you done?"

"I have a Master's from the University of Chicago and I work there in the city now."

"Wonderful! I did enjoy teaching, but had to retire six years ago due to my health. Wanted to fix up the place here, but my back gives me such fits that heavy yard work's mostly impossible."

Joe glanced at the small home, perhaps eight hundred square feet. *You call this retirement?*

"My place isn't much, but I enjoy it. About all I could afford on a teacher's salary. Two incomes sure would have helped, but the right man just never came along." She smiled. "What about you? Got a girlfriend?"

"No, ma'am. I'm trying to enjoy the single life in Chicago while I can."

"That's my only regret in life. Now, don't get me wrong; I had boyfriends over the years. Just never met my soul mate. So, why are you back in town? Visiting family?"

"Yes, ma'am. My mother's in hospice; I just learned about it a few weeks ago. My boss wasn't happy with me taking off. That's why I'm just now making it down."

"I'm so sorry to hear about your mom, Joe."

"I'm on my way out to see her now, so you take care."

* * *

Joe pulled his BMW from Mrs. Jones' driveway and headed north on

Highway 236 toward Timbo. A few miles before Highway 66, he turned onto a dirt road that disappeared into a tree-thinned valley; a new, three-story home had been built atop the ridge.

Gravel pounded the undercarriage of his vehicle as he sped along the bumpy path. Several times he swerved to prevent a loose rock from damaging his low-slung Beemer.

After a mile the woods reappeared and trees, mostly oak with scattered pine and dogwood, grew thick up to the road's edge.

At one point he made a sharp turn, Joe saw another curve a hundred yards ahead. He knew after taking the bend his boyhood home would be on the left. An ache played with his heart. He wished he were back in Chicago, then wondered about the condition of his mama.

He reflected on that last day at home, ten years ago, before his dad paid a friend to drive him to Little Rock for the flight to Chicago.

The family stood on the porch with Joe. "Here you go, Son." His dad handed him a package wrapped in a grocery bag.

He tore the brown paper with Piggly Wiggly advertisements, and found a framed family photo from his childhood.

Great, a picture.

"You were such a cute little baby," Joe's mama whispered.

"Thank you for the exquisite gift," Joe said.

"Does that mean you like it?" Dad asked.

"Yes. I will cherish it. I really must prepare for my sojourn."

"Your what?" Joe's brother asked.

"My trip."

Joe placed the picture atop the rusted lawn chair on the porch. His suitcase lay below the seat.

As Joe slowed his BMW to make the curve, he reflected over that picture. He had left it behind, not wanting future acquaintances to see his poor upbringing.

Once Joe made the turn, about twenty-five yards ahead, he saw the sparse clearing with his home. The house was hidden by oak at first, but as he closed the gap, he glimpsed an empty rutted driveway that led to a collapsed work-shed. Patches of grass and weeds grew in the yard; nearby trees soaked up any available water, so dusty areas covered much of the location.

Constructed mostly of wood, the lower half of the house had rotted from years of weather deterioration.

Joe parked his vehicle to the side, off the furrowed driveway. As he stepped from the door, he listened to distant caws of crows and felt a slight breeze as it rustled trees overhead.

Something from branches fell and toppled down the metal roof, probably an acorn. Memories of deafening rainstorms popped into his mind. The damn tin sounded like a drum solo and had made it tough to concentrate on homework.

Joe stepped carefully onto the porch planks, doing his best to avoid damaged floorboard. In one place he saw the ground underneath and remembered he and his brother had played beneath the house.

The front door was open except for a locked screen entrance. Slipping his hand through sliced mesh, Joe popped the latch and walked inside.

The layout was easily visible from where he stood. An open kitchen and combination dining/living room to his left, with three doors to his right that led to two bedrooms and a bath. A door off the kitchen opened to the backyard and nearby woods.

"Hello," he said in a lowered voice.

When no one answered, he began to walk toward his mom's closed door. A table against the wall, below a windowpane that looked out over the front porch, caught his attention. Atop it he saw his old departing gift never taken the day he left for Chicago.

The plastic Wal-Mart frame had faded over the years, but the photo remained in reasonable condition. He picked it up and realized he had never really examined the picture those many years ago during the long goodbye.

A colored image stared back at him with his parents outside in front of the house, Joe and his brother stood before them. Dad's large fingers rested protectively on Joe's shoulders as he hovered over the small boy.

How old was I here? Four or five?

A large oak had occupied much of the front yard and could be seen in the side of the photo. Two ropes from an overhead branch suspended a bench swing.

God, I read a lot of books in that seat.

Strong winds from an approaching thunderstorm had finally destroyed the tree. With its destruction also went the tree house where Joe and his brother fought many cowboy and Indian wars.

Dad always kept the home in good repair, and damage now visible along the outside frame was nonexistent in the picture. Honeysuckle and azaleas once grew thick along the side; a stray cat had rested in the old lawn chair on the porch.

Thick roots from the old oak penetrated the earth's surface in front of where the family stood in the picture. They reminded him of varicose veins that ran up grandma's legs.

Memaw ... haven't thought of you in a long time.

The siblings wore overalls with no shirts; leg seams were rolled up. Mama smiled as Uncle George snapped the Polaroid. Her pink and white flowery dress paused in mid-flutter.

We went to the music fest in Mountain View that day. I ate a ton of watermelon and J.D. won a seed-spitting contest. Kristy and I held hands....

The photo was not centered. To the right of the house in the background Joe saw a cleared field. A semi-circular indentation in the earth marked a small levee that held in check the deep end of a pond along the hilltop.

Artwork by Liz Morris

Joe's polished wingtip shoes tapped along the wooden floor as he walked from the front room to the kitchen and peered out a window. The pasture beside the backwoods was now covered in briars and small seedlings. The pond's outline appeared eroded, covered in blue grass.

A memory of a diseased dogwood in the small backyard between the house and field surfaced. Soon after he shot the dove atop a branch, his Mama had ran outside.

"Joe Douglas! How dare you kill an animal just to be killin'! Especially a dove … it's God's symbol of peace. The olive branch, Joe. You heard the preacher … the olive branch."

Joe returned to the front room; he smiled at the thought of his mother and some of her ideas. She was a simple woman, yet incredible wisdom sometimes escaped from her mouth. She did encourage him to do well in school.

With the picture frame still in hand, Joe squinted at the image and noticed two wooden rocking chairs upon the porch, hidden behind the screen. *Memaw and Pepaw were still alive then.*

His grandparents had lived near Shiloh in neighboring Cleburne County. When the Corps of Engineers built Greers Ferry Lake, it flooded the town and they moved over to Stone County to be near their children. Time took its toll on their frail bodies and they finally moved into the small house with Joe and his family. To make space for them, Joe and his brother gave up their bedroom and slept in the front room.

Pepaw told the best stories, and no one could fix a meal like Memaw. His grandfather often hiked through the forest with the brothers as Joe knocked the cedar walking stick Pepaw had whittled for him into trees and played sword with it.

A large rock outcrop on the hilltop served as rifle range. The siblings and their grandfather would set up tiny green plastic toy soldiers and shoot BBs at them. J.D. would throw rocks as bombs.

As Joe replaced the photograph back on the table, he noticed a worn leather baseball glove hidden behind porcelain figurines. Joe and his Papa had played catch for hours in the front yard near the dirt road.

"I'm so proud of you, Joe," was the last thing his father told him before Joe departed for Chicago.

With no phone and no contact plans, Joe's family were unable to inform him of Papa's death from a stroke a month later in the welding shop where he worked.

When Joe finally received word, his father had already been buried. No reason to return to Arkansas at that point, so he wrote a long, five-page letter. He lambasted his grieving family for not trying harder to get word to him of his father's death. He criticized local customs and insinuated he might never travel back home. He was going to make a name for himself.

Ten years had given him a revised outlook on life; but now he was as confused as ever. He glanced up at his mother's closed door.

"Mama." No answer.

The hospice nurse had warned him of Mama's bedridden condition.

Taking a step toward the door, he stopped. Hunger pains played at his stomach and he wished he had eaten in Clinton on the trip from Little Rock. Maybe he could find something to make a sandwich.

When he opened the kitchen cabinet, a pack of roaches scampered toward dark seclusion. He found nothing, no bread or anything, that looked safe to eat.

* * *

Joe would never forget images of downtown Chicago, with all the tall skyscrapers, as his plane landed that first time from Little Rock.

An incredible amount of paperwork was needed for Joe to win acceptance to the university. Scholarships paid a part of the enormous expense. Loans and credit cards would accumulate. But his anticipated high-paying job after graduation would allow him to pay all debts within a short time.

He checked into what would be his home for several years; the next day he stood in long lines to register. Chicagoland's population was several times larger than the entire state of Arkansas. Never had he seen so many wonderful people. Men and women wanting to excel, to be the best they could, and ascend the economic ladder.

Within the first week he drank shots at a bar with his new roommate. Alcohol had never crossed his lips back in the dry district of Stone County, Arkansas. Joe vomited on the table and was carried out. The hangover was enough to keep him from ever repeating such an event.

His roommate liked to remind him of the fiasco and called him a country boy. Teasing was too close to home, reminiscent of bullies back in pre-college days. Joe buried his emotions and hid the intense dislike for his fellow boarder while he tolerated his roommate's wild ways until he could escape.

Always looking to the future.

Joe's next roommates over the years were more to his liking, and they were able to help one another with studies. As planned, Joe graduated and was accepted into the Master's program.

Two years later he completed his graduate degree and was ready for that high-paying job.

* * *

As Joe reflected over the past few years, someone knocked on the screen door. He went to open it.

"Are you Joe?" a woman in multi-color nurse's scrubs asked. "I'm Barbara Norwood … the hospice RN." Brunette hair sprung Medusa-like and she looked as if she had been in a rush all morning. Yet her soft cheeks and warm smile could brighten a day.

"Yes, I'm Joe. Please come in."

Stepping inside, Barbara sat a clipboard with paper on the artificial round wood table beside the kitchen. Strips of brown plastic flapped loosely from the side's curved surface.

"Is she awake … have you talked with her yet?" Barbara asked.

"Not yet. I just arrived." He glanced at his mother's closed room and back to the nurse.

"Like I told you on the phone, the cancer has spread to her brain from her lungs."

"Cigarettes, right?"

"Possibly."

Joe shook his head. As poor as his family had been, Mama and Papa always found a way to purchase tobacco.

Barbara continued. "Don't be shocked when you first see her. She's lost a lot of weight."

"I'm ready."

"You can help me while I check her vitals. Let me use the restroom first and wash my hands."

Joe glanced out the front window while waiting. The table below the windowpane where his childhood picture sat also contained many other framed memories. One was lying face down in the back corner.

Picking it up, Joe saw himself standing by the large corporate sign outside the conglomerate where he now worked. He had taken the photo to send his mom.

The three-piece suit and silk tie sure contrasted with most photos of him dressed in overalls and home-sewn clothes. The climb to such affluence had been steep.

* * *

"Joe, hi. I'm Tyron Davis, an intern working for the company. Mr. Peterson asked me to meet you and show you around. You graduated from the University of Chicago, uh? That's impressive."

The two shook hands, although Joe hesitated when greeting a black man. He had seen African-Americans on TV and students from other schools, but had never conversed with one until the day at the Little Rock airport. How could he have known he should tip the baggage handler? He'd felt daggers stabbing him from the glares he received.

Few Blacks migrated to his region of Arkansas. Stereotypes he heard on the grapevine, and what his education taught him, left him confused with what to believe of other cultures.

Tyron happened to be a lady's man, Joe soon learned, and was fond of flirting when the opportunity presented itself. Joe took notes. The girls obviously liked Tyron's approach.

"Mr. Peterson thought you might like to see your new office. Follow me."

They walked down a long hallway toward a series of elevators. Tyron ran into an acquaintance. "Jolsyn! Hey baby. Why ain't you returnin' my calls?"

"I've been out of town for a week now." Jolsyn smiled. "Call me tonight?"

"It's a date."

As the two colleagues continued toward the elevators, crowds began to squeeze them like water down a funnel. Momentum carried them toward the elevator cars, opening and closing like predator teeth.

"She's pretty," Joe said, trying to avoid zigzags of pedestrians.

"Yo, that bitch is hot. Let me tell you. Want me to set you up, just give the word."

The idea sent nervous waves throughout his body. Seven years in Chicago and he'd been able to avoid a date. But why? Perhaps due to conversations with females that never flowed naturally unless he discussed business. Personal events were off limits.

When asked, he grew up in Dallas, Texas. His high school had five hundred in the graduating class. Made-up childhood details grew elaborate over the years and he needed to write them down to remember.

Apparently no job interviewers had checked his high school references. And his college information was in good shape.

While waiting outside the elevator, Joe noticed many cultures represented around him. Blacks, Hispanics, Japanese, Chinese, Europeans, Middle Easterners, there were people from places Joe knew little about.

He had never had a black friend before and liked Tyron. Perhaps changing some of his speech to sound more like Tyron's dialect would help Joe get a foot into the African-American world?

Yet everyone seemed to avoid Joe, as they had in college and back in Fox, Arkansas.

"Hey, man," Joe said. "How tall is this building?"

"Over a hundred stories high. You're on the eighty-fifth floor."

After they exited the elevator, Tyron introduced Joe to colleagues as they strolled down a long corridor. Joe shook his new co-worker's hand each time. The interaction was quick, no one stopped to chat or ask about him.

They continued until they stood at the edge of a series of floor-to-ceiling glass panel windows. Joe looked down at the ant-size cars that inched forward on the streets below.

"I've only been this high standing on a bluff of the White River and looking out over some valley. Sure is cool up here."

Tyron paused and cocked his head sideways. "Boy, you need to get out more. This ain't nothin'. I'm gonna set you up on a date. You ever been out with a black girl? That's what you need. A sista will bring you into the modern world."

Joe felt his face flush. Surely Tyron was pulling his leg, but Joe had no idea how to respond.

* * *

Barbara Norwood turned the knob and opened Mama's bedroom door. A quilt draped over the only window blocked daylight until the living room light invaded the abyss.

From the threshold, Joe saw his mom asleep in her bed across the room. An oxygen tank by the dresser connected to a mask wrapped around her nose.

Blankets hid her body, but her face looked like latex rubber over bone. World War II photos of concentration camp survivors came to mind.

While the RN conducted hospice duties, Joe took a few steps closer. Mama's arms rested outside the blanket and against her side. Long, arthritic fingers twitched as Barbara rolled her to her side to check for bedsores.

Joe noticed the gold band on Mama's ring finger.

The nurse lowered a side rail. "Would you like to sit?" she asked him. "Visit with her, ask her questions. She's not responded in several days, but we think comatose patients can still hear the outside world subconsciously."

Joe walked the remaining few steps and sat on the bed's edge. "Hi, Mama."

After a few moments, Barbara said, "Keep talking. I have paperwork I can do in the front room. Give y'all some privacy."

Scanning his mother's face, Joe saw stretched eyelids covering sunken eyes. Memories of their relationship surfaced. She had protected him from a strict disciplinarian father and always offered him encouragement at his studies. But there were so many other daily interactions. What had he taken for granted?

When he'd been teased at school, unable to fight back with his sickly, slender physique, she had comforted him, taught him that not all the world was cruel.

As he sat watching his mom die, Joe wondered how much of his melancholy was self-induced. How much control did he have over his own emotions and interpretation of his past?

An image of Mama carrying a cake toward him as his family sang "Happy Birthday" took Joe back. And on Christmas those wacky, often nice surprises. Why did he seldom smile for the camera?

How did his dad afford to give him a 22-caliber rifle when his family couldn't even pay to have a phone installed? Squirrel hunting trips offered a multitude of learning opportunities with his dad, as did fishing on the White River. Why did he rarely converse when Dad wanted to try?

Why remember bad times when there were so many good memories? Like camping along the lakeshore at Greers Ferry Lake, or a swim in the creek after a rainstorm. He and J.D. would chase goats on a neighbor's farm, and raised several litters of kittens.

Why did the presence of his dying mom bring up these recollections?

* * *

When Joe landed in Chicago that first day no one waited for him. Airport travelers hurried across terminals; he found a safe spot against the wall to decide his next move.

Paperwork from the University of Chicago explained where he needed to go, but how would he get there? It had never crossed his mind.

Surely the subway was near, but how would he know which stop to use? Maybe a taxi would be better. He'd brought extra cash. The woman from the university who telephoned him gave few directions.

Outside, a steward with an accent asked if he needed help.

Joe showed him the map he printed from the Internet. "I need to get here."

"You need taxi ... tell driver where you go." He picked up Joe's two suitcases and loaded them in the trunk.

"Thank you," Joe said. He shook the steward's extended hand and climbed into the taxi's backseat. Joe thought he heard "Cheap bastard" before the door slammed.

Traffic congestion led to delays. Joe watched pedestrians march up streets; they reminded him of ants, everyone seemed propelled by a universal will.

As he traveled, the quality of men and women deteriorated. Now Joe saw bums and homeless loitering along sides of tall buildings. Vagabonds stood on corners under streetlights asking stopped motorists for money.

The driver dropped Joe off to meet with local university officials. With a day and a half before official school registration, he decided to explore the city. A map showed the nearest subway stop.

Directions on walls seemed easy. He purchased the proper tickets for a day and jumped on the next train.

A transition occurred as his conveyance moved down the line. Advertisements grew racy with posters of scantily dressed models eyeing wary onlookers. Interested in what the city looked like above ground, Joe jumped off at the next stop and ascended a wide block of stairs.

He had always shied away from making eye contact and saying hello. Yet he remained vigilant of those he passed, prepared to return a friendly greeting. As he walked down littered streets with strong gusts against his frail body, he noticed no one said hi.

A large man in blue jeans and black leather jacket yelled, "Hey, Buddy. Want to see live action?"

Joe walked toward him out of politeness. "Sure. What type?"

"Peek inside here."

The man cracked the metal door, alcohol stickers draped along its front. Bleached blonde and topless, a woman straddled someone on the front row seats that circled a stage. Her nipples stood out like gorgeous cherries atop white-icing cupcakes.

Joe stepped back in shock. The bouncer smiled. "Five dollar cover charge … come on in."

Across the street a marquee sign atop the entrance to a theater read: On Golden Blonde. Below it were three 'X's.

Joe glanced back at the bouncer who seemed to enjoy his naiveté. As fast as he could, he ran back to the subway and hopped the next train.

* * *

"Has she opened her eyes?" the nurse asked, checking her pager.

Clearing his head, Joe looked up. "No, ma'am."

"I need to go—got to check in on one of my patients up near Fifty-Six. Is there anything I can do for you?"

Joe looked into her eyes and liked the sincerity. "You look familiar."

"We went to school together, Joe. I got my nursing degree from UCA in Conway."

"And you moved back *here*?"

"This is home, although I wonder sometimes if I made a mistake. Do you enjoy Chicago?"

Joe paused and glanced around the room before answering. "I guess so."

"You look good. It's nice to see you again. I'm sorry about your mom; hope you have an opportunity to talk with her."

"Thank you."

From the front window he watched Barbara pull her Dodge Stratus onto the dirt road and drive away. The vehicle's white exterior was coated with mud.

She had no ring on.

An imaginary conversation flowed through his mind—internal dialogues that he invented to speak with women.

* * *

Near the windows on the eighty-fifth floor, Joe saw his coworker Karen across the field of cubicles as she arose and walked toward the restroom.

She occasionally smiled at him, but that was the extent of their exchange.

Hi, Karen, he imagined himself saying. *My name's Joe. Would you like to go out?*

I would like that, Joe.

With movie-star confidence, Joe's imagination took him on a journey. He placed his palm to Karen's face and brought his lips to hers. Slowly, like he practiced on his pillow at night, he slipped his tongue into her mouth and tasted her. Their skin compressed as one and his hand moved past her blouse and found a breast with an erect nipple.

Someone slammed a phone down and brought Joe out of his dream. The stiffness in his pants felt noticeable so he turned toward the window and stared at the ground far below.

Strong gusts swayed the building.

* * *

With his suitcase removed from the BMW trunk, Joe carried it to the bedroom he had shared with J.D.

The room looked the same. His brother's leftover junk covered the dressers, shelves, and closet floor.

J.D. was the sports enthusiast. Baseball and football trophies sat on the room's only window ledge. "J.D. Douglas." Brass plates were on every award.

Joe smiled. *Why the hell 'J.D.'? Why not Jimmy, John, or Jonathan?*

He had seen J.D.'s birth certificate; the actual name was J.D. *Just initials for nothing.*

His parents embarrassed the hell out of him and he tried not to be seen with them. When his dad drove to school one day to tell Joe about grandmother's passing, Joe slumped in his seat hoping he wouldn't be connected with the "filthy man in the green hunting jacket." His father drove straight from work at the welding shop. Black burnt holes spotted the material where molten chunks of metal fell upon him. A charcoal imprint on his forehead highlighted where he had rubbed sweat away with his hand.

The fancy suits Joe now wore could be traced to such events, his wardrobe genesis from adolescent overalls and hiking boots, highlighted by an episode a few days into his new job.

* * *

Tyron's desk phone continued to ring and Joe was not able to intercept it from his telephone.

Joe stepped across the aisle between cubicles and picked up the receiver. "Tyron's desk," he said.

After taking the message, he heard his name whispered in the workspace a row over.

"Trashy hillbilly," someone said. "Can you believe those clothes? They should have mandated he take some designer course in college … learn how to dress for success. I bet you he buys his suits at Wal Mart."

Joe heard giggles, then a familiar female voice. "I catch him staring at me all the time. Gives me the creeps. As if I would ever go out with such a hideous creature. I can tell he wants to ask me out, that's why I always walk around his cubicle."

"Why did Mr. Peterson hire him?"

"They're giving him those accounts nobody wants."

Sneaking back to his desk, Joe sat. He looked at his attire.

Atop a shelf lay a photo taken in college. After staring at it, his eyes focused on a two-inch by three-inch image of Kristy taped to his computer monitor. They had been inseparable throughout elementary school.

Laughter rose from the other side of Tyron's desk. *They're still talking about me!*

His surroundings narrowed like tunnel vision in his mind, and he felt he had to escape outside for fresh air. He made small, quick steps toward the elevator. A pack of upper executives dressed in black suits enjoyed conversation.

The elevator opened. There was only enough room for the managers, so Joe waited. He felt many eyes from inside the compartment watching him as the door shut. He focused his gaze toward a panel of buttons on the wall.

Quickly, he pushed the down key, and waited on the next elevator. Two women walked up behind him. They continued their dialogue and did not include him. Their power suits ended below the knees; lovely, curved calves extended into navy-blue shoes.

Hurry up!

A series of lit numbers along the top of the shaft indicated the location of the next elevator. The car seemed to stop on every floor. He tried to keep his eyes off those perfect legs.

Another crowded car opened, room for maybe two. Joe backed up and offered the space to the women. They never thanked him.

The third elevator contained five women who immediately quieted when Joe entered. The mixture of fragrances created an ambiance of pleasure. He now believed he would never experience scents such as those in intimate contact. The control panel highlighted the descent to the fiftieth floor, where they all exited to wait for the next series of elevators that would take them to ground level.

A horde waited and it took two cars before Joe squeezed his way into a crowded elevator. The lobby swarmed with occupants. Unable to walk a straight path toward the front entrance, he strolled, increasing or decreasing his pace as men and women crisscrossed the polished marble floor. A security guard eyed him, as always, while Joe lined up to exit outside.

Concrete sidewalks and red painted curbs greeted him. Impatient drivers honked at one another and made concentration difficult.

A series of Bradford Pear trees, spaced twenty yards apart, lined the street outside his company's skyscraper. Metal crates surrounded the trunks; Joe leaned against the bark and stared down. Cigarette butts and candy wrappers littered the area inside the enclosures.

* * *

Night began its descent over the Ozark Mountains. Joe stood on the porch and listened. No vehicles had passed in thirty minutes; only birds and insects greeted his senses.

Clouds' underbellies shimmered as sunlight lit them from an angle far off on Earth's horizon. *When did I last hear Mama's voice?*

A ten year absence, and although they communicated by letter a few times annually, Joe only talked with her three or four times. Phones were a luxury, so they planned their conversations for Mama to go to the neighbor's house.

"Are you going to church, Joe?" Mama asked each time. "Maybe you can meet a nice girl in the singles' Bible Study."

"Sure, Mama."

He turned and saw his reflection in the front windowpane. Old acne scarred his cheeks and forehead where he had picked at it before the mirror, stressed at night after school. Joe reentered his mother's home and walked past her ajar bedroom door.

Seeing her still comatose, he decided to sit in a rocker and turn on an old black and white TV. Without cable, nothing but static crossed the screen.

Joe turned it off and walked back outside. Ozark forest stretched over the landscape lining both sides of the dirt road. Crows cawed and a choir of insects chattered back and forth.

The rutted path continued past the house and disappeared below a dusk-orange horizon, into a valley. He stared at the road's perspective, reminding him of railroad tracks he painted in junior high art class where the rails extended on paper to a fine point. This taught him artistic point of view. Later he would compare physics' relativity with a hodgepodge of ideas to form a holistic whole. A "Theory of Everything" the textbook said.

How he wanted to make sense of his existence.

After changing into expensive exercise apparel from a large Chicago athletic store, Joe began his long jog toward that distant dot blending the end of the road with the sky's horizon.

He passed old homes with neighbors he never tried to know. Now the elderly couples seemed dead, houses remained dark and unkempt. They appeared deserted and about to crumble. Children had moved away to larger towns. Decaying carcasses of ancient structures would soon be reclaimed by local wilderness. The cycle of life.

When he reached the plateau's edge and began his descent into the valley, he stopped. The large moss-covered oak still stood beside the scythed ditch, thick branches extended skyward like monster tentacles from an ocean's depth.

The trunk's deformity remained.

He had forgotten and did not want to be reminded. Kristy and he had been inner-tubing on a local creek after a thunderstorm. They walked home hand in hand; Joe used his free arm to roll the rubber tube along the rocky surface.

An engine roared off in the distance. They laughed and talked school and gossip, what they would do the next day.

The vehicle moved closer, they could hear it over the hilltop where the road flattened toward Joe's home.

"Sounds like someone's four-wheelin'," Joe said.

"Sure is loud."

They continued up the incline, a scenic valley behind them. The unseen vehicle echoed nearer.

Joe slipped, the inner tube rolled backward and he ran to stop it. The warning scream froze in his mind. Turning, he saw a truck with roll-bar soar over the road's vanishing point and smash Kristy into the oak. Smoke filled the air and debris flew forward. A second body had crashed through the windshield and flown thirty yards into briar bush.

A teenage passenger received an underage drinking citation; the driver was booked for DUI and vehicular manslaughter after his release from Children's Hospital in Little Rock.

No one explained the events to Joe, his mind a wandering oasis of cascading ideas imploding upon themselves.

Mrs. Douglas had told her son it would be okay.

Joe shook the suppressed nightmare from his mind and walked to the tree. A hard wooden knot had formed on the bark where the truck slammed into it.

Kristy....

They would chase each other through woods, build homemade forts in thick brush, make dams to divert water runoff after rain and jump in the muddy aftermath. They attended church together and studied in the same Bible class.

Church had never been the same; nor his religion. He attended because Mama forced his presence. What kind of God heaps such suffering upon innocent children?

Emotionally drained, Joe retreated up the dirt road back toward Mama's house.

She remained unconscious, each breath carefully calculated by her strong will. Often, Joe held his own breath when his mother's lungs seemed to stop.

Each dramatic moment her body fought on, the ultimate outcome always assured.

* * *

Rollin-Kaufman Funeral Home had taken care of the service, a simple ceremony attended by ten of Mrs. Douglas' acquaintances. Joe's attempt to contact J.D. had proved futile. His sibling's last known address in Oklahoma led to a dead end.

Leaving the subway, now back in Chicago, he stepped up the concrete ramp to street level and saw his tall office building across the way. Morning sun failed to reach the cavernous valleys hidden by massive skyscrapers in every direction.

Once signed in at the security desk, after a long wait, Joe strolled toward the hallway lined with rows of elevators facing one another across the aisle. He saw the company's CEO take the express elevator to the top level.

The ground floor was packed with morning employees heading for work. Like in a herd, they wobbled forward each time an elevator opened to swallow more colleagues.

Once he made it to the fiftieth floor, he exited and waited again for the next tier of elevators to take him to his level on the eighty-fifth.

Memories of Mama and his recent visit to Arkansas invaded his mind; he tried to block them. The future was his. No need to ever go home again.

The elevator opened and he stepped in, then the door closed. He was on his way; he was making it. To the city, the big, big city.

Westerns

Photo by David Knight

New Madrid Sunrise

Introduction

New Madrid Sunrise won 3rd Place at the 2004 Arkansas Writers' Conference, Westward Ho Award contest, sponsored by Dusty Richards. I'm not sure how many entries competed, but other winners lived in Oklahoma, California, and Texas. If you've read my nonfiction piece titled *Dusty* in this anthology, then you know I'm a big fan of Dusty Richards. His requirements for this competition were either a Western short story or two chapters of a Western novel. This is a short story.

The tale was then accepted in 2007 on *Amazon.com Shorts* under its Western genre. Daniel Slater, director for *Amazon.com Shorts*, said in his acceptance letter, "Thanks for continuing to add such fantastic pieces to your body of work on *Amazon Shorts!*"

I submitted this genre piece to the *Arkansas Review* at Arkansas State University in Jonesboro. Skeptical of a western being accepted for a literary journal, I thought what the heck. Editor Tom Williams sent a nice rejection letter that said, "Liked the history." This short line made the effort worth my trouble.

I must give credit to Joe David Rice for the idea behind the story. At the time, in 2004, we were in a writing critique group editing each other's work. Joe David was working on a nonfiction book related to the New Madrid Earthquake. I was familiar with the disaster, having studied it at the University of Central Arkansas where I majored in Geography for my undergraduate degree. Joe David pulled many hidden details of the quake from his research, and included many eye-witness accounts, I knew I'd have to write this current tale.

New Madrid Sunrise

December 15, 1811 (2:00 p.m.)

Colonel William Hagan—retired U.S. Army—sat under an open wooden A-frame structure in the middle of a flatboat as an afternoon thundershower made its way up the Mississippi River.

"Snag ahead!" yelled Captain Sarpy.

Crewmen scampered across the boat and jumped over tied down barrels. They took oars anchored to the side and maneuvered the flatboat around underwater trees that caused ripples along the surface.

"Good goin'," the captain said.

Sarpy stuffed a knife used to cut rope back into the scabbard fixed to his buckskin boots. A ragged beard grew along his chin; bushy eyebrows lent an intimidating stare. Despite his stern disposition, he could be jovial under the guidance of spirits.

It had been a long journey for Hagan. From Boston, he made his way down the Ohio River to the Mississippi, then to St. Louis where he joined Sarpy and his band of men. They were taking a shipment of goods south to New Orleans.

Cold rain gave way to an evening sundown as cloud caps lit bright white on the horizon. Wildlife along the river resumed the end of its daily cycle.

"Is that island number ninety-four?" Hagan asked over the honks of geese landing in a nearby cove. He glanced at a handheld document.

Captain Sarpy rubbed his hairy chin and looked. Thick trees covered the island and other flatboats had moored to the bank. "I'd say we be midway between Chickasaw Bluff and Natchez—so that's probably Crow's Nest Island. Rogue's Nest would be a better name."

"Why's that?"

"Officially the hellhole be number ninety-four. River rats like me, however, know to steer clear of the pirates that always camp there."

Hagan saw smoke rise skyward from the forest around the island and noticed Sarpy's vigilant crew with rifles ready.

"We be landing at the next island just over yonder," Sarpy pointed.

A small islet appeared downriver near the bend. Minutes later Sarpy and his crew maneuvered the flatboat to the sandy, but mostly muddy shore.

"Be alert, men," Sarpy demanded. "Any damn pirate set foot on *our* island, you send him to the Devil!"

Hagan smiled. A confrontation was perhaps what he needed. Fighting's what he did in the war for independence—but he was a much younger man then. Another war with the Brits loomed in the near future, and he missed the days when he led men into battle.

England had already blockaded several United State's seaports twelve miles out from the coastline. The distance from land prevented an official declaration of war.

Standing to dust off his jeans, he next grabbed his gear and placed it near the tree line where crewmen were preparing camp. His old Army coat worked too well on this mild December evening, so he swapped it with a light jacket.

Darkness soon descended except for a bright fire just feet from the Mississippi. Meals were prepared and sailors discussed whatever topic popped into their minds.

"What brings you to this part of the world," one of the crew asked.

"A rich capitalist in Boston's paying me to bring back a killer."

"A bounty hunter, ey?"

"The murderer killed my client's pregnant wife."

"What makes you think he's headed here?"

"He's French and has family living perhaps in New Madrid or Arkansas Post. He also has ties to New Orleans. I'll keep searching until I find him—dead or alive."

"What's his name?" Sarpy asked.

"Godfrey Bringier."

Sarpy stood and stretched. "Yes, that name sounds familiar. I believe he escaped New Orleans, leaving behind a considerable gambling debt."

"I appreciate the information," Hagan replied. "My client's been searchin' for Godfrey for many years." He threw a blanket over his legs. "It's been a long day—goodnight."

As the crackling campfire burned, Hagan stared at the stars, trying to make himself fall asleep. All he could think of was capturing Godfrey ... and brief moments of self imposed isolation. He was most likely too old to father children. And what woman would have him, anyway?

Drunken screams of bandits, not a mile upriver, delayed Hagan's slumber. Finally, after midnight, shrieks gave way to splashing of the mighty Mississippi.

Photo by Carolyn Boyles

December 16, 1811 (2:00 a.m.)

Screeches of birds taking flight startled Hagan and his traveling partners. Geese bellowed in the pitch-black distance; he heard squirrels, too numerous to guess how many, scamper in the unseen branches above.

"What the hell—?" he murmured.

A crewmember threw fresh wood onto the fire and flames flickered higher. Several deer could be seen struggling against the river current as if panicked, trying to escape the jaws of a bear.

"A thunderstorm?" Hagan asked.

Before Sarpy could answer, a roar vibrated across the land and suddenly the Earth shook like the apocalypse had commenced.

Within seconds, sulfur smell filled the air; lightning crackled and lit the landscape. Hagan spread his feet to maintain balance.

"Get to the boat and cut it loose!" Sarpy yelled.

Hagan watched between flashes as crewmembers stumbled to the flatboat and unmoored it to keep the sinking shoreline from dragging it down. A whirlpool sucked under squirrels and other animals escaping into the water.

Upriver, where the pirates camped, he heard men squeal as if Satan himself had attacked. A cacophony of sounds penetrated his ears. Oak, cottonwood, and other varieties of trees shattering into one another resonated like the breaking of limbs he recalled from a Carolina winter during an ice storm he once experienced as a young man.

The sky now glowed and smoke filled the atmosphere. It had taken less than a minute to produce the horrible effect. Then across the river Hagen saw a scene that brought back terrible memories he had forced down into his inner most soul. The land rolled like waves upon an ocean!

While in the military he had sailed on a ship captured by a fierce storm at sea. How the crew survived was a miracle. Feelings of that earlier trauma were relived as fissures in the earth spewed water and sand, forcing him to the ground.

Help me, God!

Hagan was not a religious man, but knew many heathens would find Jesus if they survived.

The shaking ended after several long minutes. Sulfur smells and exploding sounds lingered, and would remain within his mind for a long time. Pleas for help echoed across the froth-covered river.

"Get in!" Sarpy yelled.

Hagen jumped into the flatboat and the crew headed toward the bank. Behind them, on the opposite side of the river, they heard a roar and turned to see a giant landslide, as earth and trees slipped into the Mississippi. Top branches protruded from underneath water.

What's next?

December 16, 1811 (6:00 a.m.)

Morning daylight brightened the eastern sky. "Will you look at that," Sarpy said.

The large island where the pirates camped had vanished. The entire waterway was altered.

"The river's flowing backwards!" a crewmember exclaimed.

Hagan and the captain looked. "Impossible!" Sarpy said. "Gentlemen, the apocalypse has begun. You better make peace with your Lord."

Hagan shook his head and smiled in disbelief that he himself had entertained such religious conversion in the heat of panic. *It was an earthquake*, he wanted to say. He had experienced one before upon foreign soil while on assignment with the army. But that was a minor tremor compared to this.

Climbing to the top of the bank, Hagan gazed in disbelief at the landscape. Steam rose from cracks in the ground; the once mighty forest looked like toothpicks stuck in mud where they had smashed into one another.

As Sarpy and his crew made final preparation to depart, Hagan noticed a stranger on a horse galloping toward him. Suddenly, the animal stopped and spread its long legs. The gentleman and Hagan stared wide-eyed at each other and knew.

"Another quake!" Hagan yelled down at Sarpy.

"What—"

Earth jilted with sudden force, throwing everyone to the ground. The flatboat shook loose and floated downstream just as Hagan watched the stranger disappear into a fissure splitting the surface several feet wide.

Across the river he witnessed entire banks collapse into the Mississippi and water rush into lowlands. Again the Earth's surface rolled like waves upon an ocean.

When the calamity ended he ran to the rider and helped him up from the twenty-foot opening. The horse was not so lucky.

"Thank you, mister. Thought Lucifer had pulled me under."

Hagan returned to the shore and observed Sarpy and a crewmember mooring the flatboat back to the sandy bank. One man near drowned trying to reclaim it.

"My land's ruined," the rider said, walking up behind Hagan.

"Looks worse than the battle scene I saw at Yorktown," Hagan turned and replied.

"My home's over that horizon there," he pointed. "It's standing—or was before this last quake. Don't feel safe. The chimney caved in and there're cracks in the walls. Might sleep outside for a while."

"I don't blame you. Are we far from New Madrid?"

"Down the river a bit, maybe a day. If it's still there."

"I wish you luck," Hagan said. Turning, he cautiously stepped down the slope and over small round craters that had spewed sand and water.

"I think we're close to New Madrid, right?" Hagan asked Sarpy.

"Be there by nightfall—if the river will let us."

December 16, 1811 (5:00 p.m.)

"We be tying up there," Sarpy ordered his crew, pointing to a ledge below New Madrid.

Hagan followed the men up the steep slope and found the townspeople huddled in an open field near a fire, surrounded by tents. The sun was a memory with a lingering effect on the western horizon.

One of Sarpy's crewmembers reached for his rifle when he saw a bear lying along a tree line not a hundred yards away. Deer and many smaller varmints all stayed close to the humans.

"Put down that musket!" A balding man in ragged military dress walked toward Hagan and his new friends.

"But there's a bear—"

"Do you see it harming anyone? All the animals are acting unusual these days … can't blame them with the quakes, can you?"

Hagan extended a hand for introductions. "William Hagan."

"Colonel George Morgan. Retired, as I'm sure you can tell by my age."

"As am I."

After sizing one another up, the newcomers joined the townspeople around the fire. Young boys continuously threw broken branches onto flames.

"I founded New Madrid several years back," Morgan said. "I had just returned for a visit when the quakes hit last night."

Everyone stood when the ground rumbled.

"Another aftershock," Morgan continued. "I've done counted ten."

Female screams grew louder from a nearby tent.

"Lucky to be alive," Morgan said, reaching for his tin coffee mug lain on a log next to the fire. "Crossbeam fell and crushed her leg."

When Hagan later found himself alone with Morgan, he explained the reason for his travel down the Mississippi.

"Godfrey Bringier?" Morgan responded. "Yes, I've heard of him. Bringiers are well known up and down the river. Godfrey, though. Well … most folks leave him alone. He's sort of a recluse nowadays. Lives a few days downstream in Little Prairie … last I heard anyway."

December 20, 1811 (7:00 a.m.)

Hagan nodded to Sarpy, then guided his steed toward the edge of town. Morgan loaned Hagan the horse and tack, with a gentlemen's agreement between former officers that Hagan would return it in the same condition or purchase the lot.

Not far outside New Madrid, Hagan struggled across swamp and fallen timber. *The landscape doesn't look natural.*

Cypresses once rooted along bogs now stood several feet upon inclines. Oaks and other trees that thrived on dry land now began the long process to suffocation under several feet of quagmire.

The quakes changed everything.

Just before noon, his horse refused to budge and had steadied his legs in preparation. Hagan made sure no trees were near that might topple on them.

The roar sounded like thunder spreading over sky. Ground shook and visible wildlife acted confused.

That was a mild one.

What should have taken two or three days to Little Prairie took longer due to the damaged landscape. Near his destination Hagan happened upon an exodus.

"George Roddell," a French-speaking gentleman introduced himself. He spoke broken English.

Hagan viewed the many people spread out behind Roddell. Women and children in tattered clothes and mud-caked faces looked defeated.

"De quake take everythin'," Roddell explained. "Most mi people had just 'nough time to escape derr homes before de water flood de land. Little Prairie are no more."

The two men continued to talk during lunch under a tall oak. Hagan said, "I'm searchin' for Godfrey Bringier. I understand he's living near Little Prairie … but don't see sign of him in your party."

"Never heard of him," Roddell replied.

Hagan produced a newspaper article from New Orleans with a caricature of Godfrey. "Here's what he looks like—five years ago, anyway."

"That's Lal Penick!"

"Lal—"

"Dirty bastard stole from us. Townspeople were about to take law into derr own hands … then de quake."

"Where is he?"

"He lives with an injun bride along the river several miles south of what used to be Little Prairie. I'd be careful if I were you."

After lunch, the men shared battle scars with one another related to the quake.

"My family was running from de house toward de woods," Roddell said, "when a large crack in de ground prevented their retreat into de open field. This was hours after de first big shock … maybe de tenth shock … then de eleventh shock came and there was not a square acre of ground left unbroken. I watched from de bank of de bayou by Big Lake … couldn't do anything to help them. About fifteen minutes later de water rose round them waist deep. An old man led them to higher land, but would sometimes fall into one of de cracks in de earth that were concealed from de eyes by the muddy water that they waded through. The earth continued to burst open, and mud, water, sand, and stone coal were thrown up de distance of thirty yards—trees of a large size were split open, fifteen or twenty feet up. We waded eight miles until we get to dry land."

Hagan later reflected upon this as he made his way toward Little Prairie. Fighting the elements and searching for a killer who may be waiting in ambush took him back to the time of the war with England. *I'm getting too old for this.*

The appearance of the townspeople from the exodus took over his thoughts. He imagined what the citizens of New Madrid would think when Roddell arrived. As another tremor sent animals scampering in search of a safe haven, he calculated the days to Christmas.

They'll arrive in New Madrid about Christmas Eve. I wonder what Morgan and the people there will do?

December 22, 1811 (10:00 a.m.)

The calamity looked complete. From a natural levee, Hagan saw a vast, recently made lake. In the far distance he made out the top of buildings and homes of what had been Little Prairie. The chimneys had crumbled, but many wood-laced structures had withstood the quakes only to drown in floodwaters of the Mississippi.

It took him a day to circle around the newly formed lagoon so that he could follow the river southward. He had to wade through submerged lands where towering oaks would soon meet their doom and give way to cypress growth.

With the Mississippi on his left, he maneuvered his steed down a slight slope and across a bog when the horse slipped under water and Hagan caught his foot on a snag.

As they struggled to recover the surface, he felt his rifle and gear slip free of the thrashing animal. A hoof kick in the head stunned him; he was about to black out when his first big breath took in abundant air.

Thank you, God.

He steadied himself with an underwater branch until his composure allowed him to wade toward dry land. The horse made it first and shook the water from his coat. That's when Hagan saw *him*!

From behind a thicket, Godfrey approached with his weapon pointed at Hagan's head. "I wouldn't move if I were you, stranger."

Between groves of damaged trees Hagan now saw smoke rise in the distance, and assumed it must be from Godfrey's home.

"Who are you?"

"William Hagan."

"What the hell you down in these parts for?"

"I was in New Madrid when the quake hit. I'm surveying land to the west of the Mississippi but having a difficult time of it … as you can see." Perhaps a little white lie would buy some time.

Godfrey lowered his rifle. "Forgive me—Indians are scouring the land in search parties looking for missing men … and bandits everywhere. I don't trust anyone."

"Quite all right."

"I don't get much hospitable company around these parts. Join me for lunch then you'll be on your way."

Hagan grabbed what was left of his gear and the reins to the horse. He sensed Godfrey's acute distrust, and would have to be careful before making his move. An incredible pain in his ankle caused a limp. The swelling was already making his foot feel tight within the boot.

"What's new in the outside world?" Godfrey asked.

"Disputes with England continue, battles with natives, settlers moving West—lot of changes in store for our country."

"Your country," he sneered.

A path through the quake-tattered forest gave way to an open field along a bluff next to the Mississippi. The front porch of Godfrey's home hung precariously where the columns had collapsed; chimney debris lay scattered along the ground.

A nervous squaw with lovely dark complexion stepped outside and tried to avoid the sagging porch.

Upon closer inspection Hagan noticed her leather-like skin, perhaps an indication of hard work. Her buckskin dress matched the material on Godfrey's attire; both stank.

"That's my woman, won her fair and square," Godfrey said. He threw the game he had trapped onto a large rock and turned, with a smirk, to face Hagan. "Maybe I'll let you taste her … it's their way, you know?"

Hagan avoided the comment and glanced into the native woman's eyes. *You've suffered, haven't you?*

Godfrey threw a knife at her feet and pointed at the dead rabbits and a fox. "Clean 'em and cook 'em," he ordered.

Hagan doubted she spoke English but knew she understood Godfrey's meaning. She grabbed the wild animals and walked to a cliff overlooking the river.

A few hours lapsed; Hagan now relaxed on a bench inside the cabin chatting with the outlaw. Godfrey seemed interested to learn what changes were occurring up and down the mighty river.

The house was in shambles. Empty shelves and shattered dishes were scattered about where the quake left its destruction.

The woman sat on the opposite side of the cabin with her back to the men. Hagan cut another chunk of meat from a bone when Godfrey pointed and asked, "What's that?"

Hagan glanced at his torn, shirt pocket, an excited feeling washed over him—the same tension he always felt right before battle.

"Just an article."

"Let me see … there's a picture."

Hagan's pause led to curiosity.

"Let me see the damn thing," Godfrey demanded.

The rifle leaned against a wall, feet from Godfrey. Hagan knew he would be too slow with his entire leg throbbing in agony.

He reached for the soggy newspaper clipping and started to hand it over, when it dropped midway across the table and fell to the dirt floor.

It landed so that the soaked drawing of Godfrey faced up. "What the hell!"

Hagan lunged for the weapon but was too slow.

Godfrey head-butted him with the stock; then pointed the rifle and shot. Smoke rose from the barrel and Hagan felt a musket ball penetrate his skin above the left shoulder.

"Arrggg!"

Hagan crawled toward the door but Godfrey threw a knife that stuck in his leg. The woman stood in terror and watched helplessly from her corner.

"So, I guess you came looking for me and a reward. No one out there will ever know how you died."

Hagan watched Godfrey pull gunpowder from a pouch and slowly load the rifle. He looked for anything to defend himself.

Godfrey stepped forward with the barrel pointed at Hagan's head. "If anyone asks, I'll say you *must* have got swallowed by the river."

He smiled and began to press the trigger, when a jolt moved his aim right. The shot exploded splinters from the wall. A thunder-like roar rolled over the earth and shook the cabin like a saltshaker.

Pushing the door open, Hagan tried to crawl outside. The woman wobbled to him between shock waves and helped.

Godfrey struggled to reload and exit the home as well.

Fissures opened in the earth and the entire landscape grew laden under the familiar smell of sulfur and a hazy, poisonous fog.

Hagan and the woman continued to move forward; he glanced back and watched as Godfrey staggered toward them.

A huge explosion shook Godfrey to the ground. Then incredibly, the cliff began to crumble into the swirling Mississippi.

Hagan watched as Godfrey scratched his way inches forward only to be dragged under.

The scene turned surreal as blasts echoed throughout the river valley. To his right he witnessed Red Coats charging Revolutionary forces as cannon shots exploded upon the land. Over flooded landscape he saw vessels rock upon the sea, fire and smoke hugged the surface.

Like bubbles that escape from under water, Hagan was drawn up into consciousness. He awoke to blue skies and a swashing Mississippi River. Sweat cascaded down his face as he stared into the native woman's beautiful eyes. *That smile ... am I in heaven?*

"How long was I out?"

She nodded; he knew she did not comprehend.

After removing the knife, he stood with her help and limped to the cliff's new location. *Ten feet more and I would be down there*, he thought, looking at the littered debris along the riverbanks.

Wooden remains of Godfrey's house were partially buried within the landslide. *No one could survive that.*

The woman pointed to a mound of toppled trees near the shore. Godfrey's bloody body lay half buried in soil with a limb impaled through his chest.

January 25, 1812 (2:00 p.m.)

Fortune shined on Hagan and he caught the steamboat *New Orleans* down the Mississippi and then an ocean vessel to Boston. It had been smooth sailing—no English warship prevented *their* travel.

Leaving the severed head, wrapped in extra buckskin, with his benefactor, Hagan took his reward and headed south. *St. Louis was nice ... I might give it a try.*

The hard bench he sat upon hurt his ass as the wagon traveled the muddy road leading from Boston. Hagan reached over and entwined his fingers with hers. She now smiled more often. Perhaps they could start their lives anew ... together?

He intended to find out after he helped reunite his new love with her tribe.

Full Fledged Quackery

Introduction

Full Fledged Quackery won 1st Honorable Mention at the 2005 White County Creative Writers' Conference, Western Short Story contest.

The tale next won 2nd Place at the 51st Grand Prairie Festival of Arts' fiction-writing contest in Stuttgart, Arkansas. This was cool because all the winning stories were displayed during the festival, and Stuttgart mayor Marianne Maynard handed the money and prize certificate of award to each writer.

In its final triumph, *Full Fledged Quackery* was retired to publication in the Northeast Texas Writers' Organization (NETWO) anthology, *The Treasure Box*. One of my goals in putting a collection of stories together is to show other writers what types of entries are winning awards, and add a little behind-the-scene details. Like now, for instance. My other western in this section, *After Elkhorn*, won 1st Place in NETWO's 2007 annual contest. By winning 1st Place, it was automatically accepted for publication in *The Storyteller* magazine. By being published, this made it ineligible for publication in NETWO's anthology. I was therefore invited to submit another tale, which was *Full Fledged Quackery*. Now you know the rest of the story.

Full Fledged Quackery

Two old horses struggled up the rugged road toward the hilltop, covered wagon in tow. "Move, you sons-of-bitches!" The driver whipped at them again.

The incline leveled onto a plateau and the military hospital rose in the distance near a resort hotel. To his left the driver could see the bustling town of Little Rock across the river. The infirmary had been set up as an overflow from St. Johns'.

The war was less than a month over, yet injured soldiers continued to arrive daily. Women with children carried supplies toward the wooden structures. Bandaged men smoked hand-rolled cigarettes in shade under oak and maples. Many had stumps for arms or legs. Several wounded men took notice as the peddler stopped his wagon near the ridge, unhitched the horses, and set up.

Locals grew excited at arrival of traveling salesmen. A crowd gathered while the man rolled back the wagon-cover to display products.

He then hopped onto a wooden bench and shouted, "Ladies and gentlemen! May I have your attention? Please step up and hear about the greatest discovery since the telegraph."

The man looked distinguished, like a bank teller, dressed in black slacks and white cotton, button-up shirt, a visor around his forehead kept sunlight from his shifty eyes.

Summer heat felt smothering; sweat trickled down men and women's cheeks. Mother Earth held back any breezes, and clear sky offered little hope of an afternoon shower.

The mob grew larger as the peddler enticed his audience. "Hurry up! You don't want to miss this opportunity."

Word spread; people could be seen stepping onto porches near the infirmary. Gaunt men on crutches struggled across an open field.

The salesman held up a clear bottle filled with an amber liquid. "My colleague, son of the famous physician Ben Rush of Philadelphia, and I have mixed the greatest potion since God gave us water."

Thirty yards away, a man in a white surgeon's outfit shook his head, smiled, and looked down. The rest of the crowd continued to stare in amazed silence.

"One sip of this will chase away the common cold. 'I have a headache!' you say? Well, drink this elixir of immortality and your troubles will wash away and bring on a new day."

"How much?" someone yelled.

"Not so fast," the peddler replied. "You can't medicate yourself with this gift from God without partaking the second remedy."

He held up a canister and grabbed a handful of crushed green leaves. "You mix this with my elixir and a little water and you will feel as good as new. This special plant comes from my plantation in South America. Right now I have hundreds of natives tending thousands of these miracle plants."

A young boy had been watching quietly near a tree. "Will it help my dad?" he yelled over the crowd. "He lost both arms in the war and they sent us here. Pa's over there," he pointed toward the hospital. "He's in a lot of pain."

"Son," the peddler turned and focused on the boy. "These two medications, if used together, will make that pain go away."

Spectators began to herd toward the wagon, yelling to make a purchase. "Stop!" The man held up an arm. "One at a time. I have enough for everyone."

On the porch by the doctor, a young girl turned to leave. "Where are you going, Doris?" the surgeon asked.

"To buy some for Daddy."

"Wait," he said. "Don't waste your hard-earned money on that quack."

"But you heard what he said. Daddy needs help."

"Doris…." The doctor kneeled and placed a hand gently on each of her shoulders. "I don't know how to tell you this—I'm so sorry. Your father's fate is in the hands of the Lord. I removed the shrapnel and stopped gangrene by amputating his legs, but only God can save him now. Please, honey. Keep that money you earned by cleaning up around here. This man is a quack and his medicine won't work."

"Please! You heard what he told that boy." She began to sob. "I want Daddy to come home."

"But your home was destroyed and your mother is dea…."

Doris ran from his arms toward the peddler. The doctor stood and quelled tears that started to form.

*   *   *

Dr. Stanley entered his patient's room during afternoon rounds. Rolling up his surgical gown's blood-splattered sleeves, he walked toward Doris.

"How is he?"

Doris sat defeated on a wooden stool at the bedside of her father. The injured veteran remained in coma, sweat rolling off his body. "I mixed the medicine just like the man told me," she cried.

"Maybe it takes a few days. Your father is very badly injured."

He unraveled bandages around the patient's stumps, and examined what remained of the legs. His skills as a surgeon were superior to most physicians, having learned many tricks as a young man during the Mexican War. Another mini ball to the abdomen damaged an entire lung beyond repair. Dr. Stanley knew the father would not live much longer.

"He's going to die, isn't he?" Doris asked. She began to sob, gazing at the floor.

Dr. Stanley wrapped his arms around her and carried her outside to the porch and sat with her on a bench. She buried her face against his chest.

It was too much and he felt hot tears stream from his eyes.

A gasp escaped from the window near where they sat. "Daddy!" Doris ran inside, expecting to see him sitting up and smiling.

The two arrived together and found Doris' father with wide-open eyes and mouth contorted in pain.

"Daddy?" She walked toward the bed.

"Wait, Doris." Dr. Stanley examined the soldier; the surgeon's heart race and bile taste rose from his stomach. "I'm sorry." He swept a hand over the patient's face, closing the eyes for a final time.

*   *   *

On a second-story balcony overlooking the Arkansas River, Dr. Stanley enjoyed morning coffee with his wife.

"So you don't mind Doris staying with us?" he asked.

"Not at all. It's just as if we had one of our own."

"We did try."

She smiled and touched her fingers on his. "If you hadn't been off doctoring all over the world then maybe we could have tried harder."

Doris walked into the yard below and looked up. "I'm going into town now."

Mrs. Stanley asked, "Did you get the money on the counter for the items I need?"

"Yes, ma'am."

Pulling a scarf over her head, Doris walked behind other ladies as they descended the hill toward Huntersville, across the river from Little Rock.

In town near the depot, where trains left for Memphis, she peered down a street where saloons were located, and saw a ruckus taking shape. *I wonder what's going on*, she thought.

Rugged, intoxicated characters scurried about; several cowboys heckled a man on a wagon as he tried to sell his tonics.

It's him!

She walked closer.

"…and it's sure to cure hangovers," the peddler said.

A little boy walked from the crowd and raised his hand. "Yes, young man," the peddler pointed.

"My daddy has headaches all the time and trouble sleeping. Will it make them go away?"

"It will indeed! In fact, it's been said that my special medicine will cure anything."

Doris vacated the street and stood discreetly on a wooden porch next to the sheriff's office. A deputy walked out.

"Can he sell that stuff if it doesn't work?" Doris asked.

After spitting a stream of tobacco juice into the dusty street, he said, "No law against it."

She watched as men and women fought over where to stand in line to make their purchases. Through the crowd, she saw the boy sitting on a barrel fanning himself against rising heat. He had been the one at the hospital who asked the peddler a question.

After the horde dispersed, she observed the salesman rewrap canvas blankets back over his stock, and climb onto the wagon to maneuver horses toward the edge of town, outside a cemetery in an open field. He threw gear onto the ground and began to set up camp.

The boy remained on the barrel, then finally jumped off and made his way over to the peddler's encampment.

Doris' young mind tried to comprehend the mysterious connection. She was about to leave when she saw the boy return.

As he approached, she ran to him. "You two lied about your medicine!"

"Not me—him," he motioned toward the peddler, a hundred yards away.

"My daddy's dead and you cheated me." She began to cry.

"Stop it—will you?" He gently pulled her sleeve and led her toward an alley between two saloons. "I don't like what he does. But what can I do?"

"Leave him."

"And go where? My momma and daddy are dead. He's my uncle, the only one who'd take care of me."

The peddler suddenly appeared. "I thought I saw you go in here! What did I tell you?"

"I'm sorry," the boy pleaded.

The man grabbed him hard and gave a thumb to the side of the head. "You go do what I told you and come straight back. And you, little girl, go home!"

Doris paused with fright, then hurried out of the alley when the man moved to the side and yelled, "Now!"

Her heart pounded as she ran several blocks toward Main Street. Stopping, she turned and watched the boy panhandle pedestrians up and down the street.

*   *   *

Next morning Doris awoke to a cloudy day with threat of thunderstorms looming on the horizon.

"Breakfast's ready!" she heard Mrs. Stanley call from downstairs.

While straightening her pinafore she saw her father's pocket-watch lying on the dresser. She picked it up and felt the engraved casing. Gently opening it, she saw her mother's picture inside the shell.

Daddy never went anywhere without this.

"Doris … are you comin'?" Mrs. Stanley tapped on the door and slowly opened it. "Honey! Why are you crying?" She saw the watch in the girl's hand. "Come here."

Dr. Stanley's wife wrapped her arms around the orphan, as a mom would have.

Photo by Carolyn Boyles

At mid-morning, after breakfast, Doris sat on the sofa and shooed flies away. Several military issued pistols lay on a cabinet in the dining room. She stood and approached them.

She was familiar with the weapons after her father had given her lessons. Picking one up, she examined it. *Which one's his?* She held a Colt Army Model and Starr Revolver, but had never seen a LeMat pistol before.

Sorting through them, she found the brown leather holster with embossing she recognized.

An assortment of bullets rolled around in a drawer below the shelf. She ran her fingers through them until she found several of the right caliber. After loading the pistol, she wrapped it in a shawl and headed for town.

The peddler and boy no longer occupied the campsite near the cemetery. She glanced down several streets and did not see them. The footbridge atop Arkansas River loomed ahead and she decided to cross over into Little Rock since she had missed the ferry.

Wooden planks shook against the mighty current. Union soldiers stood guard; she looked upstream where construction of the Baring Cross Bridge had begun.

Once over, she witnessed small crowds bickering outside the Statehouse. Military occupation kept everyone in an uproar.

Further up the dirt-rutted road, she spotted the wagon near an apothecary. A druggist argued with the peddler. Sneaking through onlookers, she finally heard the pharmacist say, "I said you *will not* sell your quack medicine outside my store."

"The war's over—it's a free country." The peddler took his debate to the men and women watching. "Aren't you interested in my new medicine instead of what this man has to offer from the past?" He pointed toward the druggist.

Cheers erupted throughout the crowd and the apothecary made a quick exit into his store.

Doris noticed the boy had blended in with the group and looked as if waiting his turn to perform.

She walked up to him. "Come with me."

"I told you, I can't."

Doris exposed the pistol and replied, "I'll protect you. You can stay with me."

The boy's blond hair and cheek dimples reminded her of her brother—before cannon balls crashed through the roof where he and their mother slept. It was her family's unfortunate circumstance to live between battle lines where General Holmes and General Curtis fought each other in the battle for Helena. Her father had been conscripted as rebels forces enlisted every available male to protect against the advancing Union Army.

The peddler began his pitch and uncovered the wagon to display goods.

"Come on," she insisted.

He looked back and forth, then made his decision.

The two ran down Markham to the footbridge and crossed the river toward Huntersville. Doris could see the infirmary on the bluff across the Arkansas. A ferry passed them carrying wagons and cattle; lifeless refugees sat on barrels and stared at her.

Once over they reverted to children and decided to play along the shoreline. That evening the boy followed Doris up the road toward Dr. Stanley's house.

"There you are you filthy ungrateful rat!" The peddler rode up behind them. "I've been looking all over for you."

He slid off his mount, slapped the boy to the ground and hovered over him. "You thought you could get away?"

Blood oozed from the lad's brow where the man assaulted him.

Doris stood a few yards away, motionless with fear. She watched as the man continued to pound her new friend.

Finally, she thought of her lost family and unknown future. Her courage returned. "Stop!" she screamed, aiming the pistol toward the peddler.

"As if you know how to use that thing." He laughed and rushed toward her.

Her finger twitched and then tightened. A loud pop echoed down the hill and the peddler threw his hands to his face. Blood poured through fingers and he fell to the ground, his head slammed the rutted path.

"Come on," she yelled to the boy.

They ran to the doctor's house and tried to pretend the tragedy away. The Stanleys eyed them suspiciously, sitting in their rocking chairs on the front porch.

"Can he stay?" Doris begged.

"Oh, no," Mrs. Stanley said. "He needs to go home to his mother."

"My folks died in the war," the boy responded.

Mrs. Stanley stood and used the commotion from a nearby mob as an excuse to delay the inevitable. Dr. Stanley stepped from the porch to investigate.

"What's going on?" she asked when he returned.

"Soldiers just brought a man in—he's dead. He was that quack up here the other day."

The children gasped at one another but remained quiet.

Dr. Stanley turned toward the boy and tilted his head. "You look famil…." He walked over and examined him. "Where did you get those injuries on your face?"

The boy said nothing.

Dr. Stanley looked toward his wife. "Why don't we let him stay here awhile?"

Mrs. Stanley grinned and nodded. "We'll see. Are you two hungry? Go wash up."

"Come with me," Doris said, taking the boy's hand. "I have some clothes left over from my brother that will fit you. You can change out of those torn jeans."

The couple sat back in their rockers, an evening sun hung along the eastern horizon. Mrs. Stanley reached for her husband's hand and their fingers intertwined.

Pain of the Innocent

Introduction

Note: *Pain of the Innocent* is the first three chapters of an unfinished novel. I hesitated to include it here, but the biggest surprise of my first anthology was the number of readers who asked me to finish *Horizon Bound*, the first two chapters of an unfinished story I included there. It got me thinking, maybe some big-time New York publisher will read this and give me a contract to write the entire manuscript! I'm waiting.

Pain of the Innocent won 3rd Place at the 2007 White County Creative Writers' Conference, Tumbleweed Award. Dusty Richards sponsored this contest, his requirements were: "3 chapters, plus synopsis and query letter."

Pain of the Innocent

Chapter 1

Lara sat on her son's bed with a Bible in hand and smoothed the wrinkled quilt. "If Job can overcome his problems then so can we ... with the Lord's help."

"But he was my friend, Mama."

"Kyle—sometimes there's no explanation. We have to put our faith in Him."

"Why did those Injuns have to kill everyone?" Tears rolled down the boy's cheek.

"You can't blame everyone for the sins of a few, Kyle."

He glanced across the wood floor to the other side of the cabin. On a shelf above the fireplace rested a Springfield Musket. His father had taught him how to use it before his supply trip to Fort Smith. A Charleville Musket lay in pieces on a shelf by the kitchen. It had belonged to Kyle's grandfather but hadn't worked in years. Gossip was that it had been used in the War of 1812, although Kyle's dad never believed it.

"If they come for you, Mama, I'll get the musket."

"That shouldn't be necessary ... but thank you." She smiled, amazed at his strong nine-year-old character.

As a young-un, when all other boys were still pooping in their britches, Kyle worked the land helping his father clear trees and building rock fences with the abundance of stones scattered along Ozark's landscape.

Once, when his dad had stepped in a hole and broken his leg, Kyle maneuvered the horses around to assist with getting him home. No mistaking the young lad's precociousness.

A sense of reality slapped Kyle's world when news arrived that natives butchered his friend Richard's family. The young neighbors lived in a world of brotherly love. As far as Kyle was concerned, the slaughter occurred in the land of milk and honey—at least from what he understood the preacher say each Sunday morning.

Most Indians from Georgia, Florida, and through Alabama had been forced West, into Oklahoma Territory. Reports surfaced of renegade Osage on the warpath from Kansas Territory.

For the most part, skirmishes had been few and far between in Kyle's neck of the woods. News of Richard and his family's massacre sent a wave of panic throughout the Ozarks—it didn't appear the crisis would improve anytime soon.

KYLE FEIGNED SLEEP. He peeked at his mom who worked through her bedtime routine.

Laying kindling near the fireplace, she next set a tin pot with water on a stool. He knew she would hook this for coffee in the morning to a metal rod built above the flames.

She glanced toward him and saw closed eyes. Assuming he had fallen into slumber, she disrobed her working dress and replaced it with a gown. Before she blew out candles she knelt to pray beside her bed.

The sun had set an hour earlier and it seemed late from Kyle's perspective. The entire cabin consisted of one room. His bed was partly hidden in a corner because he had tied hemp lines from the ceiling and then laid blankets over them.

Once the candle flames were extinguished, the only light flickered from smoldering coals in the fireplace. He rolled over and stared at the moon outside his window. Shutters were left open on warm nights.

Sounds of crickets rubbing hind legs echoed throughout the forest; bullfrogs could be heard croaking from Lee Creek.

It seemed peaceful—this was the only life he knew. Of course, he worked hard during the day, and tried to make it to school when lack of chores allowed. Mom read to him at night and had begun to teach him how to study the Bible.

With Papa away, he knew he could sneak an extra hour of sleep in the morning. Fall season approached and fields had been prepared. With school not in session, he could play after completing a few tasks. Elmer, a boy his age, lived over the ridge. They resided close enough that each could hear the other's mutt bark from their home.

Still, it took ten minutes to travel between farms if roads were not muddy. The two normally met halfway at the creek's swimming hole.

With his mind preoccupied over thoughts of fun activities for the next day, he slowly grew aware of an eerie silence that descended outside, through woods. Insects had hushed. It was never this quiet unless a brewing storm approached—or wolves and bears on the prowl!

Sitting up on his knees, he peered out the opening and tried to adjust his eyes to darkness. A half moon penetrated a thin overcast night; upon a pond further down the valley, below the cabin, he saw moonlight reflect off its smooth surface.

A shadowy image cut across the scene running on two feet.

Faint screams then sounded from over the ridge and a dog barked; Kyle sat up higher on his knees and focused. The pleas were not loud and probably would not have awakened him had he been asleep.

When he saw his dog, Master, atop a rug by the front door, wagging his tail, he felt relief at first. Surely the mutt would bark if anyone approached from outside. But who or what ran past the pond?

He glanced upon the landscape again and clearly saw dark figures darting from tree to tree. The word massacre formed within his mind and he remembered overhearing details of mutilations.

A growl startled him and he stared back over at Master. The dog's tail was folded between his legs and hair on his back stood ominously like metal shavings dangling below a magnet he'd seen once at a circus. The pet barked and scratched at the door.

"What is it?" Lara asked.

Kyle turned and saw Mama resting upon elbows with her sleeping cap on. "Ssshhhh," he whispered, index finger upon his lip.

Master acted like a bear was about to storm into the cabin.

Blood pumped through Kyle's heart like it might burst through his head. He saw the musket over the fireplace and rushed toward it. With nervous hands, he poured powder from a medicine horn into the rifle's shaft, then used a rod to push a ball down the tube. After fixing the shot cap, he placed the weapon to his shoulder.

It was difficult to concentrate with Master's hysteria. A hunting knife his father used to clean game lay on the table. After what felt like minutes of waiting, Kyle grabbed the dagger and ran to Mama.

"What is it, Kyle!"

"Shhh," he whispered. "Someone's outside."

"This is not funny."

She saw fright upon his face. They pushed her bed in a corner away from a closed window. All shutters were fastened except for the one above Kyle's bed.

Master's yelps lowered to a whine, mother and son thought they heard steps on the front porch. The cabin remained dark except orange coals in the fireplace.

The dog's warnings increased again until he turned berserk. Kyle stabled the musket tight against his shoulder, resting the barrel upon the mattress. The door then crashed open and a flaming arrow shot through and embedded in the cabin's wall.

The space inside illuminated and Kyle saw an Injun bring a club down on Master, silencing the dog. Two giants stood at the threshold, a third figure peered through Kyle's open window.

It all happened so fast; he was not prepared. Squeezing his right index finger, he fired without proper aim and sent the slug into the ceiling.

When he opened his eyes he saw two men running toward him. He stood and jabbed the knife as an attacker jumped atop the mattress.

Then time slowed and his body refused to obey. A gray haze seemed to envelop his sight.

When his eyes again focused, he saw the face-painted men, smiling. He remained in protector stance, arms outstretched pointing the sharp weapon tip at whoever stepped forward.

Three additional natives now stood in the open window, watching. Kyle didn't understand their native tongue, but knew their dialogue was related to his mom and him.

The largest appeared to be the leader, everyone looked to him for direction. Kyle glanced at his mom and saw her horrific expression.

Another warrior approached the leader and spoke. Kyle only recognized the expression "Shin-gah-wah-sah" and thought it was the chief's name.

Shin-gah-wah-sah then walked slowly toward the young boy. "Drop," he said in broken English, pointing toward the knife.

When the chief reached for the weapon, Kyle swung the blade into the warrior's palm; the tip pierced the skin. "Leave us alone!" Kyle yelled.

Shin-gah-wah-sah hit the boy with the same club used to smack Master, sending Kyle unconscious to the floor. Lara screamed as several men pounced upon her. Shin-gah-wah-sah walked to the door without emotion, wrapping a cloth around his wound.

When he stopped at the threshold he looked back and saw two warriors clutching a knife, about to slice the boy's forehead back. Flames on the wall began to flicker across the ceiling.

"Stop!" he ordered in his native tongue.

Both men hovering over Kyle looked up.

"We take him … do not kill."

The warriors looked at one another in confusion.

Sensing their anxiety, he continued, "I have spoken."

Shin-gah-wah-sah then saw in the corner, behind the bed, three warriors about to defile the boy's mother. One held her mouth closed as the others pried her legs apart. A fourth man jumped over the bed brandishing Kyle's knife.

Lara eyes bulged in desperation when she looked up at him, standing between her spread knees, and swipe the blade up her cotton gown exposing bare breasts. The Injun behind her used his legs to hold her arms back and began to cup each nipple.

"Stop!" Shin-gah-wah-sah again ordered.

Heated frustration flashed across the rapists faces.

"We go home soon—you can be with *your* women. Do not harm the white woman."

With a long scar shaped from his shoulder down across his chest, the attacker hovering over Lara shot a daggerous gaze toward the chief.

Shin-gah-wah-sah frowned and matched the glare. "Pa-hu-sca ... I am leader. My Spirit has given me a sign—no more talk."

Burning ambers rained from above; the warriors scooped up their captives and exited the cabin.

Chapter 2

Jonathan Searcy stood tall, height-wise, by men standards of the 1840s; most male fingers disappeared when he shook their hands. And his reluctance to shy from controversy suggested him as a possible future leader in Northwest Arkansas.

Thoughts of his wife Lara and that goodbye kiss flowed through his mind as he approached Van Buren. The creaky wagon seemed small with such a huge man sitting on the bench seat. Two horses pulled the vehicle; a white canvas protected him from the burning overhead sun.

Eyelids grew heavy, having traveled all day south from near Evansville, skirting the border along Oklahoma Territory. At Van Buren he could see Fort Smith across the Arkansas River where it met the Poteau. Two-story barracks lined the tributary and an unusual elongated U.S. flag wafted with breezes off the waterway. A small town, consisting of wooden and rock structures, had begun to arise outside the garrison.

The first fort had been established in 1817, in what was then Missouri Territory, for the purpose of promoting peace between the warring Osage and Cherokee Indian Tribes. Tensions increased for years until it snapped with Andrew Jackson's signing of the Indian Removal Act in 1830 that marked the beginning of the Trail of Tears. One stretch of the route crossed north Arkansas—which had recently become a state—and near where Jonathan called home.

Soon, numerous tribes—Ottawa, Shawnee, and Kickapoo—were coerced from their lands in Georgia, Florida, Alabama and other southern states. The

"Five Civilized Tribes" were forced to migrate as well, beginning with the Choctaw and then Chickasaw.

Jonathan had participated in conversations over the subject and possessed mixed feelings. Somehow everyone must learn to survive together; there was no other option.

After ferrying across the Arkansas from Van Buren, Jonathan directed the wagon up a low embankment. Someone said, "Good day, Sir."

Not expecting to be addressed, Jonathan looked for the stranger among a few passersby strolling dirt streets. Soon he found him and replied. "And a good day to you, Brethren."

Dressed in an immaculate frockcoat with wool trousers, the man arose from an ornate handcrafted metal chair in front of his home and approached Jonathan. Perspiration glistened along his forehead.

"John Rogers," he said. "I thank you for bringing your business here."

The two shook hands and made introductions. "I'm hoping local military will have supplies I need," Jonathan said.

"I'm sure they will. Zachary Taylor is commander … and a close, personal friend. Perhaps I can help."

Jonathan took off his hat and wiped a palm across his forehead, then shook sweat onto the floorboard. "I do appreciate you, Mr. Rogers. I'm also hoping to discuss with the commander recent activities of natives around me and my neighbors."

"Where might that be?"

"North—about a day and a half ride … by wagon that is. I'm a half-day west of Fayetteville."

"No doubt, Commander Taylor has his work cut out for him. It seems he spends most of his time keeping the Injuns from killing one another. Now that Washington has mandated all tribes east of the Mississippi into Oklahoma Territory, it's gonna get worse."

"I hadn't heard about this."

"That's what's causing much of the recent fighting … among Natives that is. Tribes from the East are now hunting on sacred grounds of tribes in the West."

"It seems we farmers, trying to carve out a living, got caught in the middle."

"Perhaps," Rogers said. "Of course, farmers back east what's causin' those tribes to move in the first place. The way I see it, it'll continue way into the future. Soon, we'll be forcing the Injuns in Oklahoma off that land, too."

Jonathan nodded in agreement and then looked up the avenue. "Can you point me to someplace I can put up for the night?"

Rogers directed him to a two story wooden home. "Claire keeps a clean place and her price is reasonable."

"Thank you."

* * *

After checking in at the hotel and washing dust from exposed skin, Jonathan headed toward the fort. He had changed into a clean pair of trousers and shirt with vest, which he had saved for this occasion, and tried his best to comb hair—something he rarely did. He wasn't a politician, but knew importance of first appearances.

A thunderstorm had attached itself to the Arkansas River and worked its way upstream toward Fort Smith. Distant thunder increased in volume with each passing minute and wind seemed to be sucked into the towering dark cloud rising on the horizon.

Zachary Taylor addressed a line of soldiers standing at attention. He wore an off-blue uniform with sword fitted into a scabbard; officer's insignia were displayed on both shoulders.

Something wrong must have occurred because he gave the men a 'What for'. The stern look on his face exhibited a tough, wrinkled surface of someone that took life seriously.

Finally, he turned and stormed toward Jonathan. "I'm told you requested an audience with me?"

"Yes, sir … I'll be very brief." The two shook hands. "I'd like to discuss my need for supplies that you might be able to provide—I'll pay of course. Also, I wanted to alert you to native attacks on farms north of here. One family was massacred two weeks ago."

"Walk with me," the commander ordered.

They turned and headed toward one of the two-story barracks Jonathan had seen earlier from across the river. The unusually shaped flag was being taken down as a result of the approaching storm. Several spooked horses also needed to be rounded up.

Inside, Commander Taylor said, "We've got renegade Indians from several tribes warring hundreds of miles in every direction. My scouts are in contact with chiefs of most encampments, but even they can't keep all their warriors in line. I've requested reinforcements from St. Louis, but don't expect this to be approved anytime soon. And even then they may take several weeks to arrive."

"What advice can I take back home with me?"

"Divided you fall. I recommend that you either live in close proximity to one another or move into a town that can defend itself. Staying by yourself on farms is an open invitation for small bands of warriors."

"The farmers won't agree to that."

"I know, which I assume brings us to your second reason for being here?"

"Right…." Jonathan paused, worried of rejection. Many farmers back home looked up to him and he didn't want to fail them.

The commander smiled. "I didn't get where I am by being stupid, Mr. Searcy…."

"I didn't mean to imply—"

Zachary Taylor held up his hand. "I understand. You wish to arm yourself—am I right?"

"Yes, sir."

"I have two scouts leaving in the morning heading north of here to Tahlequah, and then to Fort Gibson." The commander walked to a threshold into another room and yelled, "Corporal O'Leary! This gentleman wishes to purchase weapons. I want you to assist him."

The commander strolled to his desk and sat. "Mr. Searcy," he continued. "If my scouts find what you tell me truthful, then you can keep the weapons that you have the ability to pay for. If, however, I find that you have not been honest, then you will forfeit both the weapons and cash you used to pay for them. Do we have an understanding?"

Not expecting the terse reaction, Jonathan said, "…Yes, sir."

"Forgive me for my sharp reply. But we have sons-of-bitches masquerading as farmers in need of help only to sell the weapons to the same bushwhackers we're trying to protect the people against. Times are desperate and I can't be too sure. But I pledge to you I will go out of my way to protect you and the other farmers if you're honest with me."

Jonathan nodded he comprehended, then followed Corporal O'Leary outside into a pounding rain. They skirted the wooden deck beside the barrack until they had to race to a one-story stone building fifty yards away. Lightning cracked across the river over Van Buren and musket ball size hail crashed to the ground around them.

Without an overhang for protection, the two held up their arms to shield their heads. As O'Leary fumbled with keys to open the door, Jonathan glanced at gloomy dark clouds. A ray of sunshine miraculously penetrated an opening, momentarily blinding him. When his eyes adjusted he saw directly above a murky, tumbling haze extend lower, below the thunderstorm. Wind whipped up and drops of water stung his face. He held a hand out to defend himself.

When he could finally see again, he witnessed the descended cloud dip into the Arkansas River and suck water giving it a grayish color against sunrays in the background. It lasted ten seconds and then absorbed up into the thunderstorm.

"I'll be damned," O'Leary said. "I heard about cyclones but never dreamt I would actually see one. Follow me."

Inside the only light originated from the open door. Several casket-sized wooden boxes were arranged in rows around the room. Corporal O'Leary took a metal rod and hammer to pry the lid off one. Muskets lay smothered within straw.

O'Leary picked one up and said, "Springfield Musket is what I can sell you—although those Mississippi Rifles over there," he pointed to a shelf, "will be the next big thing. If you want, I can also let you purchase a couple Wells Fargo Colt pistols."

"No—muskets and plenty of means to fire them is all I need. It's difficult getting these up where I live. Some of my neighbors still shoot the same weapons their father or granddaddy used in the war against England."

"Let's go to my desk and put quill to paper and see how many you can purchase."

Chapter 3

After a good night sleep and hot breakfast of biscuit and gravy with poached egg and coffee, Jonathan crossed the mud-caked street to the stable and paid the blacksmith for storing his horse overnight. Bags of seeds, spices, and other supplies, including books written by enlightened world thinkers like Benjamin Franklin, David Hume, and Adam Smith lay undisturbed, secured in the wagon's bed.

Reaching into the canvas, he pulled the handcrafted knife from its sheath. Kyle would love it. The new calico dress wrapped in flowery paper would look great on his wife; if he could let her keep it on long enough before he ravished her body. The thought produced a smile.

On time, Jonathan waited outside the garrison's main entrance. Corporal O'Leary agreed to store the newly acquired weapons overnight until Jonathan could retrieve them this morning.

O'Leary introduced Jonathan to the scouts, ready to disembark. The Army's presence would deter any bushwhacker or warring native tribes from confiscating the weapons for their own use.

Falling in line, Jonathan maneuvered his wagon behind Sergeant Andrews and the other scout, Billy, a Quapaw Tribe runaway. Both scouts were dressed in Spanish-American style war tunics with military issued boots and coon hats.

"I call him 'Billy'," Andrews said, "after a friend killed in a battle during the War of 1812. Billy's native name is too difficult to pronounce."

In front of the scouts, sitting on Grimsley tacks atop horses that stood in foot thick mud in the middle of the road, were four cavalrymen dressed in blue. Three had a single 'V' on both shirtsleeves with one wearing what looked to be a double 'V'. Jonathan later learned that the double 'V' represented the sergeant in charge of the detachment.

Mr. Rogers waved from his home as the group prepared to board a ferry back across the Arkansas River. Rogers wore a cutaway coat with dress brogan shoes and a derby hat. Too citified, Jonathan thought—but he liked the man nevertheless. Fort Smith was always an oasis in the wilderness, considering the turmoil bubbling all around.

A thunderstorm could be heard rumbling in the distance in the early morning heat.

*   *   *

The mud-soaked road remained difficult until south of Evansville. It was easy to see where rain had ended once the road dried and turned to dust. The warm weather for late fall produced random storms that died soon after they flared up.

Under a bluff along Lee Creek, the group camped. Tall oaks, pines, sycamores, and scattered dogwoods created thick forest. Sergeant Haywood barked orders to the cavalrymen.

That evening around the campfire Haywood asked, "With all the rumors I'm hearing of warring tribes, and what you told me—why would you want to live in the countryside, away from anyone … and with a wife and kid?"

Jonathan smiled and reached for the tin container over the fire, and poured himself another cup of coffee. "You just have to understand; it's in our blood. We're farmers—we live for the land. All we want is to be left alone by natives … *and* our government."

"The situation will only get worse. They're movin' Seminoles from Florida and Cherokees and Creeks from Georgia and Alabama through here to Indian Territory they call Oklahoma. The problem is that all those Injuns already there ain't gonna stand for it. It's awful what our politicians have done to natives, all the lies—"

"You bite your tongue!" Andrews said. "We have as much right to this land as they do. Besides, don't go pretending the natives are a peaceful, fun lovin' bunch. They've been fightin' amongst themselves since before Columbus—"

"Who?" a young corporal asked. He looked fourteen.

"The man who discovered our country."

"I thought the natives were always here?" Sergeant Haywood said.

"Ain't you ever heard of history? I'm talkin' about *our* Christian and God-fearin' race."

Billy and Jonathan looked at one another and smiled. The Quapaw native rarely said much. Although young, his skin was dark with a leathery hide appearance like those who spent long days in the sun. Black eyes seemed to be aware of every movement.

Jonathan stood and addressed the group. "I guess if the roads aren't too muddy we should reach my place by evening tomorrow. My wife's the best cook around—I'll assure you, you'll eat better tomorrow."

* * *

The road remained dusty without benefit of isolated showers. Cresting a ridge, smoke could be seen on the horizon. "That's the Stanley's farm," Jonathan told Billy. "Just a stone throw from mine; his son Elmer and mine are good friends."

Billy squinted and shielded the hot sun from his eyes. "That smoke not look good. Trouble."

Jonathan shot a look back across the valley. A hidden dog jumped from briars and hobbled toward the men, his back leg dangled helplessly. "That's Elmer's dog!"

He loaded the animal into the back of the wagon and the group continued. The trail twisted down along a limestone and dirt-rutted path, then snaked around a thick patch of woods before Stanley's cabin appeared.

Smoldering timber fallen in upon itself was all that remained, except for the rock chimney that stood alone. Sergeant Haywood and the scouts road ahead, Jonathan tried to hurry but felt shock creep through his body.

As Jonathan approached, he heard Haywood yell, "You might want to stay over there."

Too late, Jonathan saw upon on the ground, before the sergeant, decaying bodies of a woman and a boy—Elmer! He ran to them only to witness flies bathing at open wounds throughout the corpses, lips and eyes appeared to have been consumed by animals.

Jonathan took a deep breath and held it until his body forced it out. When he glanced in the direction of his land he saw ominous smoke rising above trees. A tall, white-capped cloud swirled and streaks of bright sunrays rained upon the land around his farm. The same sinister feeling he got when he viewed the tornado crept upon him.

Please, Lord.

Synopsis

Jonathan Searcy, a farmer in 1830s Arkansas, travels to Fort Smith for crop supplies, and weapons to arm locals against native uprisings. He arrives back home to a devastated farm and unknown whereabouts of his family.

The Army detachment he travels with from Fort Smith back to home, along with two scouts, find themselves forced into a struggle they had not intended. Jonathan recruits the scouts and other local farmers to ride into Indian Territory to search and rescue women and children taken into captivity.

Not only must the frontiersmen combat the warring Osage renegades, they now fight their way through a struggle between native tribes also battling one another.

As the outgunned natives take flight to escape Jonathan and his now battle-strong farmers, Osage tribesmen must negotiate through hostile Navajo, Apache, Mescalero, Ute, Comanche and other local native lands to formulate an escape.

With merciless killing of so many innocent victims among every group, Jonathan must come to grip with his ideas of western expansion and mankind's greed and struggle for existence. Nevertheless, amidst his internal angst, he vows to rescue his family along with other women and children, even if the battle takes him to the Pacific.

After long travels through rugged lands of Indian Territory, west along the Santa Fe Trail in northern Mexico (present day New Mexico and Arizona), the scene is set for a final battle close to The Old Spanish Trail near the southwestern boundary of the Louisiana Purchase (Colorado) on a plain east of the Rockies. Jonathan is reunited with his wife and son, but must comfort neighbors who have lost homes and loved ones.

The story is one of hope despite impossible odds. What transpires on the return trip to Arkansas is a possible setup for a book two.

{Return Address}

July 25, 2007

Dusty Richards
P.O. Box 6460
Springdale, AR 72766

Dear Mr. Richards,

I have written a 95,000-word Western novel entitled *Pain of the Innocent.*
Farm family along Indian Territory gets dragged into the conflict between
U.S. Government and warring tribes supplanted from their ancestral lands.

To protect themselves from renegade natives, farmers arm themselves, with
Army assistance. When the Osage capture our leading man's family members,
he must seek help from neighbors and government to plan a rescue.

The story details an epic adventure as frontiersmen travel into dangerous,
often uncharted lands to save lives of their women and children.

I am seeking representation for the marketing of this book, and look
forward to hearing from you.

Sincerely,

Steve Whisnant

Enclosures: Synopsis, first three chapters, and {SASE}

A Western Struggle
(Notes From a Young Boy)

Introduction

This short western won 3rd Place at the 2003 White County Creative Writers' Conference, Western Short Story contest.

Photo by David Knight

A Western Struggle
(Notes From a Young Boy)

Rolling grassland of Indian Territory stretched for miles in every direction. Crowns of trees in narrow valleys could be spotted in the distance as the wagon train topped each hillcrest.

Tom rested on his steed and glared at ruts marking the panhandle where travelers had passed. Recent rains muddied the trail, slowing the movement west.

He would miss his friends back near Richmond. Work in tobacco fields had been hard, but the good times in school and playing with classmates in nearby forests brought back pleasant memories.

Now, three weeks into the journey, the group had recently earned bragging rights to the halfway mark—but difficult mountains lay ahead, and possibility of renegade natives kept everyone on edge.

Why had his parents decided to move to California? Sure, the Civil War disrupted life in the South. But Richmond was home. And all Tom had heard of life out West was Indians killing and scalping anyone who tread across their land.

Robert rode up behind him. "Our Pas are gonna hunt buffalo—wanna go?"

"Sure," Tom said.

Robert wanted to be his new friend, but Tom never cared much for him. His family belonged to a strict religious sect, while Tom's dad never cared for Christian dogma.

Tom's father, Jim, stood six feet tall and could fire a pistol in his left hand while shooting a rifle in his right. Rumor had it he killed a man in a fistfight once, and his manner demonstrated that could be true.

"Wait for us!" Robert yelled, riding up to the crowd of men forming into a hunting party.

Tom noticed that his dad led the group. It was always important that Jim be in charge.

A streak of lightning over the horizon was followed seconds later by a loud crash. They had been riding two hours when they noticed a black mass of buffalo moving against the backdrop of a coming storm.

A familiar roar of rifle blasts from over the next rise soon replaced the rumble from the sky. The men slowly approached the summit of a rolling hill and then everyone saw heaps of buffalo carcasses spotting the landscape.

Gray billowing clouds of gun-smoke hung low to the ground in the distance where strangers indiscriminately shot the vulnerable buffalo. Tom saw the look on his dad's face and knew to be quiet.

"What are those cow-dungs doing?" Jim said. "They couldn't possibly eat this much meat in a lifetime. They're killing just for the sport of it."

He took his rifle out to confront the rival hunters.

"No, Jim," a fellow traveler said. "This is no way to resolve a problem. Let them be. Let's round up what we need and get back."

Fury steamed from Jim's eyes; his temper had landed him in jail on many occasions. Everyone turned his own mount around. Jim, seeing the wisdom, followed.

It didn't take long to bring down the few buffalo that would feed everyone for many days. Numerous rabbits and pheasants were also bagged during the ride back.

The thunderstorm finally caught up with them and made life unpleasant. Tom would have to get used to such events. He had heard of hardships out West—especially in California.

* * *

The wagon train stretched in a lengthy procession. They were finally on their way again after the women insisted, against Jim's resistance, they rest a few days along a lazy stream surrounded by short trees. Boys made fishing poles from branches and used worms dug from under brush to catch fish near the shoreline. Girls planned tea parties with handmade dolls.

Sometimes they heard roars of a buffalo stampede, or gunshots echo over the prairie. Strange white men followed them.

Then Tom saw scantily clad horseback riders along a distant ridge, watching … and waiting. Their long hair flapped in the wind.

Jim saw them too and motioned to his companions and a sense of heightened alert spread throughout the wagon train.

Tom had heard how citizens of the United States had migrated across the no-mans-land. Gold discovered in Colorado and California brought out the worst of the worst. What did these Indians think about 'civilized' man? That everyone was a drunk and gold-hungry creature?

Railroads also brought thousands seeking land and a new life. Many wanted to put war behind them.

A long burst of gunfire rang over the horizon; chills crept up Tom's arms. His dad took a party to investigate. Tom followed and momentarily got lost in dust kicked up by galloping horses.

"Wait, Tom!" his mom called. He pretended not to hear.

Screams and gun blasts increased as the men approached the crest of the rolling hill. Jim motioned for everyone to dismount and maneuvered them behind a row of bushes. Before them they witnessed natives bringing axes down on pleading men. The same hunters, Tom thought, who had shot buffalo for no reason other than sport.

"There's nothin' we can do here except get ourselves killed," Jim said. He seemed to eye his son with curiosity. Death was taking place a few hundreds yards away and Tom bravely knelt there as a warrior might.

Jim told the group, "We're a day's ride from the pass through the mountains. If the natives follow us we can hold them off there. The only way around is over steep cliffs—which is too dangerous—or a several days' ride side trip."

The men returned. Tom's mom asked her husband, "What was it?"

"We need to go, now!"

*   *   *

Tips of grand mountains stabbed skyward on the horizon. "God's country," Tom's mom said. She never made these remarks near her husband.

Jim continued to push the group forward and some complained. "We'll not stop until we get to the pass tonight," he said.

They arrived late. A full moon illuminated cliffs; cool breeze whipped down from the mountain. Tom slipped on a warmer jacket and slept under a blanket below his family's wagon.

Morning sun brightened the sky's edge; men and women completed chores undone due to their late arrival.

Tom awoke to snowcapped mountains under fire from the sun's rays. He marveled at their height. The hills back home had amazed him, but nothing could have prepared him for this. He glanced around and saw his dad atop his mount, an expression of foreboding overtly displayed.

With his head rested on a rolled up blanket, Tom stared at the wagon's undercarriage. His mom moved about above him, then stepped down and stoked a fire beside the campsite. A surrounding stillness unnerved him. There were horses, dogs, cows, and chickens everywhere, yet the quiet atmosphere led Tom to conclude his life would change this day. It was just a feeling, like calmness before the storm.

Images from his childhood surfaced. He recalled a quiet morning back in Richmond. Townspeople had busied themselves the day before, and then activity died down and the next morning not a peep could be heard.

Then the War Between the States reared its ugly head in his quiet little corner of the world. Distant cannon blasts announced its arrival.

Dogs yapping brought Tom out from his trance. His dad directed men to arrange wagons in a line.

"Get up, Tom!" his mom yelled.

They attached the wagon to horses and moved it into a semicircle with others; cliffs towered over them from behind. Men and women loaded rifles with ammunition.

Tom jumped atop a boulder and saw them! They rode hard like shadows across the countryside.

With a Winchester carbine in hand, Tom noticed a ledge in the rock-face behind the wagons where the trail disappeared into the mountain range. He jumped from rock to rock and climbed until looking down over the scene.

There were seventy members in his party. When he glanced at the line of Injuns bearing down on them he saw nearly one hundred warriors dressed wildly, faces painted. A few carried rifles, but most had bow and arrow or tomahawk in hand.

His father galloped up and down the line of wagons screaming orders. Children hid behind parents who steadied their rifles, ready to fight.

The attackers were thirty yards out when Tom heard his dad yell, "Take aim—fire!"

A volley of lead from musket rifles and repeating carbines sent forth clouds of smoke along the wagon line. Tom watched the front row of natives dissipate as riders fell.

He shot twice from his high vantage point when something on the right drew his attention. An arrow pierced his shoulder and pinned him to a piece of dead wood lying against a rock.

Stunned at first, he panicked. A stinging sensation spread down his side. Then instinct took over and he aimed his rifle using one arm, the other to support himself.

The archer was about to let fly another arrow when he seemed to notice that Tom had him in sight. Lead projectile knocked the man back against the cliff, just as another attacker along the ridge made his way to within range of Tom.

Tom moved the rifle to his waist and struggled to lever another shell into the chamber. Impaled to wood, movement was almost impossible. Tom looked up and saw the warrior about to release an arrow. Suddenly, the native's chest burst open and he slipped from the ledge. Other attackers behind him searched the field of battle and saw their fellow warriors retreating below.

They turned toward Tom and found he now had aim on the next unlucky soul, but he did not shoot. With survival instinct, they returned down the mountainside and disappeared over a ridge.

Tom struggled to turn and look down on the scene. That's when he noticed his father waving his buffalo rifle. What a shot, Tom thought. It had to have been sixty if not eighty yards away.

Jim barked orders to several men to remain ready for another attack, then ran up the cliff to his son. "That was brave of you," Jim said, then added, "…but not very smart to go out on your own." He took a knife from his belt-attached sheath and sawed through the arrow behind Tom's shoulder, releasing him.

Tom had lost a lot of blood and was in great pain; his fingers burned and began to throb.

"My son!" Tom's mom scampered up the trail.

"Calm down, Martha!" Jim ordered. "He's okay."

Women took care of the injured as men prepared for a possible second attack. Tom's wound was minor compared to others. His friend Robert lay next to a burning wagon, his skull exposed, likely from an ax stroke. Robert's mom cried hysterically as men covered the body and carried it off.

Jim argued with a man who lost his wife.

"I say we follow them and attack their village!" the fellow frontiersman demanded.

"No," Jim said. "You knew the risk when you signed on. God knows the awful things our society has done. We've broken all our treaties with them and kicked them off their land. I'm sorry for your loss but my job is to get us all safely to California."

Tom saw the man's wife slumped against a carriage wheel; an arrow pierced her chest. Scattered around the wagons lay dead natives. The horrible conflict caused tears to slide down Tom's face.

* * *

"…and that's the story of how your great grandfather brought us out West."

The children looked at their Papaw with awe.

Mama carried a pitcher of lemonade onto the wooden porch overlooking the Pacific. "Is he telling you children stories again?"

"Only the truth, my dear. Only the truth."

"Show us where you got shot by an arrow," a grandchild said.

Tom smiled. "Sure."

After Elkhorn

Introduction

If I had to pick my most successful story to date, it might be *After Elkhorn*. It's won or placed in every contest entered. I found the details to write the piece when I purchased literature on the Civil War battle from the gift shop at Pea Ridge National Military Park in northwest Arkansas. Using public records is a great way to research topics for your writing—hint, hint.

After Elkhorn first won 3rd Place at the 2006 White County Creative Writers' Conference, Western Short Story, in Searcy, Arkansas. An event that made this special was that Ellen Withers, Rhonda Roberts, and Lorna Stone also placed in the contest. We were all members of the same critique group at the time.

Next, *After Elkhorn* won my most prestigious prize to date when it took 1st Place in the 2007 Northeast Texas Writers' Organization (NETWO) Short Story Contest at the 21st Annual Spring Writers' Conference. I still remember checking my e-mail on Sunday, April 29, 2007, and receiving this message from Dusty Richards: "Wait till you hear the news. You took first place in Texas at NETWO contest. Congrads, Dusty." The official notification from Jim Callan with NETWO said, "We had excellent turnout, and some excellent entries. However, yours stood out and the judges rewarded you." NETWO's website stated they had entries from Oregon to Florida, Texas to Canada, and many states in between. Other winners lived in Texas, California, Washington, and North Carolina. I was very excited, can you tell? By winning this contest, the story was automatically accepted for publication in *The Storyteller* magazine (see below).

I entered *After Elkhorn* (before publication acceptance) in the 2007 Arkansas Writers' Conference Westward Ho Award and won 3rd Place. Sponsored by Dusty Richards, who had never seen nor read the story as of the NETWO contest mentioned above, he required, "Western short story or three chapters (plus prologue and synopsis) of a western novel." The number of entries was not disclosed, but other winners in this contest lived in Oklahoma, Arkansas, and Iowa.

Finally, the story was retired from its contest days when Regina Williams, editor of *The Storyteller* magazine, published the tale in the July/August/

September 2007 issue. Regina agrees to publish the winning entries from several contests throughout the country. When *After Elkhorn* won 1st Place at NETWO, she accepted it.

Photo courtesy of Arkansas Department of Parks and Tourism

After Elkhorn

The rumble of thousands of feet grew closer; morning fog hid trees lining the ridge atop the valley.

Thomas knelt, the line of his comrades stretched across a long, tree-cleared field below Big Mountain, a few hundred yards from the gorge. Their blue coats crusted with filth from the exhausting march and tiring delays on muddy grounds.

Somewhere a cannon sounded across the landscape and all hell broke loose.

"Wake up … honey, wake up!"

Bolting up in bed, Ruth swung her arm in defense, glancing off the top of her husband's head.

"Ruth! You're okay, the war's over."

Thomas lit a lantern. In its soft illumination, he saw terror-stricken eyes and sweat rolling from her forehead. "Come here."

Cradling her head against his chest, he stroked her damp hair. "You're safe, Ruth. No one's going to hurt you."

"I dreamt about you in battle."

"The war's over … goodnight."

As she sensed his return to sleep, her eyes scanned the covers. A quilt lay flat against the feather mattress where a bulge of his left leg should have been. A scar dug deep into his face and across an eyelid.

His suffering had been intense, yet she too endured internal pain. Her mind often drifted back to that horrible battle eighteen years earlier…

"Get away from the window, Ruth!" Her mother pulled her to a corner by a rock chimney as musket balls pounded the outside walls.

The door suddenly blew open and a man hobbled in, wearing a blue coat. A Northerner!

Red, thick blood oozed from his cheek; he stared at the terrified mother and daughter crouched in the corner, before unconsciousness claimed his soul and he fell to the floor.

Ruth shook her head and tried to forget those days. After turning off the lantern, she closed her eyes and prayed. Before sleep, she remembered the good times after the killings had stopped. These memories kept her sane.

GRANT STRUGGLED UP the banks of the Arkansas River dragging a fish. "Caught a catfish, Maw. Big one, too."

"Go clean it and then get ready for breakfast. Your paw is back there shaving."

Ruth watched the fourteen-year-old disappear around the side of the house. *Looks so much like his father.*

From the front porch, she glanced over the partly tree-cleared valley. Patches of oak spread out in front of her. Harvesting crops was not profitable, but it did put food on the table. Her family's bread and butter turned to raising cattle.

On a bluff across the water, where the river meandered into the horizon, stood the small town of Ozark. The rural county grew into a home soon after they moved from her childhood raisin' outside Pea Ridge, near Leetown, between Pratt's Store and Elkhorn Tavern off Clemon's Lane. It hadn't been easy...

"Help me get him away from the door!" Ruth's mom demanded. The sounds of war slowly died as the sun descended.

The teenage girl strained against the soldier's muscular frame. Finally, the two women pulled the Yankee to a collection of blankets set up in the corner. A trail of blood coated the wooden floor.

The mother's midwifery experience led her movement. "Heat up some water, Ruth. And bring me those scissors in my sewing case."

Outside, the sounds of crickets and birds gave the illusion of safety. Ruth glanced through the damaged front door and saw lightning bugs flash along the landscape in Ruddick's Field. An eerie haze hugged the tree line as the battle smoke rose off the ground.

Mom wiped a moist rag across the man's face and cleaned the wound. She next cut the wool pant leg from his injured limb. Blood continued to ooze onto the covers from the spot where a musket ball had entered just above the knee.

"Look, Mama!"

Her eyes followed her daughter's finger outside the door's threshold and saw shadowy images of approaching men against the setting sun that tried to penetrate smoke.

"Confederate soldiers, Mama. What will they do with him?"

"What about us, helping the enemy?"

A thud brought Ruth back to the present. She turned and saw her husband had knocked the chair over in the kitchen, just inside the door.

"Let me help."

Thomas leaned against crutches and balanced himself on one leg. When she picked the chair up, he slowly maneuvered into it. The thick scar on his face never tanned like the rest of his features. Heavy lifting was impossible, but he could still sit in a wagon and drive. Their son did most of the difficult work.

Ruth watched her husband tilt his head so his good eye could focus on the breakfast she placed before him. The wound to his face had glanced an eye, making it impossible to focus on objects. It was easier to just wear a patch.

"Paw! I caught a big catfish this mornin'," Grant said, entering the home.

"How 'bout that," he replied. "Why don't we cook it up for supper?"

Ruth sat across the table and smiled. "I suppose we can do that today, after you two take care of fixin' that fence."

Taking her time to eat, she watched the men attack the food. Grits and biscuits usually satisfied them. And she always had her homemade jelly.

The opened front door allowed a nice breeze that blew up from the river. Blue, their mangy mutt, hopped on the porch and sat just outside the doorway. He knew not to enter, or Ruth would skin his hide.

When the men folks finished their meals, they stood to leave. Grant grabbed his father's dishes and placed them in a bucket filled with water.

"We're going," Thomas said. Using his crutches, he hobbled over to her for a kiss, then toward the door where Blue began to bark.

She watched him struggle down the few steps from the porch, then head toward the wagon, the dog at his heel. When he turned to smile, she waved. How handsome he is … except for that scar. The scenes of their meeting continued to play daily in her head…

"Quick!" Ruth's mom demanded. "Hide these clothes. If those confederate soldiers ask, this man is one of them—do you understand?"

"Yes, Mama."

Three men wearing white wool coats walked toward them and ascended the wooden step into the house. Two soldiers grew thick, matted beards and mustaches; Ruth could not see their mouths move when they spoke. The third was clean-shaven, but allowed his sideburns to grow long down his cheeks. All three carried rifles.

A stern expression on the men sent a wave of nausea through Ruth.

They searched the one-story home before the young warrior with sideburns asked, "Who's he?"

"We don't know," Ruth's mom answered. "He crawled into our home like this. His wounds look bad … I don't think he'll live."

The soldier walked toward the injured adversary and stared. Blood dominated the blankets and had pooled onto the floor along the edges.

"We're hungry. What have you got to eat?"

Mom started to cry. "The war's taken all we have! I can't feed my daughter as it is."

The man's comrades foraged through the house and then returned. "There's nothing here to eat," one said.

The soldier with sideburns lowered his rifle toward the injured man's head. "You're not protecting some Blue Coat, are you?"

Ruth fell to her knees and sobbed. "We told you we don't know who he is! Please stop the killings!"

The soldiers laughed, then backed away out the door and disappeared onto Ruddick's Field toward Telegraph Road.

"This man's goin' to die if we don't get him to a doctor."

Ruth looked at the injured man and then to her mom. "Tomorrow, I'll run for help."

IN LATE SUMMER the Arkansas River drained too shallow for steamboats to make their way up or down from Fort Smith to Little Rock. On the front porch, Ruth sat in a rocking chair Thomas had made. She could see in the distance the outline of her son Grant playing in the stream with several friends from nearby farms.

Thomas had taken the carriage into Ozark, an event that took all day. Sometimes travelers had to wait hours to ferry across the river.

Reconstruction had brought some order to the South, but not for years later. Arkansas fared better than many states, but food and resources were scarce in the mid-1860s.

Why did he come back for me?

A honeysuckle breeze cooled her face as Ruth reminisced…

As she promised her mother, the next morning Ruth hurried down Clemon's Lane toward Pratt's store. An alarming silence kept her on edge, after the previous hellish day.

She inconspicuously approached the establishment where horsemen in blue coats passed her without a word. They looked battle weary with drooping eyes and slumped shoulders.

A large, white tent had been assembled beside Pratt's store. A man stepped out who resembled a picture of General Lee. Short, thin gray hair lined his head with sideburns connected to a well-groomed whitish mustache and beard. He wore a blue coat with twelve buttons up the front, and epaulettes on both shoulders. A sword dangled from his waist.

"General Curtis!" A soldier stopped at attention in front of the officer.

Ruth stood to the side and listened.

"Report," Curtis commanded.

"General Van Dorn and Price are in retreat down Huntsville Road. We have secured the field of battle from Morgan's Woods and Big Mountain over to Elkhorn Tavern."

Photo courtesy of Arkansas Department of Parks and Tourism

"Have Colonel Carr report to me immediately." The general glanced over and saw Ruth. "Young lady, this is not a proper place for you."

Ruth ran up to him. "Sir, we have a Yankee soldier injured in our house. He may die if he's not seen by a doctor."

"Come with me."

Ruth followed him across a rutted road to a small field surrounded by oaks just beginning to bud. A temporary hospital had been set up; Ruth gasped when she witnessed the injured, most lying on the ground under the shade. Flies encircled the open wounds of several dead men.

"Out of the way!"

She stepped back as two men carried a maimed soldier on a makeshift stretcher made from a confederate flag wrapped around two muskets.

"Nurse!" Curtis yelled.

A slender man covered with blood ran to the general. "Sir."

"See if you can help this woman."

With no further words, Curtis turned and walked away.

The nurse appropriated a horse and they rode together back to Ruth's farm. Inside they found her mom wiping the injured soldier with a damp cloth. The medical attendant leaned down, inspected the limb, then said, "That leg's got to come off."

A pair of bickering mockingbirds brought Ruth back to the present. Grant and his friends continued to play near the river. Leaning her head back on a pillow tied to the rocker, Ruth fell asleep.

AN APPROACHING BUGGY soon awoke Ruth. Glancing down the dirt path, she saw Thomas and the scar that ran from his forehead to his chin.

Mom and I had nowhere to go, our friends and relatives were killed by disease and war. He came back for me! For us. He's a good man.

Ruth stood and walked to the edge of the porch. "How 'bout some biscuits and jelly to tide you over til supper?"

"Sounds good—I'm starving."

Once he finally struggled to the top of the porch, Ruth embraced him. "I love you, did you know that?"

"You better. I gave up a leg to meet you."

"Come on in and tell me about your day."

Entering the cabin, Ruth reached down and squeezed her husband's arse. "What was that for?" he asked.

"Grant's down at the water … we have the house to ourselves."

Artwork Contributor Bios

Sherrie Shepherd

Sherrie Shepherd is an artist and illustrator. Born in Lincoln, Nebraska in 1958, she moved to Arkansas in 1962. She later attended the University of Arkansas at Little Rock and graduated with a BA degree in Art.

From 1986 to 1996, Shepherd drew a syndicated cartoon strip called *FRANCIE* about a single mother. *FRANCIE* appeared in the United States and abroad for ten years. Other cartoons by Shepherd have also appeared in magazines such as: New Woman, Cosmopolitan, Medical Economics, Complete Woman, Ladies Home Journal, Ebony and Saturday Evening Post. Her cartoons have been published in several books, *Mothers and Daughters*, *Playing By The Rules*, and *Life's a Stitch*. Her work is well documented in "Who's Who of American Cartoonists".

Shepherd's work also includes realistic and abstract work that has been collected by corporations and private collectors. She is constantly experimenting with other art forms such as photography, podcasts and writing. Shepherd's editorial cartoons can be seen in the Arkansas Times.

E-mail: artscape4@yahoo.com

Lance Waters

Lance Waters is a native of West Helena, Arkansas and also a graduate of the University of Arkansas at Little Rock where he earned a degree in Finance.

During college in 1986, he purchased his first camera, a Pentax K-1000, and from that point he has been interested in photography ever since. His passion for Christian Missions and travel lends itself well with his passion for photography. *"I felt very honored when Steve asked me to take a few shots for his new book, and was more than happy to help."*

Lance and his wife, Suzanne, reside in Little Rock, where they own Waters & Waters Realty—a full service firm that owns, manages, and sales property throughout central Arkansas and the US.

Lance on his photo for *Last Supper*
Title: *Depravity Cost*

For the Non-Religious Reader:
The photo is of a blurred man in a suit holding out a communion cup to the reader—a cup full of poison. By offering the cup to the reader, the reader will hopefully take the story more personal and be more involved. By making a Communion Cup the focal point of the photo, it gives it the religious aspect of the story—the heinous act of using a Church (representing good in the World) as an instrument of evil.

For the more Spiritual and Christian Reader:
The focus point of the photo is of the Communion Cup and what it represents—the blood of Jesus Christ, but more importantly, the COST paid by Christ for our Sinful nature which is his sacrificial death.

There is always a price paid for the evil and wrongs that people do. In this story, that is the price paid by those affected directly—the victims, their families, the businesses, and the community they lived in which the story describes. However, there is also the price paid by those who heard it and were impacted indirectly which would number in the millions.

David Knight

David Knight is chief legal counsel for Stephens Inc., a major regional investment banking firm. He has been a photographer for many years and regularly markets his work in support of various cultural and philanthropic organizations. He is an avid supporter of The Rep and just completed six years of service on its board of directors, including two terms as chairman. He lives in Little Rock with his wife, Janna, and their three daughters, Riley,

Anne, and India.

In 2005 David published his first book of photography entitled, *Faith and Good Works in Africa*. A driving force behind the effort was to capture how ministries have enriched those in Rwanda and Uganda, especially after the ethnic genocide committed in 1994. Dale Dawson wrote in the foreword, "My prayer is that by sharing our trip, those who are rich in resources will be motivated to put their faith into action and embrace Jesus' call to love others and serve the poor."

David's next incredible book of photography was his 2007 release, *In Character, a Season at the Rep*. Much of this endeavor went to support the Arkansas Repertory Theatre. Each chapter presents a different production from the theatre's thirtieth season.

Skylar Whisnant

Skylar attends third grade at Jefferson Elementary in Little Rock, Arkansas. She enjoys soccer, basketball, swimming, and softball, and plans to join Liz Morris' Fifth Grade Art Club in two years. Other events she is active in include Girls Scouts, Awana, activities at Calvary Baptist Church, being a good big sister of twins, Garden Club…. How do her parents keep up, she sometimes wonders.

Carolyn Boyles

Carolyn Boyles is a freelance writer and photographer living in Central Arkansas. Her writing has appeared in *The Storyteller*, *Audacity Magazine*, *Echoes of the Ozarks Vol. III*, *Concealed Carry Magazine*, and on *Amazon Shorts*. Her book, *A Complete Plain-English Guide to Living with a Spinal Cord Injury: Valuable Information From A Survivor*, was published in 2007.

Stewart Matthews

Stewart Matthews is an amateur photographer specializing in landscape and nature photography. He began his love of photography as the photo editor of *The Profile* at Hendrix College. Throughout the past 3 years, Stewart has taken several outdoor photography courses to refine his technique, including with Arkansas photographer and publisher Tim Ernst. Stewart has also performed free-lance computer processing for a local photography studio. An avid outdoorsman, Stewart supports the Arkansas Chapter of the Nature Conservancy and enjoys fly-fishing, camping, biking, hiking and backpacking. His hobbies also include home repairs, woodworking, beer making, and taking pictures of his two children, Steele and Riley. Stewart is a graduate of Hendrix College where he met is wife, Kristy. Stewart has worked in the public health field for 11 years and is currently a project manager at the Vital Records section of the Arkansas Department of Health.

Liz Deering Morris

Artist Liz Morris received her BA in Fine Arts from the University of Arkansas at Little Rock in 2000, and MA in Teaching from the University of Arkansas at Monticello in 2006. These degrees prepared her well where she is now a wonderful art teacher at Jefferson Elementary in Little Rock, Arkansas. Liz is the daughter of artists John and Kathy Deering (nine of their sculptors are on the Arkansas State Capitol grounds), and she is married to Jake Morris, who teaches at Mills High School.

In 2007 Liz's Jefferson Elementary Art Club had the honor to illustrate Steve Whisnant children's book, *Domino*. The Little Rock School District recognized their effort as an outstanding project.

E-mail: lizdeeringmorris@sbcglobal.net

About the Author

Arkansas author Steve Whisnant is happily married and the proud father of three daughters, including twins. Since 2000 he has won or placed in over 80 writing contests and his work has been featured in *Quills & Pixels*, *The Counselor*, *Amazon.com Shorts*, *The Storyteller*, and several anthologies around the country next to Spur Award winners and Pulitzer Prize and Pushcart nominee authors. He has also been a guest writer for several Arkansas newspapers.

In addition to serving as past President for Fiction Writers of Central Arkansas (www.fwca.org), Steve is currently the Arkansas State Representative for *ByLine Magazine* (www.bylinemag.com) and a member of the Ozarks Writers League (www.ozarkswritersleague.org) and Northeast Texas Writers' Organization (www.netwo.org).

In 2005 he released his first book, a collection of award-winning short stories entitled *Yesterday Again*. This was followed up in 2006 with his novel, *Department of Corrections (D.O.C)*. In 2007 he had the honor of releasing the illustrated version of his award-winning children's story, *Domino*. Jefferson Elementary 5th Grade Art Club in Little Rock created the artwork.

In his "day job" as the Field Representative for the Arkansas Department of Health, Vital Records, Steve trains coroners, physicians, funeral directors, nurses, and others how to complete death and birth certificates. "What an opportunity," he says, "to learn of ideas for future stories." He holds a B.A. from the University of Central Arkansas and MPA from the University of Arkansas at Little Rock.

www.stevewhisnant.com